Captain Hansen peered out the barn door. He was certain the commandant and his guards were waiting for him to make his move. He found a rock by the door and picked it up. He threw it as hard as he could in the other direction to create a distraction.

Hearing it hit some trees, he made a run for it. When he didn't hear any gunshots in the direction of the rock, he knew they didn't fall for it. He ran as fast as his aching legs could carry him, zigzagging as he went. When he made it to the thicket of trees, he kept on going. To his surprise, he never heard a shot. He didn't know how far he ran, but it felt like miles before falling to the ground exhausted. Hiding himself as best he could, Captain Hansen waited for the worst.

Whoever it was, they were headed right for him. Hansen knew he was well hidden, so if he lay still and if they didn't have a dog, they would pass by him. Soon a silhouette came into sight, and he was alone—no dog. The man came right up to Hansen and stopped. About five foot ten, carrying a rifle and a backpack, he snapped to attention, saluted, and said in a Southern drawl, "Staff Sergeant Jones, at your service, Sir."

Follow Captain Hansen and Staff Sergeant Jones, along with three others, as they make their way through Nazi Germany, each teaching Hansen valuable life lessons he'll need—if he ever gets out of Germany alive.

My Dear Nikki

Captain Hansen's Inspiring Escape Through Germany

A Novel By

GARY JAMES SUMNER

Drawings in this book are from Allison Allred:
http://akallred00.wixsite.com

ISBN: 979-8-89031-507-6 (sc)
ISBN: 979-8-89031-508-3 (hc)
ISBN: 979-8-89031-509-0 (e)

One Galleria Blvd., Suite 1900, Metairie, LA 70001
(504) 702-6708

Photo taken at Stalag VII at Moosburg, Germany. Pictured are (L-R) John Fitzpatrick (hand in pocket), Ed Stephenson (beret), Ernie Sands (bending over stove), Francis "Fran" Finnegan, John Lindquist, Charles Woehrle, Jim Houser, and Lt. Marshall Draper (kneeling) of the 15th Bombardment Squadron. Draper had the unfortunate distinction of being the first US POW in Germany, shot down on June 21, 1942. Lindquist and Houser are wearing German reversible padded parkas, probably gathered as "war booty." These men were roommates at Stalag Luft III, South Compound, Block 130, Room 10. They kept together on the march in January 1945, sharing food and emotional support. (Photo courtesy of Ben van Drogenbroek through the 458th Bombardment Group (H) web page: www.485bg.com)

Front cover enhanced by Doug Warren

"I believe those who build their lives on a firm foundation and are well rounded will be better off to withstand the turmoils of life."

—Gary James Sumner

CONTENTS

Book Three:
We All Have Mountains to Climb for Self & Country

Book Four:
For Love of Money

DEDICATION

In my lifetime, I have had many mentors who have helped me along the way to become a better and well-rounded man. This book covers the basics in four areas I feel are critical for a firm foundation. For all those who teach the love of God, family, and country, this book is dedicated to you.

WHY I TACKLED WRITING

It was a Saturday morning in November of 2012. My wife and I were listening in on a conference call from a gentleman by the name of Dan McCormick.

Somewhere in that counseling session, Dan inspired me to step out of my comfort zone and write the story I heard many years ago, a story that always helped me face my fears. I named the book *From Fear to Freedom.*

Why was it out of my comfort zone? When I sent my parents a copy of *From Fear to Freedom, my* father expressed to my mom, "I didn't know the boy could read, when did he learn to write?" Of all the compliments I've received, that one means the most to me. I love you, Mom and Dad.

My father said that because he knew how much I struggled with reading. Back in the '80s, I tried to write a short story for the fun of it. The problem was, it took me months to write eighteen pages, and it was no longer fun. I was always checking how to spell the simplest of words. I couldn't spend that kind of time because I had a family to provide for and a full-time job.

After listening to Dan, I decided to give it another go. Thank God for spell-check and wonderful editors.

INTRODUCTION

THE STORY BEFORE THE STORY

As a disclaimer, Mr. Hansen wanted it to be known to the reader, he is not one with letters after his name, what you would call, having credentials like a "PhD" and he knows he'll be criticized for it. I told him they're called trolls. You should have seen the look on his face when I told him that. "What does a mythical creature who lives under a bridge have to do with anything?"

He respects all those who have gone through the hard training for their degree and loves to read their thoughts on any given subject. He has quite a few favorites and I list some of them in the back under Recommended Books.

Mr. Hansen always finds it interesting how many times the experts would agree by saying the same thing, only worded differently. He would also find times when their opinions would conflict. Who knows who is right and who is wrong? Mr. Hansen would never throw out any opinion; he simply would put any piece of the puzzle that didn't fit on the shelf. (As you get to know Mr. Hansen, you'll better understand that phrase.)

The Purpose Of This Book

I feel it only fair to warn the reader this is not a story of escaping Nazi Germany, though Mr. Hansen shared with me some close calls that I put into this book. His main purpose was to help others learn basic lessons and principles; what he calls Christian values, that he was taught from his four guides, whom he called his guardian angels.

Without their help, Mr. Hansen doubts he would have ever made it out of Germany alive, or achieved the success he has enjoyed. They gave him, as Mr. Hansen put it . . . a firm foundation upon which to build. Mr. Hansen tells his story from a Christian point of view, and he makes no apology for it. This is his story and his gift to you.

Nikki's Introduction

Who am I? My name is Nikki Brown, and I have a question for you. Have you ever met a person who always had a positive outlook on life? Did you wonder if they were born with it, or did it develop gradually? With Mr. Hansen's help, I think I found the answer.

When I was a little girl, my Grandfather Vince told me about a POW whom he saw when he was a prisoner in World War II in Commandant Schmidt's camp. Grandpa said that any of the POWs who tried to escape from his camp were sentenced to death. They were, however, given a choice as to how they were to die. The choice was the firing squad or "something out in the woods." My grandfather watched each prisoner being led into the woods, and after about an hour, they came back. The prisoner went before the wall to be shot. No one knew what the other choice was. The commandant kept that a secret. Whatever it was, it had to be worse than a bullet up against the wall. Out of all the ones my grandfather witnessed who were sentenced to death, there was only one who never returned. He chose the unknown.

I had to find out who he was and what was out in the woods. I convinced the newspaper I was working for to send me to Germany to track down the story and tie up the loose ends. It was a miracle, but I found the commandant who held my grandfather captive.

I decided to tell Captain James Hansen's story as though you, the reader, were listening in on our conversation—what he said, what I said, and what I was thinking at the time. James told me how he had to make the choice as to how he was to die, and how he made it through enemy territory.

James could hold your attention for hours on end. We would start at nine and end by five. James knew how to work a room—the way he walked around, moving his arms, holding his hands in a way that you felt like you were right there, experiencing what he was going through by the expressions on his face. He would raise one eyebrow and lift his head as if to say, "What?" Whenever both eyebrows went up and his eyes opened wide, you were as surprised as he was. If both eyebrows went downward, look out. You didn't know what was going to happen, and you'd find yourself on the edge of your seat. His personality was one of kindness and warmth, and his laugh was infectious. When he talked to you, he always made you feel like you were the most important person in the room.

In the months that followed, I fell deeply in love with his only grandson, Ray. I think I had fallen for him the first time I saw him with that grease he missed on his forearm when he was told to stop whatever he was doing and fly me back home. Still, I was cautious. I had my heart broken once before, and I didn't want to learn that lesson over again. I made a list of the attributes of the man I was looking for, and when I was able to cross off the last one, I said yes, and we had a whirlwind of an engagement, with a wedding that could only be described as a fairytale. James was able to meet my Grandfather Vince at a family reunion held in my honor. Those two really hit it off. My grandfather passed away shortly before my wedding, but I know he was there in spirit.

Two years after the wedding, James was able to hold our first son, Raymond Jr. Needless to say, when the doctors gave James only six months to a year to live, they didn't know Captain James Hansen. A year and a half after Raymond Jr. was born, we had another son we named James; family and friends call him Jimmy. On Jimmy's second birthday, Ray and I told Grandpa James we were going to have one more to complete our family. Seven months later, Reese was born.

Though we had been blessed with three beautiful children, Ray and I felt our family was missing someone. We knew there was one more that needed to bless our home. The good Lord must have quite a sense of humor, because we had twins, a girl and a boy. The girl we named Reagen, and the boy we named Jesse. It was a hard labor, touch and go for a while. With many prayers and the loving attention of the skilled doctors and nurses, I pulled through fine. Perhaps I'll tell you about that another time. We have a family portrait above the fireplace with James holding the twins. He never felt more blessed.

It was shortly after that when James called the family into his bedroom. He knew it was his time to go. James felt a desire to ask the Lord for a blessing to each family member.

One by one, we knelt by the side of his bed. James had always tried to live close to the spirit, doing what he thought the Savior would want him to do. His oldest son, Jimmy, went first.

I was the last. As I knelt, James looked me in the eyes. "My Dear Nikki, even though it took a lifetime, I knew you'd come. When Jimmy introduced me to you, we knew you were the one I had been waiting for." He took my hand, closed his eyes, and asked the Lord to bless me with the strength and encouragement I'll need for my mission in life and more.

When he finished, I wiped the tears from my face. I gave his hand a kiss and thanked him.

We left the room in silence, not wanting to disturb the spirit we were all feeling. As I was closing the door behind me, Karen lay next to James with her arm embracing him. The last words I heard James say were to his wife, "I'll be waiting for you."

James would not allow his story to be printed until he had passed away, due to a promise he had made to a very dear friend.

This book is the last gift he wanted to give to all. Before he died, he read it once more, made a few additions, and told me how pleased he was with the way I captured the moment. He smiled and wondered where the bookstores would place the books on their shelves. Religious? Relationships? Historical? Inspirational, or perhaps in the finance section? It will all become clear as you go on this journey with Captain James Hansen.

He teased me about making this book about me and his grandson Ray, and making it a love story so it would be placed in the romance section. No, this book isn't about me or Ray. It's about the Captain and what he learned from the four men who led him to safety. They were the ones who gave Grandpa James the four foundations upon which to build his life. It will most likely be placed in the Personal Growth and Development section of the bookstore.

I wasn't sure how to break down a book with so much information. Mr. Hansen suggested each soldier get his own book, having people purchase four, making it a set. I thought of the price and what it would entail, so I found a way everyone could be happy. When he saw it, he smiled, "I love how you turned four books into one. You gave each of my guides their own book with chapters along with subtitles of each point I wanted to cover. It makes it read like a textbook . . . one of the best I've seen, if I do say so myself." James was the only one I wanted to please, so if only one person finds the hidden treasures and pearls of wisdom that James offers in this book, I know their joy will be great.

PART ONE

THE HANSEN FAMILY SECRET

THE CHOICE

It was a Monday morning. We finished breakfast when James and I retired to his study. It was time for Captain James Hansen to tell me part one of the family secret he calls, *"The Choice."* Part two is what could only be told after Captain James Hansen passed away. He shares that story in "The Hansen Family Secret Part Two" in this book. Many but not all of the family knew part one and fewer still knew part two; the reason for that will be made clear in the end. Even though the family had been anxious for all to know the rest of the story, they truly miss James.

As we walked into his study, he motioned for me to have a seat. After I sat down, he sat back in his chair and began. I smiled, took out my recorder, and turned it on.

"So Nikki, you would like to know what happened to me after the commandant locked me in the barn."

James began. "I'll start with when I was shot down. We were flying cover for the bombers when we noticed all the top turrets turned to their six-and-pointing-up mode; it almost looked like they were aiming at us. We turned to look at what they were aiming at, but the sun was in our eyes. The German pilots were known for this maneuver. They were hard to see, but coming in fast were Messerschmitt 262s, six of them, the first time I'd ever seen a jet. We were told they could go over a hundred miles an hour faster than the top speed of P-51s. The bombers aren't built for speed, and we were carrying reserve gas tanks, which I ordered to be dropped, and then for us to climb.

"Pushing the throttle wide open, we climbed. As we dove down, picking up speed, one 262 came right into my sights. I let him have it, but I undershot. My wingman, however, took him out. The 262s might be faster, but because of their speed, I knew the Mustang could outmaneuver them. We fought tooth and nail, a dogfight that should go down in history. The 262s took out three of the bombers, and there was no way I was going to lose any more. We took out three more of theirs, leaving them with two.

"One of the Messerschmitts came in on the right waist gunners of the bombers and took out one more. He flew right in front of me, and I fired. Again, I couldn't adjust for the speed. I was so angry I did what no pilot should do—I took off after him without my wingman. All I could see through my anger was to get revenge.

"As I dove down after him, he knew I was on his tail and he pulled away. I didn't give up but stayed on his tail. He had to pull up sooner or later. What I didn't see was the last jet right behind me. He did, however, get my attention when I saw the tracers whizzing by my canopy. My wingman followed him down, but he was out of range to do any good.

"There was one more short burst, and I was hit. The jet in front of me was long gone, and the one on my tail broke off. He must have been out of ammo, or else he would have finished me off for sure. I leveled off and tried to climb, but it was no use. I was losing oil pressure too fast. "My plane was too low for me to bail out, and I could see no safe place to land. I was in a real predicament, to say the least. Desperately scanning the landscape, I saw a small opening in a group of tall trees up ahead. I quickly calculated the distance, altitude, and airspeed. I didn't see how I was going to make it, but somehow I did. There must have been a headwind to keep me airborne. I kept the wheels up as long as possible to avoid any drag on my aircraft.

"As I came over the top of the last tall tree, I could feel the branches scrape against my P-51. Quickly bringing down the landing gear, I could hear the small saplings break against the wings as I touched the ground. I held my breath as the plane's wheels hit every mound of dirt that had been pushed up by whatever was making their home in that clearing. I hoped that one of those mounds of dirt wasn't a big rock. When I thought I was going to make it, the trees at the end of my little makeshift landing strip were getting closer and closer, and I wondered if I should have landed with the gear up. Then snap! The left wing hit a tree that wasn't going to give way. I spun around like a top.

"When my Mustang came to rest, I quickly took inventory of myself and couldn't believe it—nothing was broken but the wing. I knew the Germans had seen where I went down, giving me only seconds to hightail it out of there. I eluded them for a while, but they eventually caught up to me.

"I was taken to be interrogated, but all they got out of me was name, rank, and serial number. I was beaten and deprived of any real food. I was fed hard black bread and water for many days. How many days? I had no idea. My cell had no windows, and the light was left on the whole time I was there. When they could see I wasn't going to cooperate, I was to be dumped in a prison camp.

"Hundreds of POWs were crammed into boxcars, packed so tight there was no room to move. When I say there was no room to move, I mean *no room*—not even to make our way over to the walls to relieve ourselves through the slats.

"We held it as long as we could, but it gets to a point where you have to go where you stood, inside your clothes. There was nothing else you could do. I didn't think it was possible, but I slept standing up. It was days before we were let out. When the doors opened, the ones standing up against the door fell out from the weight of the others pushing against them. I remember when I could finally move my legs how hard it was to step over some of the dead who had fallen. We were given water and the same hard black bread. This time, I was so hungry it tasted pretty good.

"From there, we were divided up. Transport trucks showed up and loaded in as many of us as they could. I was the last one on. As the tailgate closed, I could see the rest of the POWs being loaded back onto the box cars. I thought to myself, 'At least there will be enough room for them to lie down.' We were under heavy guard, so we had no chance to escape. It was a bit of a drive, and we had no way of knowing where we were when we pulled into the prison camp. When we stopped, the guards ordered us down. I couldn't move as fast as they wanted, which won me a prize—a hit to the gut with the butt of a gun.

"While being marched into camp, I caught my breath and went in standing as tall as I could. I wasn't about to let them think they had gotten the better of me. We were placed in an area inside the fence where I could see the other prisoners, but none came up to us. I learned later it was against one of the many rules. No one speaks to a prisoner.

"The commandant alone lays down the law. We must have stood there for at least an hour. Come to find out, the commandant was waiting for another truckload of prisoners to arrive; there was no way someone of his great importance would make an appearance twice in one day.

"As I stood and looked around, it was evident the other prisoners were anxious to greet us and learn of any news about the war. As a prisoner, there's a love-hate feeling toward new arrivals—they love to get an updated report as to how the war is going, and hate because there is no more room in the inn. But this didn't matter to the Germans, they crammed us in. I couldn't believe my eyes. Some of the men looked like ghosts. Many of their clothes were rags, and I could see the ribs on most of them. Those who still had some fat on them must have been the newer arrivals.

"No way was I going to end up looking like that. I had a wife and a newborn baby back home that I hadn't even held yet. I was enraged to think the prisoners were being treated so badly.

"Finally, two large trucks pulled up to the gate, and the camp came alive. More guards came out of their living quarters and retrieved their dogs to greet their new house guests. As the men climbed out of the back, some were so bad off they buckled under their own weight as they hit the ground; it was then that the dogs would attack, bringing them quickly to their feet. One prisoner, out of reflex, hit the dog, and that's when we learned one of the rules the hard way—never, and I mean never, touch one of the dogs. The prisoner was so weak it only took one blow of the rifle butt to the head. It made a sickening sound, and we knew he was dead. There was nothing anyone could do. As the men lined up with the rest of us, I watched two guards drag his body behind one of the buildings, and it was the last time anyone saw him.

"It was now time for Commandant Schmidt to make his grand entrance. He came out of his office dressed to impress. Shiny, black leather boots that went below his knees. A black trench coat and matching gloves, with a crop under his arm. He stood there, letting us bask in his presence. I remember thinking he was quite a young punk for a commandant and wondered what strings he had pulled to get his job. But still, you knew you didn't want to cross him.

"There he was with his high-arched hat and stiff neck, looking us over. He slowly walked down the three steps to inform us of his rules. His first one we had already learned—never touch the dogs. With each rule, he would slap the riding crop in his glove, and when it was one that needed extra attention, he slapped it against his boot, making such a crack that most of us flinched. I could see he especially enjoyed that. As he walked around delivering his rules, he stopped in front of me and looked me right in the eye. 'Never try to escape. You will be caught, and your punishment will be death.' With each 'never' came a crack of the crop.

"We were all assigned a barrack, and that's when the other prisoners could greet us and help us to our quarters. Some of this I've already told you, so I'll make it short.

"I could feel myself getting weaker and weaker by the day and knew if I didn't make a break for it soon, I wouldn't have the strength. It was a night when the moon was a sliver, and with the cloud cover, all was pitch black. I tried talking to two guys that I had gotten to know a little to come with me, but they wanted nothing to do with it. They said they would try and cover for me at roll call. I timed the searchlights and made my way through the fence, past the guards, and disappeared into the woods. It only took until noon when the dogs found me and ripped into my leg and arm. When the guards brought me back, Commandant Schmidt came out and greeted me with a smirk on his face. 'Welcome back, Captain. Care to take a walk?'

"He took only a few guards and a dog. With my hands tied behind my back, I was no threat. I knew I was going to die. The commandant informed me on our walk that if I had made my way to safety, the punishment for *him* would have been a demotion, and then sent to one of the Fronts where all the action was. As we started our walk into the woods, the commandant told me to think about one word I would like to have my family remember me by and he would do his best to let them know.

"We walked for about thirty minutes when we came into a small clearing. There was a barn with an old dead tree in front of it. A large branch about ten feet off the ground would be perfect for a rope to be tossed over for a hanging. When we walked under it, I stopped, but they kept going. The commandant turned and looked at me.

'What, you think you are to be hanged? You should be so lucky. No, your fate is what is in that barn.' Commandant Schmidt looked at his watch. 'You have sixty seconds to decide.'

"It was a huge barn with a heavy board across the two doors, locking in whatever was inside. What could possibly be in there? Perhaps wild, starving animals, ready to eat me alive. No, not wild animals, but the dogs that seemed to love to rip the prisoners to shreds. Perhaps it was full of booby traps that would spring some kind of a torturous, slow, agonizing death. All of the worst kinds of death ran through my head. Perhaps once I was locked inside, they would set the barn on fire, burning me to death.

"It felt like ten seconds when I heard the commandant tell me my time was up. I was about to pick the firing squad, as had all the others before me.

"Then all of a sudden, I had a feeling I couldn't explain. Something in my gut told me to pick the barn. I took a deep breath and told the commandant my choice: 'I choose the barn.' I was led up to the door, and the heavy board was removed. The commandant took out his knife and cut my hands free. The guards opened the door, but I had to walk in on my own accord. Before I walked in, the commandant asked what was the one word I would like my family to remember me by. I looked him in the eye and said: 'Integrity.'

"Once I had cleared the door, I heard it slam shut behind me. The big, heavy board slid down in place, locking me and whatever or whoever inside. The slamming of the door caused what seemed to be hundreds of birds to fly around. My heart was pounding in my ears so loud I could barely hear the flapping of the birds' wings. What sort of death was I going to face?

"My imagination went wild. Dust was everywhere, and with the shadows from the birds and the dust reflecting off the beams of light through the cracks of the barn, I thought my heart was going to come right out of my chest. I stood there choking from the dust, waiting for the worst. Once the birds and the dust settled down, my eyes became adjusted to the darkness, and I saw that the back door to the barn was ajar. It was a trick: if I made a beeline to what appeared to be freedom, I knew for sure I'd spring some kind of booby trap.

"I stood trying to figure out what I should do. Should I go straight to the door? No, that would be too obvious. Maybe if I stayed against the wall of the barn, that would be safer, but which way? I didn't know what to do. I froze, dead in my tracks. Tired and hungry, I couldn't think straight, but knew I had to do something.

"I closed my eyes and took in a deep breath. As I slowly exhaled, I opened my eyes. The right side, yes, the right side is the way I'll go. With the wall of the barn against my back, I knew that at least no one could come up from behind me. Inch by inch, I carefully moved the loose hay, looking for any trip wires. I was halfway through when I heard some movement from the loft above. I stopped. I looked around for anything I could defend myself with. A stick, rock, anything, but there was nothing. I stood, straining to listen, but there was no sound—only the pounding of my heart.

"Once again, I started to move. Out of the corner of my eye, I saw a shadow, and I quickly put up my fists to fight. Whatever I saw was gone. My nose started to bleed, and I could taste it in the back of my throat. My blood pressure must have been going through the roof to give me a bloody nose. I put my head back to get the bleeding under control.

"When it finally stopped, I remember telling myself, 'If I don't pull it together, *I'm* going to be the one that kills me.'

"Again I saw movement, this time in the hay about ten feet in front of me. Was it real or was my imagination running wild? Do I go back and start over and go down the other side? I'm almost there. I kept staring at the hay, where I saw whatever it was go. Again it moved, and again I could feel the blood start to run over my lip and in the back of my throat. It was then it leaped out and ran away from me. It was a cat with a mouse in its teeth, and it disappeared through a hole in the wall.

"Blood was now streaming down my face. Trying to stop the bleeding, I started to move again. Inch by inch, I went looking all around, waiting for the worst. I thought for sure I was going to step on a landmine, or a trip wire that would spring a trap, killing me slowly. I don't know how long it took, because I was frozen with a fear that filled my mind.

"When I finally reached the door, I leaned against the wall and looked out the door, keeping my head inside. I was certain that the second I stepped out into the clearing, I would be cut down, so I decided to wait until the sun went down. I figured I would have a much better chance in the dark than I would in broad daylight.

"As I waited, I started to calm down. My breathing and heart rate slowed to a more normal rate, and my nose finally stopped bleeding. It was then that I noticed a small backpack by the door. Do I open it? What if it's a bomb? I decided to leave it alone. As I kept looking through the cracks, watching to see if I could spot anyone, I kept glancing at the backpack. I couldn't take it any longer; I had to see what was inside. I opened it carefully and saw that it was filled with jerky, black bread, and a canteen of water. I remember chuckling to myself, thinking the commandant was giving me my last meal before the execution. I picked it up and went up into the loft to hide and wait until it was dark enough to make my move.

"As I lay there, staring at the food, I wondered whether or not I should eat it; after all, it could be poisoned. I decided that if they *were* out there waiting for me, I was going to have to make a run for it. The adrenaline that had coursed through my body earlier had subsided and left me feeling weak and shaky. I knew I was going to need energy to make a run for it, and my only source for renewed strength was in that backpack. So I took a couple of bites of the jerky and bread and washed it down with a big gulp of water. I have to say, it sure tasted like a Thanksgiving feast.

"With what little we had been fed in camp and while I was on the run, I wasn't able to find any kind of food to live on. It was the first bite of real food I had in many days. I wanted to devour it all, but my stomach had shrunk so much that the few bites I took filled me up. It only took a moment and my stomach started to cramp. Fear of having eaten poisoned food overtook my reality, and I started convulsing. I wasn't positive what was and wasn't real. Fear eats at you like a cancer, and unless you take control of it, it will eat you alive. Was it poisoned, or was it my fear getting the best of me? I told myself over and over, 'The food is fine and I'll be fine.' My stomach calmed down, and I was able to eat the rest of the bread.

"I waited there for what seemed like an hour. In that time, I was able to finish off one of the pieces of jerky and half of the water in the canteen. Having regained some strength, my spirits lifted. I climbed down from the loft and made my way toward the door. It was dusk, and I remember looking through some of the slats, trying to figure out which way would be the best to make my break.

"The light was perfect. It was time to make my move, dark enough to make me a harder target to hit, and lit enough so I could see my way without running into a tree. I found a rock by the door and picked it up. I threw it as hard as I could in the other direction to create a distraction. As I heard it hit some trees, I made a run for it, carrying the backpack of food and water with me. When I didn't hear any gunshots in the direction of the rock, I thought, 'Great, they didn't fall for it, and I am about to be cut down.' I ran as hard and as fast as my aching legs could carry me, zigzagging as I went. When I made it to the thicket of trees, I kept on going. To my surprise, I never heard a shot, or anyone following me. I don't know how far I ran, but it felt like miles before I fell to the ground exhausted."

That was the story I sent off to the newspaper that sent me to Germany to track down the commandant, and if at all possible, the POW who chose the unknown. I'm not going to take the time to tell that story. If you want to know how I accomplished that task, you'll have to read *From Fear to Freedom*.

PART TWO

THE HANSEN FAMILY SECRET

BOOK ONE

YOU'RE NEVER ALONE

ONE

A SOLDIER NAMED JOHN

It was the next day when we walked into James's office. I was about to receive *part two* of the Hansen family secrets.

"Nikki, I remember my mother telling me that whenever I had a close call and could have had gotten hurt badly, it was my guardian angels looking over me. It seems she was always telling me that. My dear, as you already know from talking to my son Jimmy, there were four who helped me escape Nazi Germany, or as I like to call them, my *guardian angels*. Each gave me a foundation to build upon, and without a firm foundation, the building would be weak and could fall. I was taught line upon line, concept upon concept, as I put the pieces of the puzzle together that would shape my life.

"My first mentor gave me a spiritual foundation on which to build. The second mentor taught me about relationships and personalities. The third reminded and taught me why America was and is so great, and what our forefathers went through for you and me. The fourth mentor gave me the foundation as to how to control money and not let it control me. Money is not the root of all evil; it's the *love* of money that's evil. And believe me; I know plenty of people who fall into that category.

"Let me tell you about John. Now, where did I leave off yesterday?"

I looked at my notes. *"You ran for what felt like miles before you fell to the ground exhausted."*

"Thank you." James took in a deep breath and let it out slowly. I could see him reflecting in his mind back to that day. "I didn't know where I was. All I knew was that the prison camp was to my back, and that's where I was going to keep it. When I couldn't go any farther, I found a large tree that had fallen over and I laid myself up against it, covering myself completely with branches. I tried to relax, but it was no use. My heart and mind were racing so fast, it was amazing I could even hear him coming."

"Who was coming? A guard from the prison camp?"

"That's what I was afraid of. Whoever it was, they were headed right for me. I knew that I was well hidden, and if I lay still, whoever it was would pass by me—that is, if they didn't have a dog. I watched and waited. Soon, he came into sight, and luckily he was alone—no dog. Whether friend or foe, I could not tell. It was too dark to make out his helmet or rifle. I could see he had been looking at my tracks and followed them. He came right up to me and stopped. He probably heard my heart pounding. There was enough light that I could make out his silhouette through the cracks in the branches that covered me. He was tall, carrying a rifle and a backpack. I thought I was a goner for sure.

"He stood there. I wasn't sure, but his helmet looked like one of ours. Were my eyes playing a trick on me? Then he did something that took me totally by surprise—he snapped to attention, saluted, and said with a Southern drawl, 'Staff Sergeant Jones, at yer service, Sir.'"

To hear James talk with a Southern drawl took me by surprise. I couldn't help but smile. *"How on earth did he see you if you were so well covered up, and without a dog?"*

James smiled. "I asked him that very question the next day. He said, 'Branches—the way I had them piled up—looked more like a beaver dam, something you jus' don't see in the middle of the woods.'

"Nikki, you can't imagine how good it was to hear that drawl instead of a German accent. He then knelt down in front of me and removed the branches from my face. I have to tell you I never so wanted to kiss a man in all my life, but in this case, I would have made an exception, had I the strength."

I smiled. I knew what he meant.

"John smiled. 'You're a hard man to track down. I noticed some blood along the way. Where are you hurt?' That's when I noticed the throbbing in my leg and arm where the dogs had bitten me on my first escape attempt. He helped me remove the rest of the branches.

"As he dressed my wounds, he told me he was there to help me get through my trials. I thought it strange that he would use the word *trials*. I expected him to say, 'rescue me,' or 'get me to safety'—something like that, but I figured it was a Southern term. I later came to understand that he chose the word *trials* for a reason.

"Nikki, he helped me in so many ways that I will never be able to repay. He looked me right in the eyes. I'll never forget it. Even in the dim light up close, I could see that his eyes were blue as he told me that if I did what he would tell me, I would survive. He said it with such confidence, I believed him, and for the first time in a long time I had hope. He said he would watch over me while I got some shut-eye, my heart was still pounding so fast from my ordeal that I thought it would be impossible to relax, let alone get any sleep."

Hansen Learns to Relax

"John looked at me. 'Sir, I know what you're likely thinkin'. Rest maybe, but sleep? No way. Am I right, Sir?'

"I nodded my head. Who is this guy, some kind of mind reader? Not likely. It wouldn't take a mind reader to figure out what would be going through anyone's head, after what I'd gone through. Then he said, 'Sir, if you let me, I can help.'

"I was exhausted; all I could do was nod my head. He took out of his pack a green wool army blanket and covered me with it. Then, in a very slow and calming voice, he said, 'Close your eyes, Sir, and jus' focus on your breathing. I want you to take a deep breath in through your nose. Can you feel the cool night air?' I nodded again.

"John continued. 'Good, now slowly, exhale out through your mouth. Good, another cleansing breath in through the nose and out through the mouth. Now jus' breathe normally. Only think about the air going in and out of your lungs, nothing else. You'll find your mind wants to wander. That's normal. When that happens, don't worry about it; jus' get your mind back to your breathing. Good, now picture yourself on a beach and the tide's coming in. With each breath you're taking in, there's a nice, warm wave covering your feet. As you exhale, see the wave going back out to the ocean, taking all the stress from your feet. As you inhale, the next wave is covering your knees. Exhale, and feel all the stress from your knees being taken out to the sea. Continue to breathe in. Here comes the next wave. It's going up to your hips and back out. All the stress goes with it. Once more as it's going to go up to your chest. Can you see it as you breathe in?' Again, I nodded.

"Nikki, I was so relaxed I couldn't believe it. John told me to take one cleansing breath and take in all the smells of the forest around me and let them cover me like a blanket of protection. As I inhaled, I noticed a slight hint of mint, pine, and all kinds of vegetation. John told me to keep breathing.

"The sounds of the night sang me to sleep while he stood guard."

As James told that story to me, I was breathing right along with the story, totally relaxed. I could almost smell the ocean and the scent of pine trees, along with each of the sounds he was describing. I felt as though I were in the woods right there with him, that's when it dawned on me: when his son Jimmy gave me a tour of the corporate office, he showed me the . . . "Pondering room," where someone could go and relax amid sound effects. So that's where James got the idea. He continued:

"In the morning when I awoke, I looked around and found myself alone. I figured the soldier was my imagination that had gotten the best of me, but then I noticed the blanket around me and the bandages on my leg and arm. I couldn't remember the last time I had slept so soundly. But where was he? Did he get captured during the night trying to save me? I wanted to call out, but that is something you don't do when you're on the run.

"I reached into my pack, pulled out the last piece of jerky, and washed it down with what was left of the water. Never before did a dried-out piece of meat ever taste so good. It tasted like . . . freedom.

"Then to my right, I saw him again. He came up to me and sat down. In a low voice, I told him, 'I thought you were a goner.'

'No, Sir,' he said, 'I was on guard behind you jus' over the ridge. How'd ya' sleep?'

'Like a baby, thanks to you, Staff Sergeant Jones!' He gave me one of those smiles where you lift one side of your mouth.

'Our journey is going to take a while,' he said. 'How 'bout you call me John?' He looked up through the trees. 'We're burning daylight. We'd best be on our way.'"

"Let me tell you, Nikki, I was wound so tight the first hour or so, I thought I could see a German behind every bush and tree. Every little sound made my heart skip a beat. Once I stepped on a large stick that snapped so loud, I about came out of my skin. John turned around and started to laugh.

'It's a good thing you don't have a gun, or you'd have shot that stick.'"

The way James said it, I started to laugh.

James smiled, "Oh, it's funny now, but at the time I was in no mood, and I reprimanded him in a voice as stern and as loud as I could without giving away our position to the enemy. John stood, trying not to smile. Let me tell you, that is not the kind of response a captain would expect from a staff sergeant. You're to come to attention and wipe that smile off your face. John tried, but he couldn't. He was there helping me and there I was chewing him out for a little joke. I thought what it must have looked like if there were a bystander watching the whole scene. I could see the humor, but it was still hard to humble myself and apologize, but I did, and together we had a good laugh."

Another Lesson in Relaxation

"John smiled, 'Sir, I think it's time to play a game.' I looked at him and answered, 'Game? Have you gone mad? This is not the time or the place to play a game.' Then he said to me, 'Forgive me for saying, Sir, but you're more nervous than a long-tailed cat in a room full of rocking chairs.'

"I looked at John and told him that was the dumbest saying I'd ever heard. John smiled and wiped the sweat from his brow with his hand. He didn't take any offense at what I said. 'That's an expression my daddy taught me when I was jus' knee-high to a grasshopper. It may be dumb, but it sure paints a picture.'"

I interrupted James. *"That's the saying you told me when we first met; I was wondering how a California man had so many Southern sayings. You got them from John."*

James nodded, then continued. "So there we were, somewhere in Germany, and I'm shaking my head, all the while John's smiling.

'Something else my daddy taught me—sometimes you jus' need to relax 'n blow off steam. He told me a story about a great leader. One day, this leader was out playing with a bunch of kids, laughing and running around with them, acting jus' like one of the kids. He loved playing with them, and they were having a fine time too. Two gentlemen were takin' in this whole scene and thought it was beneath their great leader to be actin' in such a manner, and they let him know it. He smiled and asked them a simple question: "Gentlemen, you're experienced trappers. What would happen if you were to leave a trap in the set position all the time?" They answered him, "It would lose its strength and be of no use to the trapper. Everyone knows that." He smiled, put his hands on their shoulders, and said, "And so it is with us all."'

"John then put his hand on my shoulder."

'Sir, now is a fine time to loosen that spring from your trap.' I laughed inside, thinking he told me to loosen the spring from my mouth.

"John put down his M1 Garand rifle and picked up a stick. 'Ever play the game stick pullin'?'

"I looked at him. 'Stick pulling? Sounds like a game you made up.'

'No, sir, it's an old pioneer game, and I don't often lose, or if you want, we can Indian leg wrestle.'

"John took off his pack and sat down on the ground, his legs stretched out, holding the stick with both hands in front of him. I followed his lead and took off my pack, sat down facing him, knees bent, feet against his. I grabbed the stick he was holding. 'Now what?' I asked.

"John smiled. 'Now we pull. You try to pull me up to my feet, and I'll try to pull you up. That's how come we call it *stick pullin'*. Ready, set, go!'

"Nikki, I gave it all I had. I really thought I'd pull him up without any trouble. I knew I outweighed him and I definitely outranked him. After about ten seconds, John smiled and asked, 'Have you started?'

"And with a burst, I was up on my feet. I couldn't help but smile. 'So that's how it's done,' I told him. 'Now that I know, look out, you're going down.'

"I must have tried to pull him up for a good five, ten minutes, but each time, John stood me on my feet. It was a lot of fun, and by the time we were done, even I was laughing. It felt like the weight of the world had been lifted off my shoulders, at least for a little while. John told me that a little diversion of loosening the spring, so to speak, would come in real handy later in my business life."

"James, when Jimmy gave me a tour of the corporate office, I saw a mural on the wall of the gym with two soldiers holding a stick. That was you and John, wasn't it?" James gave me a wink.

TWO

HALF EMPTY OR HALF FULL?

"John said a lot of things that day that I didn't understand but would come to make sense of later. We walked for a few hours before we stopped again. John looked around and said, 'This looks like a good place to rest up.'

"John put his rifle down, took off his pack, reached in, and pulled out a tin cup and a spoon—the kind we had been issued back in boot camp.

'You'll need these, Sir.'

"I took the spoon and almost without thinking, bent it in the handle so I could hook it to my belt. I covered it with my shirt so light wouldn't reflect off of it and with it on my belt, it was easier to get to, not to mention by doing it this way it wouldn't clang together with the cup in the pack when I walked. John then pulled out a C-ration and put half in his cup and half in mine. Then he took out his canteen, reached over, and gave me half of his water.

'There you go, Sir.'

"As he handed me my canteen, I took it and said a most ungrateful thing; every time I think of it, I shake my head. I actually said, 'Half empty is better than empty.' Can you believe it? Not even a thank you. John looked at me and smiled.

'I like to think of it as half full is better than empty.'

"I was so embarrassed that I didn't say anything. Lifting the canteen, I thought about it and had to admit, half full was a much better way to look at it. I swallowed the water and once again my pride, and I thanked him."

Relax and Focus

"As we ate, I thanked him for helping me get some sleep. That trick had worked, and I asked him where he learned it. He gave me that half smile of his and said, 'That was something my mother taught me one time when I had a bad case of the chicken pox. I was havin' a hard time sleeping, so she taught me that *little trick*, as you put it. Sometimes I picture myself as a block of ice melting in the sun. There are all sorts of mental images you can use.'

"I told John the beach scenario worked great and that I was from California, so I could relate to the waves of the ocean."

"James, when Jimmy showed me the pondering suite, he thought your favorite sound effect was the ocean. So that came from John as well."

"Jimmy told you that, did he?"

"That and more, but please go on."

"John said that little technique always worked for him. It helped him to focus. I told him, 'Relax and focus? Sounds like a contradiction to me.'"

'Not at all, Sir. Think about last night, jus' before you slipped off to sleep. What do you remember?'

"I thought for a moment and then told him I could remember the faintest of smells, and being able to hear the smallest of sounds, as though they were right up against my nose and ears. John looked at me as if I was supposed to figure out what I had said. It took a moment, but I had one of those ah-ha moments that must have been written all over my face. John looked at me and raised his canteen in a toast-like manner.

'That's what I'm talking about, Sir.'

"John took a drink and continued.

'I use that little technique for a couple of things. When I'm fixin' to take a cat nap, or when I have too many things bouncin' around in my head and need to sort things out. It slows my mind down so I can get it all in order. I start my day with it too. I ponder about what I want to get done that day. At the end of the day when I'm ready to go to bed, I go over what I got done and what I didn't do and how to do better on the morrow.'"

Hansen's Just Not Sure

"I asked him, 'Why the routine?'

"He said, 'Sir, may I ask you a personal question?'

'Go ahead.'

'Sir, are you a God-fearin' man?'

"John caught me off guard. 'Can't say that I am,' I told him. He looked genuinely surprised."

'Really? Even when you were coming in for a crash landing, you didn't call on God for some help? Or when you were looking for a clearing to land your plane, spotting one up ahead, you didn't ask God for some help? A little headwind perhaps, to keep your bird up jus' a little longer?

'Or when you came over the top of them trees and touched ground, snapping the saplings like a lawn mower cutting grass, bouncing up and down as the wheels hit every mound of dirt pushed up by the critters that made their homes in the ground?

'Or as you were watching the larger trees at the end of your makeshift landing strip getting closer and closer, you didn't think to yourself, *Please, God, no?* Or when your left wing hit one—breaking it off, spinning you around like a top, until it came to a stop, you didn't toss out a *Thank you, Jesus?'*

"I looked at him. 'Yes, but that's different.'"

"James, wait a minute, how on earth did he know all that?"

"Nikki, I asked John that very question. Smiling, he looked like the cat that swallowed the canary.

'Your wingman followed you down, and as soon as he got into friendly airspace, he reported where you went down.' That's when John told me, 'I'm part of a special search-and-return-home team. We found where you landed and saw your plane with a busted-up wing. With your wingman's report and my tracking ability, I could read the signs, and the rest was easy to put together.'

"I thought for a moment about John's question, 'If I were a God-fearing man . . .'– in all seriousness I looked at John. I remember telling him, 'Before the war, I thought I was religious. At least as a kid I would go to church on Christmas and Easter with my parents. As a teenager, I'd go to different churches with whatever girl I was interested in at the time, but I found myself getting more confused than anything. I told him I didn't think religion should be so hard to understand. After all, we're talking about one God with one Bible, but for me, everything seemed to be conflicting—and I mean everything, from what God looks like to how many gods there are, and whether to be baptized.

"Some say if Jesus was baptized, then we all need to be, or we'll go to a lake of fire and brimstone, never consumed, just burning for eternity. Others would say you don't need to be baptized. Just look at the thief on the cross; all he needed to do was acknowledge that Jesus was the Christ and he would be with Jesus in paradise. Even those who believe in baptism can't agree on the 'how to' from the age to the method. Some sprinkle water while others pour a pitcher of water over you, while still others dunk you completely underwater.

"Churches may disagree one with the other, saying that theirs is the true church and bad-mouthing the others. And then there are other religions that say Christ hasn't come to earth yet, or that there was a man called Jesus, but he wasn't the Messiah. What's a guy supposed to believe?' I could see John take a deep breath and let it out.

"John looked at me, 'I know what you're talking about, Sir. Those kinds of questions have been around since the beginning of time. Back in AD 325, Constantine called a council of Catholic bishops to meet at Nicaea. All the religious disagreements were causing some pretty severe political problems, and he wanted them resolved once and for all. The argument was that Jesus Christ was the highest created being, but He wasn't divine, so the Nicene Creed was adopted saying that God, Jesus, and the Holy Spirit were one and would be known as the "Trinity."

'I know what the answers are for me and why it's so important to have a spiritual foundation to build upon. I also know atheists and agnostics whom I trust because they have a moral foundation and believe honesty is the best policy. I'll gladly share with you what I have found to be true, but don't take my word on it, or anyone else's, for that matter. Your journey in life is to find out for yourself.'

"I told John, 'I'm not so sure about churches. I've talked to people who left their church because someone offended them or hurt their feelings. Why would anyone at a church do that?' It seemed like John had a story for every question I had.

"John looked at me. 'I once knew a great man who said, "Sooner or later, you'll be offended at church. If not, you're not going enough." That may have been paraphrased, but you get the idea.'

"I smiled and nodded my head. John added, 'Church isn't for perfect people. It's a hospital for sinners. If we had to be perfect, there wouldn't be anybody sittin' in the pews on Sunday. Last time I checked, none of them could walk on water. Sir, sometimes even people we work with can offend us. Maybe we could jus' give them the benefit of the doubt that they didn't mean to offend or hurt our feelings. Maybe it'd be good to ask ourselves if we did anything that could have caused them to act that way, and if so, we ought to be the ones to apologize.

"I have to tell you, Nikki, I really didn't like hearing that. When someone says or does something that offends me, I need to stop and think if I had done something that could have caused them to act that way. I thought about it and could see how it could be true.

"I sat and thought for a moment, then asked, 'If there is a God, with all the evil things that I've seen in this war, why doesn't He come down and put a stop to all this madness?'

"I went on for about ten minutes with questions like these, but John didn't say anything. He listened and let me vent. Then John put my mind at ease like only he could do. He put his hand on my shoulder once again, looked me right in the eye, and spoke."

'Sir, there is one thing I know, and it's this. God lives. His ways aren't our ways. We have to have faith, He knows what He's doin'. After all, He is God. Jus' know this: He loves you, and He has a plan, even if you can't see it right now. He hears and answers prayers. He doesn't always tell us what we want to hear, or as quickly as we'd like, but He always answers. It's our job to open our heart to hear what He has to say.'

"John said it with such conviction that all I could say was, 'I hope you're right. I wish I could have that kind of assurance.'"

'You can, Sir, jus' have a little faith.' We gathered up our things and continued on. We walked in silence for the rest of the day, as John let me ponder what he had said.

"The next time we came to a stop it was for the night. John reached into his backpack and took out another C-ration. There was a stream nearby, so we filled our canteens and sat down to eat. John started to build a small fire, and I became—to say the least—*a little worried*. 'Aren't you afraid we'll be seen with a fire?'

'No, Sir, building a small fire at dusk will be fine. It's jus' light enough so the flames won't be seen, and by putting it up against this tree, the smoke, what little there will be with this here dried wood—well, Sir, it's dark enough that once it goes through the branches, it'll break up so it won't be seen. Jus' make sure when you build a fire there aren't any rocks around to reflect what little light there is off them. Also, never look into the flames; it makes it so you can't see very well if in an emergency you have to look into the darkness. Besides, I'm fixin' to put it out jus' as soon as we heat up some water. The hot food will help us keep warm during the night.'"

THREE

HANSEN LEARNS ABOUT THE FOUR

"I noticed John always paused before eating each of his meals, but I said nothing. While we ate, I asked him about his team and how big it was.

"He told me four—himself, Hart, TJ, and Richman; they were put together because of their unique skills. John was the tracker—I think he could track a snake over a flat rock. After they came across my plane, they followed my tracks and the tracks of those who were hunting me down. They could see where the Germans caught up to me and where I put up quite a fight. I told John, 'It took ten Germans to bring me down. If there had been only nine, I would have made it.' John almost laughed so loud he could have given our position away. Good thing he had swallowed his last bite; otherwise, he probably would have spit it out all over me. Once he stopped laughing, he said, 'That's funny; the tracks we were following showed three Germans and one dog.'

"Okay, I may have embellished a little, I admitted. John speculated that there were a few possible places they could have taken me, so they split up in pairs. Whichever team found me first, one person would stay and help me, while the other one would get on back and tell the others. From there, they would split up and go to their assigned rendezvous places. By traveling in a small group, there would be less chance of being seen.

"When I asked John if he had a map, he gave me one of those 'you've got to be kidding' kind of looks. 'Of course, Sir, if you want to get someplace you've never been, get a map or find a mentor, someone who's been there to show you the way. Jus' make sure you have the right map or mentor.'"

"That was the saying Jimmy told me before he showed me the map room back at the corporate office."

"Yes, my dear, that too came from John. After we ate and cleaned up, I asked to see the map. John took it out of his right front pocket and laid it out. It was too dark by this time to see anything, so we took the one blanket and draped it over us to block the light from John's flashlight. I held the flashlight, which had a red lens—less likely to be seen, and it's easier on the eyes to adjust to the darkness after you turn it off. John used his Ka-Bar as a pointer."

"What's a Ka-Bar?"

"Sorry, in the military we use terms and acronyms so much I forget not everyone knows what they mean. A Ka-Bar is a single-bladed type of knife."

"I feel like I should have known that. The next time I see Grandpa Vince, I'm going to ask why he never taught me that one."

James continued, "The map showed four prison camps they thought I might be in. John and TJ took two, and the other team took the other two. I could see an X through one of the camps. John and TJ waited at that camp for over a week looking for me. They would take turns and climb a tree at the edge of the clearing before dawn and stay there all day looking through binoculars trying to spot me from all the other prisoners. Once they determined I wasn't in that camp, they went to the next one.

"Good thing they left when they did, because as they got to a vantage point to overlook the camp, I was being led out through the gates into the woods. They were on a large hill that the commandant and the guard led me around to the barn. Through the binoculars, they could see everything. As soon as it was safe, TJ left to report to the other team, and John headed down to the barn, but of course, I was no longer there.

"John looked at me. 'Sir, I've been meaning to ask you something. When I got to the barn, I thought for sure I was going to find you dead inside, and my mission was going to turn into a recovery of the body. When I saw the back door open, I couldn't believe it. What was inside, and how did you get out?'

"Nikki, I looked at John and told him all my fears were inside—the fears of my imagination. John nodded and smiled, giving my leg a tap. 'I'll bet that's a lesson you'll keep for the rest of your life.'

"John turned his attention to the map, pointing to where known enemy troops were, and showed me the route we'd be taking. John estimated it would take about four months. When I started to complain about how long it was going to take, he chuckled. 'Jus' be glad we're not going the same route Moses took. That route went on for forty years.'"

Have Faith and Hope

"After we turned off the light, I asked John, 'Why me? Why was I so important to go through all that trouble? I was one of thousands.' John folded up the map, put it back in his pocket, and explained, 'God only knows, Sir; I get my orders and follow them.'

"I didn't know either, but I was grateful for the company and the help. I'd been thinking what he said about faith and asked him, 'What the heck is faith, anyway?' He got a look on his face as if to say, 'I was wondering when you'd ask.'

'Well, Sir,' John said, 'it's like it says in the Bible. To put it quite simply, faith is something that you hope for, but jus' can't see.'

"I must have had a puzzled look on my face. John looked at me and said, 'I can give you a perfect example. When you had the choice between the barn or the wall, why did you pick the barn?'

"Before I could answer, John added, 'You had faith and hope that somethin' in that barn would be better than certain death. Deep down inside, you hoped for freedom, but you couldn't see it, right?'

"John could see I was thinking it over when he continued, 'You, Sir, put your faith to the test. You had the courage to go through the doors. All the others let fear stop them. Satan uses fear to stop us from many things. God uses faith. I believe there are two kinds of fear; one is good, it keeps us safe, and the other keeps us from bein' great.

'Faith and fear can't be in the same room. It's like when Jesus was walkin' on water in the middle of a storm. His disciples had gone before him in the boat when they saw Jesus comin' toward them. They thought it was a spirit. Needless to say, they didn't know what to make of it, and they were scared to death.

'When Jesus called out telling them not to be afraid, Peter wanted to walk on the water too. I wonder what must have been going through the other disciples' minds when Jesus told Peter to come. Peter, he put one leg over, and then the other, and he also started to walk on the water.

'Can you imagine the faith Peter must have had to do that? He was doing fine as long as he kept his eyes on Jesus, but as soon as he took his eyes off him and looked at the storm, Peter started to sink. When Peter took his eyes off the goal, to be with Jesus, Peter let fear in, and faith left.

'Peter called out for help; Jesus reached down and pulled him up. I always smile when I think of what Jesus told him: "O, thou of little faith, wherefore didst thou doubt?" Peter had a whole lot more faith than I could ever muster up. Yes, Sir, I believe if you keep your eye on the goal and it's righteous, with God's help, you can achieve it.'

"I told John that I'd heard that story before, but I never thought of it like that, so I asked where I could find it. He told me it's in the book of Matthew in the fourteenth chapter, toward the end.

"Nikki, my dear, do you remember what I told you about F.E.A.R?"

"Of course, the 'E' can stand for several things. False Evidence Appearing Real. As a reporter, I can't tell you how many times I see this. Another is False Emotions Appearing Real. I'll never forget my first interview. I let my emotions get the better of me. I had no evidence that the person I was going to ask for an interview was going to treat me badly and rudely, yet I let my mind take me there. It took me hours to get up the courage to make that phone call, and when I was done, even though I didn't get the interview, it wasn't nearly as bad as I had made it in my mind. Another thing you said the 'E' could stand for was 'environment.'"

James smiled, "You remembered. Humans, for the most part, are social creatures. We socialize with others to feel like we are a part of a group or community. Sadly, many put too much time and energy into wondering and worrying what others are thinking about them, when all the time, they are thinking the same thing about how everyone is judging them. Quite ironic, don't you think?"

"I told my grandfather about what you taught me, and he reminded me how he taught the same principle when I was growing up. He used to say, 'You show me your friends and I'll show you your future.' That was his way of saying that if you don't have good friends who support you in doing good, then get new friends."

"Your grandfather is a wise man."

"I like to think so." A thought came to mind. *"James, did you get that F.E.A.R. advice from John?"*

James smiled, "It has his name written all over it, doesn't it? John also told me something I have remembered from that time on: 'Sir, you can make up any word you want for each letter, but for me, the F always stands for False.'

"Nikki, John told me that out of all the different words and meanings you can assign to each letter, the one I express to my family the most is 'False Emotions Appearing Real.' Satan wants false things to appear real. He does not want you or any of God's children doing the right thing."

He paused to let that sink in. "Something else John told me: 'That old serpent, the devil, has many tools in his arsenal, all very effective. Discouragement, self-doubt, anger, hatred, and jealousy—the list is longer than your arm. The one I think he likes best is fear. Fear can stop us from doing so many things that could lead to greatness.'

"Nikki, I like to have what I call "Personal Interviews" with my children and grandchildren. A week before their birthday, we make a day of it. Whatever they want to do, we do. Rock climbing, long bike rides—it doesn't matter, as long as we can do it together. At the end of the day, we go to dinner and then come home to this very office. Here I share a little more about what happened in Germany as I was being led to safety. In these interviews, I have the opportunity to find out what's on the children's minds and what's going on in their lives.

"When, and *only* when I felt they were old enough and mature enough, I would give them the final part of the Hansen family secret, which I'm giving you.

"My dear, by the time we are through you'll be given the final part of the Hansen family secret to share with all, but only after I'm gone."

I was so intrigued I almost asked what it was, but I quickly caught myself. If Mr. Hansen had been waiting all these years, I could wait for a few months as he prepared me.

James continued. "When I have these interviews, especially with the boys when they're getting to the age where the opposite sex is starting to stir up the emotions, I remind them of False Emotions Appearing Real, and what they think is love is most likely lust. That's one of Satan's favorites, stirring up false emotions.

"Nikki, John went on to tell me that fear is real, at least to the person who's experiencing it. They may be afraid of the monster under the bed that's not real, but to them, it is. They have to muster up the faith and courage to look and find the truth for themselves."

"James, you also told me that sometimes fear is real, and you need to take action."

"Yes, I did. Let me go a little deeper. The feeling of fear and a warning can be confusing."

Talk about confusing; it must have been written all over my face.

"Let me try it this way." He paused for a moment. "You've had a feeling like a knot in your stomach telling you that you shouldn't be in a certain place or you shouldn't be doing what you were doing, right?"

"Of course."

"Nikki, we all have that feeling, or what some call *fear*, what John labeled as a *warning call* from the Spirit of God to the Spirit inside us all. When we listen to that heeding, we become more and more sensitive to its messages. Sadly, too many ignore those messages because of peer pressure. They push them aside until they can no longer feel those messages."

I was starting to understand that James was giving me a piece of his puzzle. I was excited. I felt like a little girl going on a treasure hunt, finding the pieces of the family secret.

FOUR

FAITH IS LIKE A SEED

"One night, John wanted to teach me a little more about faith. We finished our dinner and cleaned up when he asked me if I had any farming experience. I looked at him and said, 'Not unless it could be done on the back of a surfboard.' I think he liked that one.

"He said, 'Faith takes time, like when a farmer plants a seed in the ground. Does he put that seed on jus' any kind of dirt? No, of course not, he puts it in soil that he's prepared. Does he come back the next day to harvest what he planted? Heck no, it takes time and effort. Faith works a lot like that. Plant the seed of faith, and with your effort, and God's help, it'll grow. You jus' have to do your part.'

"That reminded John of a sermon he once heard about two men who thought they would put the faith of a mustard seed to the test and move a mountain. I, of course, didn't have a clue as to what he meant by that and told him so. John reached into his pocket and pulled out his Bible. He turned to Matthew 17:20 and told me that a mustard seed is about the size of the head of a pin, and Jesus taught if you have faith as the size of a grain of that mustard seed you'd be able to move mountains. So that night each man looked at the mountain and said, 'In the morning, that mountain will be gone.' When the first guy woke up, he opened his curtains and saw the mountain still there and said, 'I knew it'd still be there.' The other man woke up, saw that the mountain was still there, so he went and got a bulldozer, and moved it himself.'

"I told John that to me, neither one had faith, but John saw it another way.

'Well, Sir, the moral of the story is this: God lets us figure things out for ourselves to accomplish what we want and need. Where one man wanted God to do all the work, the other man went to work. God gave us a brain to come up with ideas, to bounce them around in that thick head of ours, and then to take them to the Lord to see if what we came up with is the right thing to do. If it's a good idea, He'll let us know by the way we feel; it'll jus' feel right. God gives us the tools and opportunities, but it's our job to put into action the gifts he gave us.'

"John paused and picked up his gun. 'I'll take the first watch and let you ponder on it. Get some shut-eye, Sir. I'll wake you when it's your shift.'"

Too Close For Comfort

"I laid down, making myself as comfortable as possible. John had given me a lot to think about. As I lay there, I could hear the babbling stream next to me. It reminded me of the times my father and I would go hiking in the woods, fishing the streams. It wasn't long before I was fast asleep.

"A few hours later, I awoke and took John's place and let him get a few hours of shut-eye. As the sun was coming up, I woke John up with my hand over his mouth. A troop of Germans was coming up fast! I can admit it now, I was scared. I'd been in a prison camp and I sure as heck didn't want to go back. John, on the other hand, was as cool as the other side of a pillow. He looked at the situation, saw a small gap in their formation, and we crouch-walked as fast as we could, about fifteen feet into a large bush, and covered ourselves with the green blanket.

"John whispered, 'Have a little faith and we'll be fine.' He then gave a quick prayer that we would be safe and that they might pass without seeing us. John no sooner said Amen when we could hear them coming from both sides. I could see John slowly take off the safety from the M1. They sounded like a herd of buffalo trampling through the woods, and they came so close we could hear them breathing. Slowly, the sound of their boots faded off in the distance.

"They didn't see us. We waited for a long time after they were out of earshot in case there were stragglers. We slowly climbed out of our hiding place and looked to see if there were any more coming up from the rear. The coast was clear, and John hit his knees and gave a prayer of thanks. I didn't know if it was an answer to prayer or not; I did know I was glad to be alive and safe for the time being."

A Lesson in Fasting

"I started to fold up the blanket and stuff it in the backpack. 'Let's get out of here.' John took out his map and studied it.

'That troop must have come from here, and here's the direction they were headed. We need to divert and go around them.'

'Fine, as long as we get going.'

John shook his head, 'No, Sir, we're stayin' put, and I'll give you two good reasons: It's best if we let those guys get a day ahead of us; maybe what caused that troop to go by so fast is the possibility the Allies are pushing them this way, and if we wait, they could come to us. And the second reason, which I think is the best reason of all, is that today is Sunday, and Sunday is a day of rest. We pushed ourselves pretty hard yesterday. We're safe here and we need the rest.'

"I wanted to keep going. I knew I outranked him and could have ordered him to keep going, but I knew John really was the one in charge. Somewhere in the back of my mind, I remembered what John said: He would get me home if I did what he told me.

"I reluctantly agreed, and we went back to the tree where we were. 'Well, if we're not leaving, at least we can eat.' John reached into his pack and handed me a C-ration.

'You can have my portion, Sir. I'm not eating today.'

'Why not? Are you sick?' I asked him.

'No, Sir. Today is the first Sunday of the month and my family always fasts on the first Sunday. I know they're fasting and praying for me. It's a way we can be close. Not only to my family, but to God.'"

My first Sunday with the Hansen family had been on the first Sunday of the month. James could tell by the smile on my face that I had discovered another piece of the family secret. *"So that's why your family fasts on the first Sunday of the month."*

He gently nodded, then continued. "I, of course, didn't have the foggiest idea what he was talking about. 'Fast?' I asked. 'We're not even going slowly, we're stopped.' John shook his head in disbelief.

'Fasting is going without food for a few meals. Back home, Mom and Dad would take us kids to the part of town where the down-and-out were and the meals that we would have eaten. We made them into sack lunches and gave them to the needy.' John chuckled as he looked around, 'Sir, it looks like you're the only one around, and you look like you need it.'

"I took the C-ration and opened it, telling him, 'Far be it from me to break a family tradition.'

"That day, we spent getting to know one another better—where we were from, what our families were like, and of course, who our favorite baseball team was. If a prisoner came into camp and didn't know the names and stats of his favorite baseball team, we figured he was a German spy, and no one would trust him. Our close second favorite thing we liked to talk about, of course, were the girlfriends who broke our hearts and the ones that didn't get away. I could talk about Karen for hours on end. I did get around to asking John why he was fasting and why on the first Sunday.

"John looked at me. 'Several reasons, Sir. It doesn't have to be the first Sunday, any day will do. Dad found the first Sunday's jus' easier to remember, is all. Fasting for me helps keep me humble. If ever you start to think you're the center of the universe and the world revolves around you, try walking on water or jus' go without food for a while and you'll see jus' how almighty you are.

'Everything I have I feel was given to me by God, even the stuff I take for granted, like the air I breathe, so going without food for a few meals and giving it to someone else helps remind me who's really in charge; it keeps me grounded, so to speak. The scriptures talk about prayer and fasting when someone's sick or afflicted. Back home, if we found out that a loved one was sick or in need of emotional help, we'd fast and pray together for that person.'

"I shook my head. 'I don't understand—why a group?'

'Think of it like this: if you have a battery that doesn't have enough power to start your car, you use another to jump start it, right?'

'I'm with you so far.'

'And let's say that battery doesn't have enough power either, so the more batteries you can hook up, the more power you get. Fasting kind of works like that: a group of people, all with the same goal, asking God for help.'

'So, since there isn't a group, why do it now?'

"John smiled, 'You don't have to have a group; you can also fast by yourself. If you want an answer to prayers, or jus' get closer to God, it helps focus your mind and spirit on being open to getting answers. I guess you could say that it shows God you're willing to sacrifice a little for his help.'

"Nikki, I may have been out of line, but I asked him what he was fasting for that day. John looked at me, and I'll never forget what he said.

'I'm asking the Good Lord to get you home safely.'

"I didn't know what to say, so I smiled and nodded. John took out his pocket Bible and started to read to himself."

FIVE

ANOTHER KIND OF MAP

"After a while, I asked John, 'I've noticed you like to read the Bible whenever you get a chance. How come?'

"He put down his Bible. 'Sir, do you remember what I said about maps?'

"I nodded. 'Well, Sir, the Bible is like a map to me. Life is short. If I die as a young man on the battlefield, or as an old man in my bed, I want to get back home to my Heavenly Father, and the scriptures are like a road map. As long as I follow the right path, I'll return with honor. There isn't anything I want to hear more than, "Well done, thou good and faithful servant: thou hast been faithful over a few things. I will make thee ruler over many things; enter thou into the joy of the Lord." That's in Matthew 25:23.'"

I wanted to interrupt James but didn't. I couldn't believe it, another piece of the puzzle. The plaque in James's kitchen, next to the door that led out into the garage which read, "Return With Honor" had John written all over it. James continued.

"John told me he loved to read the stories of what happens to the people of each time period, how they would be blessed when they kept the commandments, and a whole passel of trouble they would get into when they didn't. He often wondered if archaeologists would ever find more scriptures. I had to stop him right there.

The Lost Ten Tribes

"'I know I don't know much about the Bible,' I told him. 'But I *do* remember one of the preachers talking about in Revelation how it says there won't be any more scriptures.' John nodded.

'I know that scripture in Revelations. It means don't add on to or change what was said. If you took that literally, you'd have to go to Deuteronomy 4:2, and everything after that would have to be taken out because it says the same thing there. Not only that, the New Testament wasn't put in chronological order, and Revelation wasn't the last book written, so any scriptures in the New Testament that came after Revelations would also have to be removed.' After a few minutes, he asked. 'Have you heard of the Lost Ten Tribes of Israel?'

'I may not know much about the Bible, but I had heard of the Lost Ten Tribes.' John smiled, and then he gave me something to think about.

'I can't help but think, if God led them away, he'd have a prophet to lead them—keepin' them on the straight and narrow like he did with Moses and all the other prophets. I'm sure they would have kept a record of what they went through, after all, that's how we got the Bible. It jus' makes sense to me that one of these days someone will find some old scrolls, or clay tablets with writing like they never saw before, and have it translated by some professor, and we get to find out what happened to the Lost Ten Tribes. Jus' because we don't know what happened to them doesn't mean God lost track of 'em.'

"John opened his Bible to John 10:16. 'Sir, this is what Jesus told his disciples after he was resurrected: *And other sheep I have that are not of this fold: them also must I bring, and they shall hear my voice; and there shall be one fold, and one shepherd.* I always thought He was referring to the Lost Ten Tribes, and when that day comes—whatever is written on scrolls, or clay, or whatever, it makes no difference to me—it will fit like a glove with the Holy Bible. Figurin' that God being the author and all, at least it makes perfect sense to me.'

A Lesson in Prayer

"I sat thinking about it while John went back to his reading. After a while I asked, 'You never did tell me why the routine of that morning and night thing.' He looked confused.

'That morning and night thing?' It took a second to sink in. 'Sure, I know what you're talkin' about. A routine helps me to keep myself on track, or you might say helps me develop a habit. There are lots of scriptures that tell us we ought to pray, you know, ask, knock, seek, and ponder—that kind of thing.'"

"James, is that why you like to use the word ponder?"

"Do I?" James said, kind of surprised-like. I smiled and nodded. "I suppose I could say, *I'll think about it,* but *pondering* to me is much deeper."

"I'm sorry I interrupted you. You were about to tell me about John's routine and prayer."

"That's right, John said, 'I like to start off my day with a morning prayer. So, I gather my thoughts, ponder over them, and lay out a plan for what I want to get done. Then I ask for help that I might notice the opportunities I come across. At the end of the day, I go over all that happened, what I was able to get done, what didn't get done, and things I could'a done better at. I ask for forgiveness for my shortcomings. Seems like I spend a lot of time on that one. But mostly, I'm grateful to God for all the blessings that were given to me that day.'

"Nikki, I couldn't help myself. Once again, I put my foot in my mouth. 'Blessings?' I said. 'What kind of blessings? We're stuck over here in Germany with the enemy all around trying to kill us!'

"John smiled. 'Yeah, those blessings. We're in Germany, a place I've never been before and I doubt I'll ever see again, and the enemy that hasn't caught us. Heck yeah, blessings!'

"I looked at him like he was crazy and then smiled, 'Is this one of those cup half-full things?'

"John smiled back and continued. 'Before I talk to God, I need to be in the right frame of mind.'

"Then John taught me something I had never really thought of before. 'Think of your brain as a car with gears. If you drove around in first gear all day, never taking it out of first gear, what would happen?'

'The RPMs would have to increase to have any speed, and you'd wear the engine out before its time.'

"John nodded. 'Right you are, Sir. That's why I had you stop and we played stick pullin'. I was putting you in a different gear, so to speak. I was afraid if you were wound any tighter your brain would blow a gasket and we'd have to spend the rest of the day looking for all them springs in the blades of grass.'

"I sure laughed at that one. 'There are lots of benefits to putting yourself in different gears that you'll learn along this journey. Jus' like putting your car in a different gear so you can go faster with less effort, so it is with our brain.'

"John looked at me. 'Do you remember what it was like when you were coming in for that crash landing and what you were experiencing? That was your brain in first gear with the RPMs going through the roof. Can you imagine being in that gear all day? You wouldn't last long, that's for sure. So sometimes we jus' need to slow down and listen.'

"I didn't understand. 'Listen for what, the sounds of the night?'

'If that's what you want to focus on, then yes, but if you're prayin' to God, then you need to listen to the thoughts that come to your mind. In order for us to be able to communicate with our Heavenly Father, we need to be in a different frame of mind, or in a different gear. We need to slow it down. That's where I find using that technique I showed you helps me to collect my thoughts and ponder on what I want to pray about. When I'm in this slower gear, I find I get deeper learning and understanding. That night while you were concentratin' on your breathin', did your mind wander?'

'Did it wander? I wouldn't call it wandering; I'd call it more like a two-year-old running all over the place.'

"Nikki, I loved it when I could make John laugh, and he got a chuckle out of that one. 'I knew it did, Sir. To be able to keep your mind focused for a period of time takes practice. Everyone, and I do mean everyone, has a hard time focusing at first. Think of your brain as a muscle that needs to be exercised. Let me ask you this: When you first went into boot camp, do you remember what everyone looked like? Some were physically fit with toned muscles, while others not so much. Some had a hard time finishing the obstacle course, while with others it was like a playground, and they breezed right through it. For others, it took a little longer than most, and some washed out altogether. Those that stuck with it eventually got fit. Our brain works the same way: with practice it gets easier to stay focused.'"

The Brain Has Two Parts

"I told John, 'This pondering thing sounds a lot like meditation.'

'Some might call it that, Sir; but some meditations teach you not to pray; you don't need to call on a higher power. Jus' meditate and empty your mind. Pondering for me is filling my mind: I believe God wants us to learn and grow and to ask Him for help.

'Did you know our brain has two parts? The conscious and the non-conscious. The conscious is the part that has filters and is aware of our surroundings. It filters and questions every thought we have. That's the part of the brain that questions whether or not there is a God. Our Heavenly Father put it there for a reason. He wants us to work for it, to learn. He wants us to find all the pieces of the puzzle we can in this life and put those together the best we can. Sometimes, the pieces fit easily and make sense. Other times, they jus' don't. Jus' because you can't find where a piece fits, you don't throw that piece away. You jus' put it aside until it does fit. You might ask yourself, what if it never does fit? Well, in that case, no harm, no foul.'

"John chuckled. 'Maybe someone put that piece in from a different puzzle jus' to throw you off.' Then he added, 'The conscious part of the brain doesn't shut down until we go to sleep.

'Now the non-conscious or subconscious of the brain never shuts down. It's working 24/7 and it has no filters. It lets everything in. Ever go to bed with something on your mind that you needed a solution for and wake up in the middle of the night with a great idea to fix the problem?'

"I found myself nodding my head as I said, 'Sometimes.' John smiled and let it sink in."

Write It Down

"John told me, 'That was your subconscious mind that you put to work on the problem. Was it such a simple solution to the problem that you jus' knew you'd remember it in the morning, but when morning came you couldn't remember it to save your life?'

I nodded.

'May I suggest you keep a notepad by your side so when you wake up in the middle of the night you can jot it down? I'll bet you didn't know Thomas Edison would put himself in a light sleep jus' so ideas would come to him?'

"Nikki, I never knew that. Did you?"

I couldn't help myself and answered with a Southern drawl, *"Can't says I did."* Just as James liked to make John smile, I enjoyed making James smile as well. He continued.

"There was something I noticed while we were walking during the day. From time to time, John would take a notepad from his pocket and write something down. I asked him at that time if he was writing down the thoughts that came to him.

'Not jus' thoughts, but things that happened that I wanted to remember.

'Back home,' he said, 'I have a journal that I would take the short notes from and in more detail put them in that. Then, if it's a problem I'm working on, I ponder about it. I find doing this also helps me slow down the RPMs, so to speak, before I pray. Think of it like this: when you wanted to communicate with another pilot, you tuned your radio to a certain frequency, right?'

"I nodded.

'So when we want to talk to our Heavenly Father, we need to tune our minds to the right frequency or vibration so we can hear not with our ears, but with our heart and mind.'"

SIX

HANSEN LEARNS TO PRAY

"Nikki, I sat there thinking it over and it made sense, but there was something I needed to know. When I went to all those different churches, they all prayed a little differently. Even John prayed like I'd never heard. It was as best as I could describe it: Older English, and I asked him if he was a Quaker or Amish. John smiled.

'Good people both, but I'm not one of them. My mother loves the King James Bible, and she taught me to pray using Thee, Thy, and Thou.' Then he added, 'I had a buddy back in boot camp who is Jewish, and if you think I pray different, his prayers are in Hebrew. Jewish prayers are beautiful songs, sung to God. He taught me what some of the movements are and what they mean. Some of the movements help the person to meditate.'

"Nikki, I learned that John felt that by using such English words, it showed respect. It wasn't the Thee, Thy, and Thou that was different, it was also the way he started his prayers. Once again, it was his mother who taught him to pray in the same manner that Jesus taught in Matthew. John took out his Bible and turned to the Lord's Prayer. John told me to look at it as an outline. I never thought about it like that, but it made sense; after all, Jesus was a teacher of men.

Then John taught me the outline in the Lord's Prayer. He sat next to me, pointing to the verse, and said,

'Jesus tells us to call on God by addressing Him as Father in Heaven, and then thank him for the blessings He's given us. Next, we need to ask for forgiveness for our shortcomings as we forgive those who have wronged us. Then we ask God for the things we need. After all, He did say, *Ask and Ye shall receive.'*

"Then John lets me know he closes his prayer in the name of Jesus because of His Atonement.

"Nikki, at that time I didn't know. I told John it seemed like every time I prayed there was never an answer. You should have heard John's incredulous tone. 'Really? Never? You don't think the fact that you walked away from a crash landing without a scratch wasn't an answer to a prayer?'

"All I could say was, 'I guess so.' He looked at me like I was from Mars. Then, with a little pride in my voice I said, 'Or maybe it was my flying skills. I am a pretty good pilot.' John had a way of humbling a guy.

"He looked at me and said, 'Forgive me for saying, Sir, but you're not that good of a pilot. You do remember being shot down. You had help landing that plane, whether you want to admit it or not. I think God has a plan for you, and He's not done with you yet.'

"What do you say after that? I sat there and had to admit he might be right. I didn't know what is and isn't an answer to a prayer. I asked him, 'How do I know?'

"John thought for a moment, and then he shared a story with me. 'I once heard of a man who demanded God to answer him and show himself in the form of a light so he would know, and he got his answer.'

'Really? What happened?' I asked.

'He got struck by lightning and got killed, deader than a doornail.'

"I almost bought it, but John couldn't keep a straight face. 'Yeah, that was a story I jus' made up. But it does have a moral to it. Never, and I mean never, demand God to do anything. You jus' might not like the answer.'

Answers to Prayers

"I had to agree and asked, 'But short of being struck by lightning, how do you know?'

"John said, 'Answers to prayers come in many ways. Think about it this way: When you come into a dark room and flip on the light switch, you get an immediate response, right? Sometimes answers to prayers are like that, like when you came in for a crash landing.

'But mostly it's like the beginning of a new day, where the light is so faint you can barely make out the horizon. There is no immediate light, like when you flipped on the light switch, but a gradual increase until the sun comes up over the horizon, giving full light.' John looked at me and asked, 'Were you ever in need of something and someone came along and helped you?' I nodded.

'You might not think that was an answer to your prayer, but it was. I think most of our prayers come through others. I also think sometimes we are the answer to someone else's prayers, by helping them.'

"I smiled, and in a drawl, replied. 'I'll have ta' give that some ponderin'.' John, being the good sport that he was, smiled back.

'My mama has a saying she taught me. If you want answers to prayers, first wear a hole in the knees of your pants, and then wear a hole in the soles of your shoes.'

"Unsure of what John meant, I must have had a look on my face that told him.

'Here's another way of looking at it, Sir. Many times, answers to our prayers don't come while we're on our knees, but while we're on our feet, serving the Lord by serving those around us. There's nothing wrong with serving others. After all, didn't Jesus humble himself to serve his disciples when he washed their feet?'

"John went on to say, 'For those who haven't found God yet, but believe in a higher power than themselves, they might call it the power of the Universe, or infinite intelligence, some unknown. When they need or want something, they put that thought or prayer out into the Universe. Make no mistake about it, when anyone receives anything in this world, it's from God. When we ask for guidance, God wants us to work for it, and by that I mean—'

"John paused. I think he was looking for a way that I could grasp it. 'Let's suppose you have a dilemma and you need help. God wants you to work things out in your mind by first gathering all the information you can. Weigh out the pros and cons. Ponder over it and come up with what you think is the best solution. Then ask God if you're right. If you're right, you'll know by the way you feel, and if you're wrong, you'll have a—'

"I could see John was searching for the right word that I would understand.

'Sir, best I can describe it would be a fog or confusion or stupor of thought. Things won't be as clear, and you'll jus' have to go back to the drawing board and keep at it until it feels right in your heart and mind.'

"Nikki, I got to the point where I loved the way John talked and explained things. I asked him, 'So am I supposed to ask God about everything?'

'Heck no, there are some things that you jus' shouldn't trouble God with. There's this lady back home who asked what to do for everything, from what shoes to wear, to whether or not to have tomatoes on her sandwich. The good Lord gave you a brain, for Pete's sake. Some things you should jus' figure out on your own.'"

A Still Small Voice

"Then John asked me a question. 'When you were facing the barn, what made you decide to go through the door?' I had to think about that one. I told him it was something in my gut that felt right. John looked at me.

'Some call it a gut feeling; others call it the Spirit talking to your spirit. I like the way the prophet Elijah refers to it as a "still small voice."

"I remember telling John, 'I didn't hear anything. It was only a feeling.' He pointed his finger at me.

'Precisely! Have you ever been in a situation when all at once you had an impression to stop, and for no good reason you stopped, only to barely miss what could have been a major catastrophe?'

"Let me tell you, Nikki, my eyes were wide open, and I nodded. 'Sir, that was the Spirit talking to your spirit.'"

When James told me that, I had to interrupt. *"Oh my gosh! Last week I was driving on the freeway when I got a strong impression to move over into the next lane, and not a moment too soon, because the truck in front of me lost part of his load and I could have been seriously hurt or even killed."*

James told me how grateful he was that I had obeyed that warning.

"Nikki, that was the first time I ever heard of that process. I told him I thought that when God spoke, it's in a voice of thunder, or when He shows himself, you know, like in the Bible stories, a burning bush and all that.

"John waved his hand like he was swatting a gnat. 'Nah, where's the faith in that? When God does appear to man, it's always been to His prophets or those He's fixing to call as His prophet. For them, they no longer have faith, but a sure knowledge. Whenever God shows himself like He did to Moses or speaks to a young boy like Samuel, there's always a reason.'

"I told John that may have been in ancient times, but not anymore. He had a comeback for everything I could throw out. John looked at me incredulously. 'Why? Did God lose His power? Or maybe He jus' doesn't care about us anymore? Or maybe we're so advanced He's jus' not needed anymore?'

"I sat and shook my head, thinking about it. I looked at John. 'I don't know what to think anymore.' John once again put his hand on my shoulder. He could see the quandary I was in.

"He assured me, 'God hasn't lost his powers or abandoned us. We're His children and He cares about each of us. He's the same yesterday, today, and forever. He loves us and He does talk to us. You jus' have to know how to listen. We learn piece by piece until the pieces fit.'

"I bowed my head and took a deep breath. 'I hope you're right. Heaven knows I want you to be right.'"

The Funnel Story[i]

"A few days later, we were taking a ten-minute break to rest. John always took whatever time he could to read the Bible, and I was curious as to how many times he'd read it, so I asked. 'I reckon six or so.'

'Six or so? That's a lot.'

"He smiled. 'I suppose, but when you're a P.K. it's not.'"

"James, I've never heard the term P.K."

"Neither had I. So, I asked him. It turns out P.K. is a 'preacher's kid.' His father was a pastor for a small congregation back home. I told him what little I knew about the Bible was a bunch of rules telling you what you can't do. John put down his Bible and thought about it. 'I suppose you could look at it that way. Let me tell you about a good friend of mine, Matt.

'When Matt was a little over sixteen he wanted his freedom, what you would call want'n to spread his wings. Matt thought there were too many rules in his father's house, so my friend's father took Matt out to the woodshed. Mr. Wright didn't give him a lickin', but a lesson. His father had a way of explaining things in a loving way so Matt could understand. He took a funnel and a five-gallon gas can from off the workbench and asked my buddy to pour gas into the car. As my friend was doing it, his dad asked him if he found that task to be hard or easy.

'Of course, he said it was easy. Then he asked him if it would be hard or easy if he turned the funnel around the other way, and of course, he said it would be hard if not impossible.

'Then his father took the funnel, wiped it off, held it up to Matt, and explained, "I want you to think of this funnel as if it represents life and this large opening represents freedom, the kind of freedom you want at this point in your life, but trust me, you're not ready for it yet. If I let you do anything and everything you want and let you run free, what kind of man would you become? What kind of father would I be? At this point in your life, it would be too tempting to take the easy road. Drop out of school, take odd jobs for peanuts. Far too many have chosen that road. This world is full of lazy, dishonest people who break their word as easy as they break our laws—slowly going down the funnel as it gets smaller and smaller."

'"Society gives those who choose the easy path some leeway, hoping they will straighten up and fly right. But if they don't, society comes together and says enough is enough, and their freedom is taken away, and they're locked up in the narrowest part of the funnel. They made their bed, and now they have to sleep in it. You'll find that the choices you made earlier in your life determine opportunities that will open up. Poor decisions, and jus' as this funnel gets smaller and smaller, fewer opportunities are available. What kind of a job could you have? Who would hire you? Your choices would become very limited for the rest of your life."

'Then Matt's father turned the funnel around, pointing at the narrow part and said, "Now I know you feel like I'm putting a lot of restrictions on you, you feel like you're living in the small end of this funnel, you feel you should have more freedom, but I'm doing it out of the love I have for you. Once you get through this narrow part in your life, though it may feel like forever, it's not. You'll be on your own soon enough, and you'll see that life will be opened to a vast number of opportunities available to you—jus' as this funnel opens up. I want you to have your freedom, but I want you to be ready, so you'll know what to do with that freedom when you get it."

'Matt's father, Ted, helped him understand that he wanted him to be free and out on his own, but he had to be ready for that responsibility.'

"John looked at me. 'God wants us to be happy. The rules, as you put it, are commandments to help us stay out of trouble.'

"I had to admit that made sense, and with a bit of a laugh I told him, 'Thanks. Now every time I use a funnel, I'm going to be thinking of that story. So what happened to Matt?'

'Matt understood why his father had rules, and he and his father became very close. When Matt and I were in high school, he found he had quite a knack for numbers and finances, so when we went to college, he took classes that would help him for a career in either accounting or investment financing.'

"Nikki, Matt and John only got in a year and a half before they both went into the service. John went to Germany and his buddy Matt went to the Pacific Theater."

A Lesson in Reading

"I was with John for about a month. He taught me a lot. John is the reason why I have so many books on so many different subjects. One of John's sayings is, 'The more you read, the more you'll know and be well-rounded.' He taught me the importance of reading the same book many times over in a lifetime. 'You'll always find something new that you missed before, something that will apply in your life at that time. Reading is like exercising your brain.'

"John also suggested reading several books on the same subject. 'You'll always find something new that says the same thing, only worded differently. That'll cause you to see it in a whole new light. It's another piece of the puzzle.' John taught me not to read a book only to read it, read it to apply what you learn to your life. If you only get one new idea from that book, then it's worth the time and money. John would sum it all up by saying, 'Leaders are readers.'"

A Lesson in Gratitude

"Another thing I learned while I was with John was to appreciate what I have. After about a week or so into our journey, we came across another little stream where we stopped to rest and eat. I was carrying the rations since John was carrying the gun and ammo.

"As we were eating, I started to complain. 'I sure am tired of the same thing over and over. What I wouldn't give for a nice juicy steak with all the trimmings!'

"As John poured the water into my cup to rehydrate the meal, he took his spoon from his belt and started to stir it. Looking into his cup, never taking his eyes off the food, 'Could be worse.'

"Nikki, at the time I didn't see how, and I let him know it. That was probably the dumbest thing I could have said. Not another word was spoken as we sat there and ate the C-rations. Later, when we stopped for the night, I reached into the pack, and the C-rations were gone. I must not have secured the flap and somehow, they fell out. I was panic-stricken. I remembered taking quite a fall. That's when they must have fallen out. I told John, 'They're gone; all of them! We have to go back.'

"John shook his head. 'It would be a waste of time. Even if we could retrace our steps, the animals would have gotten 'em by now. We'll jus' have to eat off the land as best we can.'

"For the next few weeks or so, we ate the most disgusting things that would make a billy goat puke. One time, we were feasting on some grasshoppers and I couldn't help but laugh out loud. John looked at me like I was crazy and asked, 'What's so funny?'

'I was thinking about what I said that I couldn't see how our food could get much worse.'

"Together we both had a good laugh. That's when I learned that sometimes you just have to laugh at life. I was about to help myself to seconds when I saw a rabbit to the right of John and about ten feet behind him. I picked up a rock and gave a quick prayer that we might have rabbit for dinner. That rabbit was the best meal we had eaten in a very long time. You can bet I never complained about another meal, no matter how bad it was.

"That night before John was going to take the first watch, I told him how grateful I was for his help and that I didn't have to go through this trial alone. John smiled. 'Sir, with God by your side, you're never alone.'"

BOOK TWO

WHY PEOPLE DO WHAT THEY DO

ONE

A SOLDIER NAMED HART

"In the morning when John and I were getting ready to leave, another soldier came into camp. He walked up, John gave him a salute, and then they hugged with two slaps on the back like brothers who hadn't seen each other for a long time. He handed John some papers, and after John read them, they came over to me and explained, 'I'm needed elsewhere.'

"Then John introduced me to Master Sergeant Mark Hart, the second of the four who were going to lead me out of Germany. John told me, 'Hart will get you through your next trial, Sir. He knows this terrain better than anyone. Pay attention to him and you'll come out finer than frog's hair.' John reached into his pocket and took out his Bible. 'Let me give you my map, Sir. I think you'll find it useful.'

"I knew how much that Bible meant to John and I couldn't accept it. But he insisted. Then John taught me one more lesson:

'When someone offers you something, learn to be a gracious receiver.'

"That was John, generous to a T. I shook his hand and thanked him. Nikki, at that point in my life, I think the only man I had hugged was my father, and that was only when I left for the war.

I was a little surprised when John gave me a hug and said, 'You're welcome, Sir.'"

"James, is it because of John you and your family are such huggers?"

"Yes, I suppose it is."

James sat back in his chair. I could tell he was reminiscing in his mind about John.

Then he continued. "John threw his pack around his shoulders, gave me a salute, and disappeared into the woods. Master Sergeant Mark Hart stepped up and gave me a salute: 'I passed a large troop a few miles back. Let's move out, we're burning daylight.'

"I couldn't help but smile—'we're burning daylight'; gee, I wonder where he got that?"

Forgiveness

"I picked up my empty pack and told Hart I'd lighten his load. I put the new rations into my pack and you can bet I made sure to latch it tight. We walked for a few miles or so when we came across a dirt road. Hart took out his map and showed me our route. 'We need to cross here, Sir.'

"As he was tucking the map back into his front pocket, we could hear them coming. The sound of those lumbering giants is so distinctive it always made the hair on our necks stand up."

"Let me guess, tanks?"

"Nikki, my dear, your grandfather taught you well. Tanks—how many was hard to tell, but definitely more than one. How close? Hard to say with the way sound bounced off the terrain. They could be miles away or around the bend. Our best cover was right where we stood, so we quickly hid ourselves. It was only a matter of minutes when we could see the lead tank. As the tanks were getting closer, we could feel the ground shaking beneath us.

"We could see the dust cloud being kicked up. Quickly, we took out a cloth and wet it down to cover our mouths and noses. Five tanks, two panzers, three tigers—the sound was deafening. We could have screamed at the top of our lungs and they wouldn't have heard us. Needless to say, we didn't try that little experiment. I've got to tell you I was scared out of my boots.

"When the tanks passed and the dust settled, I started to stand up. Hart saw them first and grabbed me by the arm, forcing me back down. He put his finger to his lips and then pointed to the road. A large group of enemy soldiers was following behind the tanks, far back enough so as not to be walking in the dust. As they walked by, the fear I had turned into hatred and rage and I could feel the anger coursing through my veins. I wanted to jump out of my hiding place and take out as many as I could with my bare hands. After they passed and it was safe to come out, Hart had a look on his face that I wasn't expecting. It was as though he was disappointed in me.

"Hart looked at me, 'Sir, your worst enemy that you have to face right now is you.' I looked at him as though he had lost his mind. He added, 'That kind of hatred is like a cancer, and it will eat you alive. If you think about it, they are doing what you're doing: fighting for their country.'

"I almost yelled at him out of reflex, but not wanting to give our position away, I kept it to a dull roar. I let him have it. Who did he think he was, anyway? I pointed down the road. 'You're comparing me to them?'

"Hart had these big eyes that could really disarm you. 'Sir, think about it. Yes, what their leaders are doing is wrong and downright evil. Yes, there are those who know it and want to follow them. But I'll bet most of those men who passed us are only following orders out of survival. They don't want to be here anymore than you do. They have no choice. If they didn't fight, they could be put into a concentration camp or even killed. Others do it for the same reason you do, because they feel it is their patriotic duty. They have families like you do, and all they want is to get back home alive to pick up where they left off.' Then he asked me what I did before the war.

"I calmed down a bit and told him I had been going to school to get my degree in business. My wife and I did odd jobs to make ends meet. I graduated and was looking for a job when Pearl Harbor happened, and my wife and I knew it was what I had to do: I volunteered to serve. Because I had a college degree, I was eligible for the US Army Air Corps.

"Hart pointed down the road. 'Don't you think someone in the troop that passed by was doing the exact same thing you were doing? With a wife and family, enjoying life, looking toward the future until a madman took control of their lives? I'll bet you dollars to donuts they have the same dreams we all have.'

'Dollars to donuts? You've been hanging around John too long, that's for sure!' I was still upset to say the least. I looked at him and said, 'After all that I've seen that has happened in this war, do you expect me to forgive and forget what I know to be evil?'

'I'm not saying that at all, Sir. What I'm saying is this. The hatred that you showed to all those men, without knowing any of their circumstances, is not healthy. You have to let it go. Not to pull out the *Judge not lest ye be judged* card, but it's something to think about.'

"Nothing was said for the rest of the day; I didn't feel like talking. It wasn't until later that night after we ate that I broke the silence. 'Hart, I've got to tell you, I'm having a really hard time with letting it go.'

He nodded, 'I understand, Sir. All I can tell you is I have seen what happens to those who let it eat at them over a lifetime. It makes for a miserable life. As I was growing up, my father would point them out to me. You can see it in their faces a mile away. Their countenances are cankered with a dark spirit. They rarely smile, always seeming to be angry and bitter at the world, only thinking of themselves. You know they have problems in everything, from marriage and family relations to their business life. Even their health can be affected.'"

Prelude to War[ii]

"I sat there, thinking about my anger and hatred. I looked at Hart. 'How did this whole war get started anyway?'

'Well, Sir, if you had asked John that question, he'd have taken you back to Cain and Abel. But since you asked me, I'll shorten it by a few thousand years. Since the Bible uses the snake as evil, then so will I. Only this snake has three heads: Japan, Italy, and Germany. Cut off one head and it can still live.

'You asked how this whole thing started. Looking back, I'd say Japan started it with the invasion of Manchuria on September 18, 1931. The League of Nations investigated and gave the Japanese quite the tongue-lashing, but nothing more. Since nothing happened, Japan took over Shanghai in '32.

'Next was Mussolini's turn. His people were growing restless because fascism wasn't paying off like he said it would. He needed a distraction. The Romans used what was known as "bread and circus"—entertain the people with grand colosseums to keep their minds off their troubles so they won't rise up. So, what did Mussolini use to distract? What all bullies do: they pick on the weak.

'Mussolini looked around and saw Ethiopia as a prime target. Mussolini knew that nothing would happen, so in 1935, he invaded small, defenseless Wal Wal in Ethiopia.

'The Emperor of Ethiopia went to the League of Nations and asked for help. Help was granted, but not in a way that could do any real good. The decision was to stop trading with Italy.

'With no real help from the League of Nations, Ethiopia went to war with what they had. Their Air Force was one old plane used for transporting the Emperor. With no machine guns or tanks, the men went to battle with spears and a few old rifles. It was a blood bath for the Ethiopians.

'Now it was Hitler's turn. He saw that nothing happened to Japan or Italy and knew nothing was going to be done. So in March of '38, he invaded Austria—the land of his birth. Can it really be called an invasion if you're invited in to take over? Since Austria was going through hard times, its people looked over and saw how prosperous Germany was, and since Austria had once been a part of Germany, ninety-eight percent of the people voted and welcomed Hitler to be their ruler. Little by little, Austrians lost their freedom and liberty, from travel to the loss of their guns.

'That went so well that a year later, Czechoslovakia was next. Hitler said he only wanted a small part where Germans resided and would leave the rest alone. And like before, the League of Nations did nothing.

'Six months later, on September 1, 1939, the Nazis invaded Poland. England and France stepped in, and WWII began.

'The United States helped with supplies, but as far as putting boots on the ground, we didn't feel it was our war to get involved in. The Great War—WWI—was still fresh on everyone's minds. That is, until December 7, 1941, when the Japanese attacked Pearl Harbor.'

"Nikki, I had so much anger and hatred toward Germans and all those who caused so much pain and suffering, I couldn't see how I could ever let it go, and I told Hart as much. Hart shrugged it off. 'I don't know what to tell you, Sir. Maybe this is one of those times that are talked about in the Bible, where you need to ask for help.'"

Fasting, Hatred, and Charity

"The next day was the first Sunday of the month. Hart took out a C-ration and handed it to me. 'No thanks, I think I'll go without today.' Surprised, because he knew how much I loved to eat, he asked me if I was sick.

"I told him I thought I'd try this fasting thing so he put the C-ration back into my pack. I didn't know what the heck I was doing, and I think Hart knew it.

'What is it you'd like to fast for, Sir?'

"I shrugged my shoulders. He didn't say anything. He sat there patiently looking at me. I finally spoke. 'I guess—I guess I thought I'd ask to get rid of this anger and hatred and that I'd like to get back home to my wife and son, whom I haven't even held yet. I don't want to bring that kind of hatred spirit home with me. Is that asking God for too many things?' Hart gave me an approving smile.

'I'm sure God can handle that list. Would it be all right if I join you?'

"I didn't know what to say, since I'd never fasted before. I remember John saying something about batteries and the more the better, so I simply replied, 'I could use all the help I can get. I simply don't know how to start or what to do or say.'

"Hart nodded, 'Well, Sir, I think you've already done the hardest part—knowing what to ask for. Now all you have to do is ask God for the help. Did John teach you the outline of a prayer?'

"I took out John's Bible. 'He did.'

'Well, Sir, I think if you talk to God from the heart, those are the prayers God likes the most.'

"So I said my first prayer while fasting. Hart said I did fine, and he was sure God heard me."

The Origin of Hatred

"Nikki, my dear, that day we spent talking about why man does what he does and how evil takes control in one's heart. Hart said that John told the team a story, how we all have two animals living within us. One is good and the other is evil. The one that dominates is the one we feed. John also told them that evil exists when good men do nothing. And when evil raises its ugly head, only Satan smiles."

I was excited to hear the same story my grandfather told me when I was a little girl. I wanted to interrupt, but I didn't. James continued.

"I asked Hart, 'Where does all this hatred come from, anyway?' Hart shook his head, 'It has never ceased to amaze me how man's inhumanity to man has no bounds. You can trace it back before the beginning of time.'

"Nikki, I thought he meant back to the time of Adam and Eve, but he was thinking even before that. Hart told me about a time when the team was talking to John about this very thing one night. John told them about how his father would teach his congregation about a war in heaven. Satan was cast out with a third part of the stars of heaven. Nikki, this was all new to me, but it's right there in Revelation Chapter 12. Hart said that John's father loved to read Isaiah. That's where he found the answer as to why Satan was cast out with his angels.

"Lucifer, one of Satan's many names, wanted to exalt his throne above the stars of God. He wanted to be above the heights of the clouds. He wanted to be placed above God. Talk about power hungry and having too much pride and ego. The war in heaven was fought over two different ideologies. If you think about it, most, if not all wars are fought because of that. I took out my Bible and started to thumb through it. I asked him where it was and he told me I'd find it in Isaiah 14:12–15."

I couldn't believe it! The same story and the same chapters and verses my grandfather taught me. *"I know that story. My grandfather taught me such stories when I was a little girl."*

"I wish I had a grandfather like yours. I thumbed through the pages, but I couldn't find Isaiah, so Hart gave me a hand and I made note of it. Nikki, Satan and his followers have been down here ever since, putting all kinds of evil in the hearts and minds of mankind. I think Satan looks for those who love power. I can't prove it, but I think politicians have the type of personality that loves power and control. It takes a special kind of person to handle that kind of power and know when it's time to get out.

"Nikki, over the many years, I've looked at politicians with a different lens. There are those who want to elevate themselves above others, and they'll use any means possible at their fingertips. Class warfare is a favorite, pitting one group of people against another, taking from one and giving to another. Nikki, it's through the struggle that we become stronger and grow.

"Sorry, I got off on a tangent. Where was I? Oh yes, Hart tells me, 'Satan goes up to Eve and tells her she didn't need to obey all of God's commandments. He told her she should eat the fruit of the tree that God said not to. Eve did put up a good argument by telling Satan if she did, she would surely die. And, of course, Satan had a good comeback by telling her she would not surely die, but become as one of the gods, knowing good and evil. Last time I checked, Sir, neither Adam nor Eve is still alive. Satan will tell you a hundred truths to get you to believe one lie.'"

TWO

CHARITY

"That day while we were fasting, I could tell by looking at Hart that he was thinking something, so I asked him what it was. He thought for a moment then said, 'Sir, one of the best things I've found to help change a heart about someone is to serve them. You know? Help them out.'

"I was a little confused. 'Do you mean charity?'

'Charity has two meanings, Sir. One is where you give something to another, and it could be of value or of little value, like when someone on the street asks you for spare change. You could give that person a dime, or all you have.'

"Nikki, I have to tell you, I had a hard time with that one and so I came back with, 'But what if that person is lazy and by giving them a handout, it isn't really helping but enabling them?'

'Well, Sir, I guess that's where you'll have to rely on that gut feeling to make your decision. Perhaps you can help in other ways, like giving them a job.'"

"James, you said Hart told you there were two meanings of charity. One was giving them a handout or a hand up, what is the other form of charity?"

"Nikki, I asked that very question. Hart smiled. 'The other charity is the pure love of Christ. There are plenty of scriptures that talk about it. 1 Peter 4:8, "And above all things have fervent charity among yourselves: for charity shall cover the multitude of sins."

'1 Timothy 1:5, "Now the end of the commandment is charity out of a pure heart, and of a good conscience, and of faith unfeigned. The list is quite long."'

James quoted them so eloquently I knew he had made them a part of his life.

"Hart told me to take a look at John's Bible, the one he liked to call his road map, and look up 1 Corinthians 13. As I turned to it, I could see John had marked up all the references to 'charity.'

"Hart explained, 'I asked John once that out of all the references to charity, which one was his favorite? He looked at me, you know, with his head cocked a little to the right, and said, "I reckon Paul sums it up best in 1 Corinthians 13."'

"The way Hart said it, I could swear I heard John's voice. We both had a good laugh. We spent the rest of the day going over other scriptures that talked about charity in the Bible John gave me."

Sometimes It Takes Time

"After we ended our fast and cleaned up, I told Hart, 'Every time I think of this war, I still have a lot of anger. I thought fasting was supposed to take that away.'

"Hart looked at me. 'You're not putting God on a timetable, are you? Because He has His own timeline, maybe you'll be given an answer right away, or maybe that's something you'll have to work on for the rest of your life.'

"I definitely didn't want to hear that. I wanted an answer at the end of our fast, if not before."

Devastation That Evil Causes

"For the next few weeks, we came across several towns, or what was left of them. Some had been abandoned, and in others, the people were living underground in cellars with no light or ventilation. The villages were mostly filled with women and children and a few old men. The one thing these towns had in common was they were all in a state of ruin. From a distance, we could see through the binoculars the devastation that the allied bombers had left.

"Why would any man let so much destruction and devastation happen to his people? The blindness caused by an obsession with power and control is the only conclusion I could come up with. The few towns left standing suffered their own economic devastation. There was very little food, and we could see that the people were starving. Hitler's thirst for power and control over others could only come from the devil himself. It was easy to understand why so many people wanted to come to America to get away from dictators and other rulers."

A Gut Feeling

"As we were traveling, we came across a small house. It looked more like a shack or a tool shed. Smoke was coming from the chimney, so we knew someone had to be inside or nearby. We looked around and saw no activity. We were down to our last two meals and needed supplies. Hart and I talked it over. If we were to ask for help, whoever was inside could do one of three things: (1) they could help, (2) they could send us away, or (3) they could give our position away and we would be captured, which would be sure death. Hart left it up to me to decide; after all, I was the ranking officer.

Hart asked, 'What does your gut say?'

"We sat there, staring at the small home. I didn't know what to do. Hart could see me pondering over the dilemma when I stood up and said, follow me.

"We walked up to the house and knocked on the door. A woman who appeared to be in her late twenties came to the door. We could see the obvious fear in her eyes. I tried to communicate to her that we needed help, but it was evident by the look in her eyes she was becoming more and more frightened. Hart stepped in and in perfect German explained to the woman our plight. She relaxed a little and opened the door enough so she could look outside to see if anyone was around, then motioned for us to come in quickly.

"Inside were two small children about the ages of five and three. She told Hart that she was there alone, that her husband was drafted into the war and sent to the Russian front with very little training. In his first battle, he lost his arm. He was lucky, his friend who was next to him lost his life. He had gone into town to try to get work to feed his family and would, God willing, be back in a few days.

"She had nothing to give. She told Hart, what Hitler had done was wrong, she paused . . . and told Hart, 'Not wrong . . . evil.' If she had any to give, she would gladly do so. I looked at the children who looked as if they hadn't eaten in days. I reached into my pack and took out the last two meals we had. I walked over to the counter, picked up two bowls, and placed them on the table. Opening the meals, I emptied them into the bowls. There was a teapot of water on the stove, so I fixed up the two meals and motioned for them to come to the table. I took the spoon from my belt, took a small bite, and rubbed my stomach while giving an *mmmm* sound to show the mother that it was good. I then smiled, put my hand on her shoulder, and we let ourselves out.

"Outside, Hart asked me why I did what I did and that those were our last two meals. I told him it looked like they needed it more than we did. I then told him that I've lived off the land before and I can do it again and by that, I meant we could do it. He nodded with approval. I then added that I figured those were the meals we didn't eat when we were fasting, and they rightfully should go to someone in need.

"I'll never forget what Hart said as he put his hand on my shoulder, 'You know what I think, Sir? I think you answered someone's prayer and it looks to me like someone's having a change of heart toward Germans.'

"I gave him a slight smile. 'I wouldn't say all Germans, but maybe some.' That's when it dawned on me, he spoke German. He told me his mother's side of the family came to the United States when she was a little girl, about the same age as the oldest girl we had fed. His grandparents settled in the States where other Germans settled and never did learn English. His mother taught all the kids German so they could talk to them. Many of the Germans where he grew up were very sympathetic toward Hitler and his cause. It wasn't easy for Hart to tell his grandparents he wanted to serve his country, but he knew it was the right thing to do. He saw little action, except once. Mostly, he was used for translation purposes.

"Nikki, for the next two weeks, we ate better than we ever had. We caught fish in about every stream we came across, and when there were no fish, we had squirrels or rabbits that we would snare. We even had some kind of large bird we came across while it slept in the tall grass. I couldn't believe the luck we had. I knew it was more than luck, and I was learning quickly to always give credit and thanks to whom it belonged."

The Landing Site

"We were going through some thick trees when Hart asked me, 'Does this place look familiar?'

'No,' I said, 'should it?' I panicked. 'Don't tell me we've been going in circles.' Hart smiled.

'Maybe if we were a hundred feet up, you'd recognize it.'

"We went past a few more trees to where it opened up to a clearing, I could see young saplings that had been snapped in half.

The trail led right up to my busted-up Mustang. I looked at Hart. 'How on earth?' Hart replied, 'This is where we picked up your trail, Sir.'

"I had to get to it. I had left something behind I had to have. I started to follow the landing path, but Hart stopped me. He suggested we stay in the tree line, because you never know who might be watching. As we were making our way to the wreckage, I noticed a large mountain and commented to Hart that Germany has some beautiful scenery. I'm sure that from the air there were some breathtaking views, but I was too busy looking behind every cloud to really notice.

"Hart stopped to look at the mountain as well. 'It is beautiful, and I'm glad you think so, because that's where we're headed and you're going over it.'

"With that, he slapped me on the back and kept walking.

The risk of the task didn't really set in until much later.

"When we made our way to the plane, I climbed in the cockpit and removed a picture of my bride, Karen, holding our infant son, Jimmy. I hadn't been able to hold him yet; he was born after I left for Europe. I sat there for a while, looking at her pretty face with her long auburn hair, longing to hold her and the baby, knowing that if I ever got back home, that new baby smell would no longer exist. I stopped myself and thought, 'What's this *if* business?' And I started thinking of our future.

"Hart's voice so startled me that my whole body shook.

'Sir, we need to be going. We've got a mountain to climb.'

"When I jumped down off the wing, Hart grabbed my shoulder and told me not to move.

"Were the Germans coming?"

"Nikki, I didn't know, but that was my first thought too, either that or a snake. Hart told me he thought he heard a click. He took out his Ka-Bar, and with the blade, he gently pushed it into the dirt under my feet. Metal on metal has a very distinctive sound. I had stepped on a land mine, but what kind? Pressure plate or timer?

"Hart cleared the dirt around it and slid the blade under my foot and the pressure plate. Together, we dismantled the trigger, rendering the land mine useless, and put it back, in case the Germans came back to check on it and plant another one if it were gone. Hart figured they must have planted it after the four of them had come by, because they walked all over the area when they came across the plane.

"That night, I was looking at Karen's picture when Hart came over. 'May I?'

"I handed him the picture. Hart looked at it and smiled. 'Sir, you must be a great salesman to have such a beautiful wife. Let's hope your kid gets her looks and not yours!'

"Hart handed me back the photo and I couldn't help but laugh. 'No doubt, when I married Karen, I definitely married up.' Hart asked how we met, and I told him at a dinner party. She sat across the table from me and I couldn't take my eyes off her."

THREE

WHY PEOPLE DO WHAT THEY DO

"As Hart was handing back the photo he tells me, 'Sir, I know it's not my place, but can I give you some advice on relationships that everyone should know about?' I looked at Hart and told him he wasn't old enough to give advice on relationships. He took no offense. 'That's true, Sir. I'm not, but my father is a psychologist, and every night around the kitchen table he would teach us things, like how we should treat each other. He taught us what makes men and women so different, and I'm not talking about the birds and the bees' kind of difference. They're called the opposite sex for a reason.'

"Nikki, I judged the book by the cover and apologized. Hart smiled, 'Apology accepted, Sir.' He started to chuckle, and I asked him what he was thinking.

'I was thinking of my father. Whenever he speaks before an audience, he likes to open with a joke. When his audience is a group of married couples, he tells them that in all his years of talking with women, he would ask them to describe the perfect husband. Invariably, they would describe another woman.'

James saw me chuckle and pointed his finger at me. "It's funny because it's true."

He then leaned back in his chair. "But, in all fairness, I suppose if you were to ask a man to describe the perfect wife, he'd describe the attributes of another man."

The Stradivarius[iii]

"Hart's father loved to teach his kids by using objects. One night after we ate, he turned to me and said, 'Sir, I'd like to tell you how I came to own one of my prized possessions. One day when my brother, sister, and I were teenagers, my father came home with an older gentleman for dinner. Dad was carrying an old beat-up violin case. After dinner, Dad called everyone into the family room, opened up the case, and told us he was going to auction off this violin. I wouldn't have given you a nickel for it, but Dad, in his best auctioneer's voice, started the bidding at a quarter.

'Mom raised her hand and shouted out, "*One quarter!*" Then my sister got into it and bid fifty cents. The next thing I knew, my brother Harold bid a dollar. It looked like it was going to go for a dollar, because it had already gone past the nickel that I wasn't even going to put up. It was then our dinner guest stood, picked up the bow, and took the violin from my dad. The old man took out his handkerchief and wiped off the dust.

'Taking his thumb and plucking each string, he tuned the old violin. Reaching into his pocket, he pulled out some rosin and tightened the bow. He raised the violin to his shoulder and rested his chin on it. Swaying back and forth, he played the most beautiful music I think I had ever heard. When he was through, he handed the instrument back to my father, who recommenced the bidding.

'My sister went to five and my brother shot right back with ten. I knew I had more money than my brother and sister combined, because I was the saver in my family. Before my sister could make it eleven, I shouted out fifty! Dad was using the bow as a pointer, and in my direction, he said, fifty going once, fifty going twice. Then, Mom shouted out, one hundred! I couldn't believe it!

'My own mom was bidding against me. She looked at me, "I know how much you have; I want you to value it should you take the bid."

'I don't know if it was what she said or the way she said it, but I went all in. I raised my hand and offered $223.50!

'Dad shouted, "Sold! For two hundred twenty-three dollars and fifty cents." I was more than happy to go to my sock drawer and get the money. I handed my dad the money and he handed me the violin. I sat down to admire my purchase but began to get buyer's remorse. What had I done? That was my life savings that I was going to buy a motorcycle with. After everyone had a chance to look at the violin, Dad had a lesson for us.

'"When all of you first saw this old, beat-up violin, you didn't think it was worth very much, and that's why the bid only went for a few dollars. But once it was put into the hands of a master, the value went to many times that. My friend Vinnie is not only a master violinist, he is also a master craftsman. He is going to take this violin back to his shop, and when he is finished with it, the value will be well over fifty thousand dollars. This violin is a Stradivarius."

'I couldn't believe it; I gently put it back in the case and gladly handed it back into the hands of the Master. He thanked my mother for a lovely dinner, then turned to my father and thanked him for all he had done.

'After he left, I asked my father what he had done for him. This is where the true lesson came in. Dad gathered everyone together and told us he was able to help save his marriage. You see, Sir, that's when I found out that my father not only taught us with objects, he used them in his counseling sessions as well. My father could tell that his wife felt she was neglected and unappreciated. So Dad, knowing what he did for a living, also knew how to relate to him and spoke his language, you might say.

'Dad had asked the man what his favorite violin was.

'"Why a Stradivarius, of course," was his answer.

'Then my father asked him, "How would you feel if you came across a Stradivarius and it had been abused and neglected because the owner didn't know what he had?"

'"I'd want to take the strings from the violin and string him up," was his answer.

'My father looked him right in the eye, pointing to his wife, and in a soft voice said, "Your wife is a Stradivarius, and you've neglected her." He looked over at his wife and saw the tears streaming down her face, and it hit him like a ton of bricks. He had no idea the pain he had caused. For some reason, we guys are clueless when it comes to women; they speak a different language.'

"Then Hart asked me, 'Sir, when you were told what to do by a prison guard who only spoke German and he hit you with the butt of his gun for not doing what he said, how did that make you feel?'

'I wanted to deck the guy.'

"Hart smiled. 'I'm sure you did, Sir. It was a lot easier to get along with the ones who spoke your language, wasn't it?'

"Then Hart said something I'll never forget. 'When it comes to the opposite sex, both need to learn the language.' I told Hart, his father must have quite a successful business with that technique. 'He does have quite a few arrows in his quiver, but I think that is one of his favorites. Sadly, he can't help them all. There was this one couple he worked with who had been married for close to fifty-five years. They had been having trouble in their marriage for the last ten to fifteen years. What started out as contention, turned into contempt.

'They had gone to several marriage counselors without any success. There was one psychologist where the husband felt they had made some progress with, when his wife walked out in the middle of the session. She felt the psychologist was taking his side and he couldn't accept that his wife was hurt and still didn't feel heard.

'After a few sessions, my father could tell they both felt they had to be right. The pain on both sides was very deep. My father told them, "When it comes to matters of the heart, the one who insists on being right all the time, loses. You only win when you both win, a true win-win scenario."'

'Was your father able to help them?'

'I haven't heard. I was heading off to boot camp when my father told me about the couple. He wanted me to know he has a much better chance to work with contention, but when it falls into contempt, there's not much hope. So I'll pass that little bit of information along to you, Sir. Don't let contention turn into contempt.'

"Hart stood, picked up his rifle, and told me to get some sleep while he took the first watch; we were going to cover a lot of ground tomorrow."

Understanding the Different Personalities[iv]

"By the time the sun broke on the horizon, we had already covered about eight miles, and that was all the ground we would cover that day. There was so much activity with enemy troops that we found a good hiding place and we didn't move or make a sound for the rest of the day. Once the sun went down and it was safe to come out of hiding, we relaxed a bit and fixed something to eat. It was a cold camp that night, let me tell you. No way were we going to build a fire, no matter how small.

"Hart broke the silence by asking me if I ever thought about why some people let fear stop them from doing things, like talking to others, while for some, it's no big deal. I hadn't given it much thought. My mind was more on the fear of getting caught. He was trying to get my mind off the enemy, and I appreciated him for that.

"Hart continued, 'It's true. For some, it's easy to talk to total strangers. It's part of their makeup. Did you know there are four different types of personalities, each with its own name?'

"Nikki, I knew people had different personalities, but I didn't know they had names. 'Yes, Sir.' Hart said, 'They're called Sanguine, Choleric, Melancholy, and Phlegmatic.'

"I laughed and told Hart the only word I understood was melancholy.

'I know what you mean, Sir. My father tried for a week to explain it to us. Leave it to Mom to explain it to Dad that we weren't college kids, only kids. So, with a little help from my mother, Dad brought us into the family room one night and sat us all down. In the middle of the room, he had taken the card table from the closet and set it up in the middle of the room, covering it with a tablecloth to hide something round under it. I thought for sure it was a ball. Dad always was a little theatrical. He was dressed in a tuxedo and Mom had her hair up. She was wearing a fancy dress, pearls around her neck, and long white gloves. So there we were, sitting on the couch, wondering what on earth they were up to. With a few waves of his hands, Dad yanked off the tablecloth and tossed it to Mom, exclaiming, *"Tada!"*'

"James, was it a ball?"

"I asked him the same question."

'No, Sir.' Hart replied. 'The round thing was a globe and it kind of made a tent to hide other things on the table. Some of the strangest things now lay on the table. None of it made any sense at all to us kids. They had gathered some of our toys, some stuff from my dad's desk, and something that we kids were forbidden to touch—a gondola that had two dolls sitting with the guy's arm around the woman, and another doll standing on the back, wearing a hat and holding a pole. Dad had bought it for Mom on their honeymoon in Italy. Mom and Dad devised a plan to help us understand the different personalities by putting them into countries.'

"Nikki, I couldn't help but laugh. I could see his mom and dad and all the kids standing around that table. I remember telling Hart that it must have been fun growing up in that house."

FOUR

THE FOUR COUNTRIES

"Hart smiled. 'It was a little crazy and embarrassing sometimes, but fun nonetheless.' He continued, 'So using things we could relate to, Mom and Dad taught us about the different kinds of personalities. Mom picked up the globe and slowly turned it while Dad talked. "The world has many different countries with different customs, traditions, and ways of doing things, along with words and phrases that can have very different meanings."'

Control Country[v]

'Dad continued by picking up the toy bulldozer that belonged to my oldest brother, Harold. As my dad picked up the bulldozer, he said, "The personality that lives in the first country we're going to talk about loves to drive a bulldozer. They live in *Control Country.*" He never named names, but we knew he was talking about Harold.

'Dad smiled, then continued. "These people love to bulldoze their way to the top where they want to go. Everything is either black or white when it comes to the ways of *Control people.* Their number one cry is *Get It Done!* Their eyes can be steely and intense, their motions abrupt, and they can put out some pretty strong vibes.

Their voice can carry the sound of impatience, and they are usually more interested in talking than listening."

'All of us kids started laughing and pointing at Harold. Mom stepped in and said, "We're not naming names." Dad then told us, "The statements people make who live in Control Country can come across as intense. Their words can be quick, abrupt, and to the point. The people of Control Country share the belief that it is necessary to *control* their environment."

'Mom picked up one of my sisters' dolls and started to walk it across the table, while Dad took the bulldozer and ran over the doll. Mom, in her little-girl voice called out, "What are you doing? You ran over me." Then Dad, in a voice to show he was clueless as to what he did, says, "Huh? Sorry. You got in the way. I was too busy getting things done."

'Dad reached over and picked up a conductor's wand, got all serious, and cleared his throat, tapping the wand on the table. Then, raising her arms, Mom pretended to get ready to play a violin. Dad started to conduct and Mom began to play. After about ten seconds, Dad turned to us kids and started to bow. Not knowing what to do, we sat there. Dad had a stern look on his face and Mom started to clap. Suddenly, Dad turned happy, and Mom encouraged us to clap as well. The look on Dad's face was now ecstatic as he bowed.

'Dad put down the wand and explained to us, "Those who live in Control Country need appreciation. So when you clapped, that showed appreciation, and that's what makes them feel good about themselves."'

Fun Country[v]

"Nikki, I don't mind telling you, Hart had me on the edge of my seat, wanting to know what his father did next."

"I have to admit I'm on pins and needles as well. What did he do next?"

"Hart leaned in and told me his dad picked up a model airplane and continued. 'The next personality we're going to talk about lives in . . .' After a long pause, he threw out his arms and shouted, *'Fun Country!'*

'Then everyone got so into it; we all started clapping our hands and shouting, "*Yeah!*" Dad went around the room, flying the plane up and down, all the while making an airplane sound. "The plane is Fun Country's favorite mode of transportation, and they all want to get to fun as fast as they can. They love to be the center of attention."

'We all turned to my sister Louise, who stood up and took a bow. "Thank you, thank you," she said as she blew everyone kisses. As she sat down, she said, "Don't blame me, blame Dad! I get it from him." Dad smiled, took another bow, and continued.

"We in Fun Country don't say, *Get it done.* No! Our favorite cry is *Let's Have FUN!* Those who live in Fun Country tend to be constantly on the move, looking for a good time. If you were to tell us to slow down, we would look at you like you're crazy and demand, "Why?" Like Control personalities needing appreciation, we in Fun Country need attention and want approval for the way we act. If we don't get it, we can become depressed and despondent. We don't even mind telling embarrassing stories about ourselves. We don't care if we get noticed for our strengths or weaknesses as long as we get noticed.'"

Perfect Country[v]

I couldn't help cutting in, *"James, I know so many people like that. What happened next?"*

"His Mom picked up the train from the table, held it lovingly, and said, 'This is my favorite mode of transportation, because unlike the plane that can go in all directions, the train goes on tracks that are exact and precise. I like predictability. The country I live in is

Perfect Country. We don't say, *Let's Have Fun* or *Get It Done.* We say, *Get It Done Right.*"'

'Then Dad picked up the magnifying glass from the table. "After you kids do one of your chores, do you feel like Mom gets *this* out to see if you did it right?" In unison, we all said, "Yes!"

'Mom explained, "That's because I live in Perfect Country, and it drives me nuts to see a job not done right. We who live in Perfect Country are very sensitive, so when you kids tell me I'm nuts or crazy for wanting a job done right, it hurts my feelings. Those of us who live in Perfect County want others to be sensitive to our feelings." Let me tell you, Sir, we kids were starting to understand Mom a lot better and why she would cry so easily.'"

Peace Country[v]

"James, what country was next?"

James winked. "Peace Country. Hart's mother asked him if he would like to pick up the gondola, the very one that all were forbidden to touch. Hart added, 'I didn't know if it was a trick question or not, but she gave me a nod and said it would be all right. I carefully picked it up. You should have seen the looks on the others' faces.

'Mom said, "The people who live in *Peace Country* love to travel in a gondola, floating gently on calm waters. They like their country because it's a land where you find harmony and cooperation.

"If you listen closely, you will hear the land of Peace in their voices, not a lot of highs and lows. They can be what you would call *laid back*, but they're not lazy. They get their work done with low energy output. They have very good social skills, since they are so willing to be cooperative. Their greatest need isn't appreciation or approval or even sensitivity to their feelings. No, their greatest need is to be respected for who they are."'

"Nikki, I only knew Hart for a short time, but that sure described him to a T. I told him I would sure like to meet his parents, who sounded like they really worked together as a team."

'They do work together well, but don't think they are problem-free. Like everyone else, they have their challenges, but they know how to work through them.'

"While we were together, Hart shared with me in more detail each of the personalities, their strong and weak points, and how different combinations of personalities work best together—what I needed to know about the differences between men and women and what makes them tick. Hart taught me what to look for when others could be going through a rough patch and how to help them at different times in their lives."

FIVE

THE WIRING OF THE TWO BRAINS

"One night, Hart looked at me and said, 'When I told you men and women speak a different language, I didn't tell you why. It's because of the way our brains are wired. Have you ever gone into a building that's under construction, with wires crisscrossing, overlapping, touching other wires all over the place?'

"I had, and I knew what Hart was talking about. He went on, 'Now, think of them as bare wires stripped of their protective coatings. You and I both know that's very dangerous. It could start a fire. But for some reason, that's kind of how women's brains are wired, from the left side to the right of their brain, with no protective coating, all the wires touching each other. That would kill us men. Women are more left-brain, right-brain oriented than men are, and that's why they can multitask so much better than we can.

'We're not brain damaged—though women may think we are. No, our brains work differently than theirs. That's all. We're more left-brain oriented, like wires with a protective coating. Without a coating, we'd probably short-circuit and blow a fuse.

'We like to do one thing at a time. Think of our brain as a big dresser with all different sizes of drawers; each drawer with one article in it. For example, you can have lots of socks, but the rule is the socks go in one drawer.

'If a woman wants to talk to a man about socks, no problem, we pull out the sock drawer, and we can talk about socks. If she starts to talk about pants, we have to stop her, put back the sock drawer, and pull out the pant drawer. One might ask, 'Why not take them out at the same time?' The answer is simple—they might touch. And there's one hard and fast rule we men live by: *Never take out two drawers. They could touch.* Henceforth, there's a short circuit waiting to happen.'

"Nikki, you're shaking your head, but it's true."

"James, I'm not shaking my head because I don't believe you. It's because I do believe you. I'm starting to understand how men think . . . And I think men are crazy." I was laughing as I said it, and he couldn't help but laugh along with me.

"Hart not only told me how different the two brains are wired, but why women can remember even the smallest of details. Things like, not only what she wore to church last week, but what the other women wore as well, and wouldn't be caught dead wearing it two weeks in a row. It's because of the emotions they attach to things. We men, on the other hand, could probably remember if we wanted to, but we don't. For the most part, we don't care. Women can sometimes get upset with men because we don't have the same emotions they have. Both men and women need to understand that. When they do, things will be a lot calmer at home."

I didn't know that most men couldn't multitask the way women can, but I was starting to understand.

"Nikki, we men for the most part, compartmentalize, like the dresser with the drawers, while women, on the other hand, can have ten drawers open at the same time because of the way they're wired. Women look at men like there's something wrong with us. They think, *If I can multitask, you should also be able to.* Women, for the most part, can't understand that when we men are doing something, there's only one drawer open, and that's the one we're in at that time.

"Hart started to chuckle. 'I heard a story about a woman who went to visit a good friend. While they were visiting, the friend noticed the husband sitting, staring off into space. The friend asked if her husband was all right, to which she replied, *He's fine. He's working on growing his mustache.*'"

When James told me that story, I smiled.

"Nikki, my dear, we're not that bad."

"Maybe not, but it does paint quite the picture."

"Yes, it does. Hart had a way of painting many pictures to help one to understand. He told me, 'If a woman wants a man to do something, she needs to make sure she has his attention. If he says, *Yes, dear, I'm listening* while he's reading the paper, it doesn't mean he is. He needs to get out of the *reading-the-newspaper drawer* by closing it and opening the drawer that says, *listening drawer.* If he doesn't do it himself, then she needs to go over, have him put down the newspaper, and get his attention eye to eye. That way she'll know the right drawer is open.' It's hard for women to understand, but that's the way most men are wired. She might even have to write it down for him, since he'll most likely have to be told more than once. Don't ask why—it's the way most men are wired.

"Nikki, there's something else you should know about men. We are programmed by nature: we are visual creatures. This is an area where most women can't wrap their heads around. If a woman wants to try and understand it, the first thing she needs to understand is the power of the visual.

"I know women can find a total stranger attractive, but trust me, there is no comparison. Those who are in marketing know this all too well. If the product is for a man, you can bet there is a beautiful woman trying to sell it to him.

"If a woman goes to the beach and she notices her man with wandering eyes, for the most part, she will take it personally and think he wants a total stranger more than her. Wait a few minutes and ask the man what the woman he saw looked like. For the life of him, he has already forgotten. The old adage 'out of sight, out of mind is true.' But even though we men are stimulated by the visual, it is never an excuse to act inappropriately."

The Five Love Languages[vi]

"There was another night when Hart asked if I remembered when I got the 'Birds and the Bees talk?' Nikki, that's something every kid remembers. Not because of the information, but because of how uncomfortable it is hearing it from their mom or dad. Hart smiled, 'I'll never forget mine. Mom and Dad called me into Dad's office and told me about what they felt I needed to know. But my mom and dad always have to take it to the next level. That's when they told me about what they call, "The Five Love Languages." These languages, like all other languages, have to be learned. Sometimes, if they're lucky, both spouses speak the same love language, but mostly, they have to learn a whole new language in giving love.'

"Nikki, I have to tell you I was confused, but intrigued. Hart could see my confusion.

'Sir, let me ask you, what is it about your wife that you do to show her you love her?'

"I have to tell you I had to think about it for a moment.

'I suppose it's when I tell her I love her, and when I help around the house. You know, do the dishes, vacuum the floor, and take out the garbage, that kind of stuff.'

"Nikki, Hart asked me a question that I really had to think about. He asked, 'Do you know if that's her love language, or yours? You named off two of the five languages of love: affirmation and acts of service, and they may very well be her top two, but they may also be your top two; thinking if that's what you like, then she must like them, too.'

"Hart could see I was in a quandary. 'Perhaps if I explained the five in this way: The first is Affirmation. Everyone likes to hear something nice about themselves. For some, one compliment can last a long time.

While for others, affirmation is their number one love language; and to keep full what my father calls "their love tank," they need to hear it more often. Tell your wife how nice she looks or how much you appreciate the dinner she took the time to make. A note for the guys who like to use sarcasm . . . if it was a simple meal that she only had a few minutes to throw together, don't even think about it. Make the affirmations real, because people know when others are not real.

'Quality Time is the second. If I were to guess, women are more likely to value this one more than men. My father knows this is my mother's number one love language. Dad will stop what he's doing and give her his full attention. He even goes shopping with her. His buddies will ask him if he likes to go shopping. His answer is always, "Heck no. But if I want my love tank full with my number one love language, then I'm sure as heck going to give her hers."

'One time, Dad was interviewing a couple who was having trouble and found out the wife's love language was quality time. Dad knew they lived near a lake and told the husband to take her for a long walk around the lake while holding hands. On their next visit, Dad asked how it went. The husband said, "I thought it was going great, but I could tell she was getting upset. I didn't know what to do." The wife looked at my dad, folded her arms, and told him, "It was nice, yes, there we were, holding hands, and then I noticed in his other hand he was holding his fishing pole."'

"Nikki, I couldn't help but laugh. I remember telling Hart that's something most guys would do. He smiled and agreed, then continued. 'Receiving Gifts is the third. Again, women, for the most part, love little gifts, and they don't even need to be expensive. A note saying you love her, or a single rose, goes a long way.

'Acts of Service is the fourth. Some would say that acts of service should be listed in the gift category, and I suppose they have a point, but I'm going to keep them separate in this example. Helping around the house to take the load off is always a good thing. If your spouse's two top love languages are gifts and services, you can kill two birds with one stone. I should probably mention that when it comes to gifts and acts of service, be a gracious receiver.

'My mom is a perfectionist. In the beginning of their marriage, whenever Dad would help around the house, Mom would go right behind him and redo what he finished, complaining all the while she redid his act of love. She would say, "If you're going to help, do it right." That one took them a few years to work out.

'Physical Touch is the fifth. Men will almost always list this as their number one because of the way we are wired. Knowing this, Dad would probe to find out what their second was. Dad would chuckle and say, "Men are knuckle draggers. When they came home to the cave dragging in their kill and plopped it before the women, he would stand waiting for praise and affirmation." That's when Mom would smile and say, "Not much has changed."

'It was my mother who told me my father's primary love language is affirmation, with a close second to physical touch. Mom, seeing how uncomfortable I was, turned up the heat. "You do know your grandparents still…" I quickly raised my hand and shook my head. Mom and Dad couldn't help but laugh. Mom, smiling, turned to Dad and told him that they had tortured me enough, and she was going to start dinner while he finished up.

'Sir, it still makes me uncomfortable telling that story, no matter how old I get. That's something a kid doesn't like to think about.' We both laughed and then shuddered.

'Dad found that for the most part, the women who listed touch meant "non-sexual." Holding hands, locking arms as they walked together. A hug can go a long way."'

BOOK THREE

WE ALL HAVE MOUNTAINS TO CLIMB FOR SELF & COUNTRY

ONE

A SOLDIER NAMED TJ

"It was two days later when Hart and I finally came to the base of the mountain. As the sun was going down, we built a small fire to cook a rabbit we caught earlier that day. We spent that evening going over everything that Hart taught me. When it came time to turn in, he told me he would take the entire watch because of what I was going to be doing on the morrow.

"The sun was starting to break when a tall, slender, young Black man walked into camp. By the smile on his face, I knew he must be one of the four. Hart gave him a big old bear hug. I heard him say, 'Good to see you, TJ.' Turning toward me, Hart introduced Corporal Gardner to me. He saluted and I returned the salute. 'Call me TJ, Sir, everyone does.'"

"Forgive me for interrupting, but I know that there was segregation in the army at that time. How is it that TJ, a Black man, was part of the team?"

James, with a small smile and both eyebrows raised, "Nikki, my dear, I'll be honest with you, when I first saw TJ, I had the same question. Once I got to know him, I asked him about it. TJ smiled, 'Didn't John tell you we were put together because of our unique skills?'

"I thought back to when I first met John and remembered him saying something like that.

'Sir, the one who put us together couldn't give two hoots and a holler what we looked like. He knows who we are and what we can do. Our mission is to get you home.'

"I couldn't help thinking that John had rubbed off on TJ as well, given his two hoots and a holler. When he said their mission was to get me home, that was good enough for me. After Hart introduced us, TJ started going through his equipment, and he asked me if I'd ever done any climbing before, I remember shaking my head. 'Does climbing trees count?'

"He smiled. 'That's all right, Sir. Follow me and do what I do and you'll be fine.'

"Hart turned to me, 'Good luck, Sir, and whatever you do, don't ask him how he got the name TJ.'

"I asked, 'You're not coming with us?'

He shook his head. 'No, Sir, this is a two-man job, and I'm needed elsewhere.'

"With that, I shook Hart's hand and thanked him for all he had done and taught me. I couldn't help myself and gave him a hug as well and told him I hoped to see him again. 'You're welcome, Sir. Have a little faith that our paths will cross again, and I'm sure they will.' He saluted and I returned his salute.

"I turned and saw TJ picking up the last of the climbing gear. I asked him where his gun was. He told me that where we were going it would only be in our way. I turned back to Hart to say one last goodbye, but he was already gone."

Mountains Out of Molehills

"As I turned to TJ, he put his hand up to block the sun as he looked at it. He told me we needed to get going if we were going to make it to our first camp before nightfall. He gave me what he thought I could carry.

"For the first hour or two, I could keep up with only a few rest stops. Then we came to a point where I looked at the mountainside and it was straight up.

"I looked at TJ and told him there was no way I could ever climb the face of that mountain. The first lesson that TJ taught me happened when he asked me what I wanted more than anything in this world. I reached into my pocket and pulled out the photo I was carrying. I told him it was to be with my wife and son. He smiled, 'That sounds like a pretty good goal to me, and the only thing stopping you was this mountain. Sir, we all have mountains in our lives; some are bigger than others, and some are molehills that we like to make into mountains. What shapes our character is how we tackle that mountain.'

"Nikki, whenever I'm facing a fear, I ask myself, what kind of fear is this? Is it one trying to keep me safe, or one that is keeping me from being great?

"TJ told me to close my eyes and focus on my goal. I can still hear him tell me I could do this if I really wanted it bad enough."

The Right Mentor

"Nikki, as I stood there, my eyes closed, he said, 'Sir, open your eyes. I've climbed this mountain before and I can help you, but I can't carry you. You have to want it.' I concentrated on my wife and son. I could see her smile and even smell her hair and the perfume she wore. I took another look at the picture, put it back in my pocket, looked him in the eye, and said, 'Let's do this.' TJ slapped me on the back.

'That's what I wanted to hear!'

"Softly under my breath I said, *F.E.A.R.* TJ heard me; 'You got that from John.' Looking up at the face of the mountain, he added, 'Only one thing, this fear is real, and if you don't do what I say and do, this mountain will kill you.' He stretched out his arm . . . 'Shall we?'

"I smiled nervously and replied . . . 'Lead the way.'

"TJ took the rope he had wrapped around his arm and shoulder and tied it around him first, showing me a knot that climbers use. Then with about ten feet of rope between us, I looped the rope around me and tied it off. TJ led the way. It was hard, and to say the least, scary, but I did as I was told.

"TJ went up to the end of the rope, looking down, he instructed me. 'Keep your body close to the wall, Sir. Let your legs do most of the work and try to keep your hands from going above your head as little as possible. That way, your heart won't have to pump harder to get blood to them.'

"We were quite a ways up when I grabbed a rock that came loose. I watched it fall to the earth. After watching about five rocks do the same thing, TJ stopped and told me, 'Sir, you're letting distraction slow you down. If you stop and watch every rock fall, we'll never make it to our first stop. Think of each rock as your past; don't look at it, what's done is done. Focus on the present and the future. We have to keep moving to get to the place where we're going to spend the night. If we don't make it there before the sun goes down, we'll have to sleep tied up in ropes, and believe me, that's not fun.'

"I thought about it and knew TJ was right. I asked him, how many times he had climbed this mountain.

'Several times, Sir, so if you're ready, let's keep moving. You don't want to lose your momentum.'

"We made it to a small ledge where we could sit and rest our arms and legs. They were starting to shake, and that's a dangerous sign. Once I felt a little better, TJ encouraged me to keep going. Starting up again was hard. I went about five feet and lost my footing and let out a yell. TJ quickly braced himself as I slid against the face of the mountain. The slack of the rope tightened as I hit back on that small ledge. I started to lose my balance, but TJ pulled on the rope and threw me back up against the wall. I got my balance, and TJ climbed back down to see if I was okay.

"TJ looked at me. 'I thought we were a goner for sure.'

"I looked at him. My heart was still pounding and I confessed, 'That makes two of us.' I was so scared and cut up from frantically trying to stop myself that the pain was now starting to hit me. As I looked down, I started to shake.

"TJ shook his head. 'Sir, I know you're hurt, and you'd like nothing more than to stop. We can do that by tying ourselves to this small ledge.

'You can't see it from here, but another fifty feet is a breathtaking spot, with plenty of room to lie down and rest for the night with a warm cup of food, but we have to leave now if we're going to make it before nightfall.'

"TJ painted such a pretty picture in my mind that I found myself telling him to lead the way."

Negative vs. Positive

"It took a lot of work and effort, but we finally made it to the first camp, a ledge about eight by eight. I dropped my pack. It was hard to know which hit the ground first, me or the pack. After I caught my breath, I stood and looked up at how much farther we had to go, and I started to complain. After about a minute, I noticed TJ wasn't responding. I looked and saw him sitting on the edge, dangling his legs over the ledge. 'Did you hear anything I said?'

'No, Sir. Once I start to hear someone complain about something I can't help with, I tune it out. It's negative, and I'd as soon not hear it. I'd rather look on the positive side.'

'What's so positive about almost killing ourselves to see how much further we have to go?' TJ didn't say a word. He sat looking at the view; the shadow of the mountain was starting to cover the valley below, and I sat down to his left.

"TJ pointed. 'Take a look over there where the edge of the shadow is reaching that small opening in the trees. Can you see it?'

'I think so. What am I looking at?'

'That's where your plane is. Now look down.'

"I looked down. I could make out the side of the mountain we had climbed.

"Then, we both looked up to where we had to go. 'Kind of puts things into perspective, doesn't it, Sir?'

'Yes, it does, TJ. Yes, it does.' Then I added, 'I guess this is a half- full kind of thing.' TJ agreed.

"As we sat enjoying the view, I said, 'Looking back on everything, I want to thank you for saving my life and getting me here. I couldn't have done it without you.'

"TJ gave me a light pat on my back. 'You're welcome, Sir. I think life is a lot like mountain climbing. It's a lot easier with help from someone who knows the way, though I didn't used to think so. I used to think I didn't need help from anybody. I thought I could do everything on my own, but after a few hard falls, I will tell you, the student was ready for the teacher to appear. Someone came into my life and showed me that there was an easier way. This mentor showed me how to look at a mountain and size it up. He would ask me what I wanted and taught me how to plan for that task. Yes, Sir, it sure helps to have a clear goal in mind and someone to help you get there.'

"TJ took out a C-ration and looked at the sky. 'If we want a hot meal, we'd better hurry. If we wait much longer, someone might see the light coming from the mountainside and have a greeting party waiting for us when we come down off this mountain.' TJ reached into his pack and pulled out a small handful of twigs, enough to warm up the water in the tin cup. After we ate and cleaned up, TJ said, 'Let's get some sleep, Sir. At least no one will have to stand guard.'

"Nikki, for the first time, in a long time, I was able to take off my boots and air them out. Being on the dodge, you never know when you may have to jump up and run for it. It sure felt good. We tied our boots to our belts so they wouldn't fall over the edge in the middle of the night. I took out the green army blanket that we both shared. TJ had me sleep against the face of the mountain, while he took the cliff side. He told me it was most likely I would do some twitching from my first climb and could roll off the edge to my death. He was right; I think I had muscle spasms all night.

"The sun was already up when we started to stir. After we ate, TJ said, 'This ledge is a lot like life. We can stay here and do nothing, but we'd die from starvation sooner or later. We can go back down, only to start over again, or we can move on. It's your call, Sir.'

"I laughed. 'I don't know about you, but I've got a wife and baby back home waiting for me.'

'Sounds like a good goal to me, Sir. What are we waiting for, Christmas?'

"I shook my head. 'You guys have more sayings than, than—' TJ cut in.

'Than a hound dog has fleas?'

"I gave a half smile. 'I haven't heard that one before, but I guess it'll do.'

"TJ replied, 'Blame John for all the sayings. He's from the great State of Texas, and when you've been around him for as long as I have, it rubs off on you.'"

The Right Path

"TJ once again led the way, teaching me more and more about how to climb the mountain and what to avoid. TJ pointed, 'You see that part in the mountain that looks like a trail? It looks like an easier way to go, but it's not. I've been down that path, and I can definitely tell you to stay clear of it. But if you want to try it, you're the ranking officer.'

'No need to go where you've already been. You lead and I'll follow.'

"When we finally reached our next stop, TJ dropped his gear and rested his hands on his knees to catch his breath. I dropped without even taking off my gear. Instead of an eight-by-eight ledge, there was a crevice cut out in the rock from the weather, about ten feet deep and seven to eight feet wide that started out six feet high and sloped down to about four feet. It was like a little cave where we could get out of the wind. Once I was able to get up, the view almost took my breath away again. After staring in awe for a moment, I asked how much farther.

"TJ said, 'As far as distance goes, tomorrow about noon we'll be at the halfway mark. But you've picked up this climbing thing quickly, and we'll be able to make up a lot of time. So yes, we are halfway there.'

"TJ picked up his pack and went to the back of the small cave, where there lay a small pile of branches. I could see ashes where a fire had once been built. TJ pulled out more branches from his pack, added them to the pile, and started a small fire. With the slope of the cave's ceiling, the smoke was able to escape easily. The shadow on the mountain would make it impossible to spot. We were far enough up that what little light the small fire gave off, it too would never be seen.

"From one of the side pockets of his pack, TJ took out a few candles and put them aside.

'We'll use these tonight. This fire may not be enough to keep us warm, but it'll heat up a cup of water. Last time I was here, I left more wood than this, so it looks like someone else found it and put it to good use.'"

TWO

HOW TJ GOT HIS NAME

"Nikki, while we ate a nice hot meal, I asked, 'What does TJ stand for and why did Hart tell me not to ask?'

"TJ smiled as he held the hot cup with both hands to warm them. 'My parents are big fans of the Founding Fathers. My dad wanted to name me George Washington Gardner, but my mom liked the name Thomas Jefferson Gardner, so she could call me TJ for short. I'm told they flipped a coin.'"

"James, it was obvious his mother won the toss."

"That's what I said, but TJ double-glanced at me. 'Don't really know for sure, Sir. To hear Dad tell it, he flipped, and Mom called tails in the air. Before Dad could catch it, Mom snatched it out of the air, slapped it on the back of her hand. "Tails! TJ it is," she announced, and put the coin in her pocket before Dad could see it. Then she walked off.'

"I gave a laugh and told him it was a great story, but I said, 'I still don't understand why Hart wouldn't want me to ask you.'"

TJ's Love for the Founders and the Constitution

"TJ gave me one of those 'ah, I understand looks.'

'Probably because Hart knows I love to talk about the Founding Fathers and the Constitution. Once I get started, it's hard for me to stop. Since being named after one of the Founding Fathers, I became curious about their contribution. As I studied with my father, I was truly amazed at what we uncovered about these uncommon and fearless men who are responsible for the freedoms that so many of us in America take for granted. As we did our research and uncovered one incredible story after another of these great men, I came to love them for their sacrifice. I was even more astonished as I went through school that very little was taught of these unusual men and the women of that time.'

"I was beginning to understand what Hart meant. TJ continued, 'For example, did you know that George Washington lost his father at the age of eleven and nearly joined the British Navy at fourteen? Have you ever heard the story of how he couldn't be killed in an ambush in the French and Indian War? How he held together a destitute army through many bitter winters?

'At Valley Forge, many men suffered to the point that they joined the British just to get food. About three thousand men deserted and went home. Around two thousand froze to death or died of starvation and disease. Some two thousand of Washington's officers resigned their commissions. When the men could take no more, a few of his officers went looking for the General. When they came to his quarters, Martha told the men he had gone off to the nearby woods and pointed in the direction she saw him leave. They were coming to tell him that everyone was quitting because they felt that the American people weren't worth the sacrifice.

'When they came upon Washington, he was kneeling in the snow, his horse beside him, and he was praying. In that small clearing in the woods, they heard his plea to God, and they knew they had to stay. Quietly they went back and convinced the troops to stay, and stay they did, even though all they had to eat were fire cakes, which consisted of flour mixed with water and salt, cooked on a flat rock. Not as a side dish but as the main course, day in and day out. They were so hungry they would boil anything leather—belts, vests, shoes, anything they could get their hands on to quiet the hunger pains in their stomachs.'

"I raised my hand to stop TJ, 'Wait, they boiled their shoes? There are no nutrients in cured leather; why would they do that?'

'You're right, Sir, not the way we tan leather today, but back then …' TJ smiled, 'Did your mother ever tell you, "Just wait until your father comes home. He's going to tan your hide?"'

"Nikki, I really couldn't help but laugh at that one. I told TJ more than once. Then he explained, 'That saying came from the way they tanned leather back then. What they would do is take the hide and stretch it over a hard surface. Then after scraping as much of the fat off as they could, they would beat it with a stick or a flat board, beating the fat that was left into the hide until it was soft, then adding salt to cure it.'

"Nikki, did you know that's where that saying came from?"

"I've heard of that saying, but I have to be honest with you, I never knew where it came from."

'Yes, Sir,' TJ said. 'The soldiers were trying to get the fat and salt from the leather. They would even cut the leather into small pieces to chew. Their clothes were nothing but threads, and it didn't have to be that way. American merchants had plenty of food and clothes on the shelves, but the army was going without because the soldiers didn't have any money. Even if they did have money, it would have been Continental money, which was considered almost worthless. They were fighting without pay. Many times throughout the war, Washington would dip into his own pocket to pay for supplies. He may have started out wealthy, but by the time the war was over and he went back home, things were financially quite bleak for the Washington household.

'In a letter to James Craik, he tells how embarrassing it was to owe money for medical services and how he had to put off the sheriff three times when he came knocking at his door to collect taxes that were overdue. You can only imagine how he must have felt when he received a seemingly polite request for prompt payment of an overdue rent for his pew at the church. When he was elected to be the first President of the United States he had to borrow money to make the trip to New York. And to think there are those who accuse him of profiting from the war.'

"TJ thought for a moment, then added, 'If it wasn't for Washington, I doubt there ever would have been a Constitution. At the Convention, he was the glue that held things together through that difficult time. Headstrong men representing their States, making sure they didn't get railroaded, talk about a difficult, if not impossible, job. When I told this story to John, he said, "It must have been like herding cats." Washington wasn't even going to be there because he was in so much pain. Having a sheet put over him at night gave him great discomfort. Washington couldn't see how he could travel, and besides, he didn't have the funds to do so. But his love for his country gave him the will, so he tied his arm in a sling close to his body and made the long and painful trip.

'Sir, did you ever stop and think that if it wasn't for the Constitution, we wouldn't have freedom of religion?' I had to admit I hadn't given it much thought. 'Only in America could that have happened. Up until that time, wherever you were born, whatever religion was being practiced, that's what you practiced. You had no choice. In different times in history, some places even outlawed religion altogether, like Russia.'

"I sat there shaking my head. 'TJ, now I see why Hart said not to ask how you got your name, but I'm glad I did. I don't think I've heard half of that.'"

The Refiner's Fire

"TJ laughed, 'I could talk for days on end about how our country got started and the trials it went through. How we were on the razor's edge of defeat on many fronts. It seems that men and women who exhibit strong principles and character are those who, at some point in their lives, have had to go through the refiner's fire. Men like you, Captain Hansen, who are willing to fight for their country and lay down their lives if necessary. Men and women who stand up for what they know to be right, even if it's not the popular thing to do. Women who sacrifice for their families—they are the glue that holds the family together. I once heard of a Mexican saying that goes something like this: *A home is not built on the ground, but on the Mother.* The history pages are full of their stories—stories that would make strong men weep.'

"I sat thinking about what TJ said. I'd heard the expression *refiner's fire,* and I was pretty sure I knew what it meant, but I asked him if he could go into more detail.

'Sure,' he says. 'And I know just the story to tell you. One time, Dad took the family to the state fair. There was a silversmith pedaling his goods. He sure knew how to draw a crowd by showing the people how he made his wares. He took a piece of silver over to the forge and heated it up. He told the crowd that in refining silver, one needed to hold the silver in the middle of the flame where it's the hottest, so it could burn away all the impurities. With his dark glasses, he told the people that he could not take his eyes off the silver while it was in the fire. If the silver was left for even a moment too long, it would be worthless. We were in the back of the crowd, and I was the youngest, so Dad put me on his shoulders so I could see.

'Mom had a question, but since the silversmith wasn't looking at the crowd, Mom shouted it out. "How do you know when it's ready?" I remember jumping and almost pulling my dad's hair out as he cinched up on my legs.

'The silversmith, never taking his eyes off the prize, raised his free hand, pointed it in the air, and said, "That's an excellent question!" It was then he pulled out the silver, took off his dark glasses, looked at the refined silver, and said, "When I can see my image in it." He picked up his hammer and started to mold it, putting it back in the flame to heat it up from time to time until he formed a bracelet. He quoted Malachi 3:3 as he worked the silver: "He will sit as a refiner and purifier of silver."

'He went to his display of goods, and holding up a finished bracelet, he challenged, "If any of you feel you are going through a trial in life that feels too heavy to bear, remember, God has his eye on you." That silversmith sold a lot of bracelets that day; I know it's one of my mom's favorite pieces.'

"I thanked TJ for the story. I was curious about the part where TJ said George Washington couldn't be killed and asked if he could tell me more about that."

Washington and the Indian Chief[viii]

"You should have seen TJ's eyes light up. He truly loved to tell stories. He cleared his throat.

'In 1755, during the French and Indian War, there was a Battle of the Monongahela, but it was more like a slaughter. The British were coming to take back a fort that the French took over about a year prior. The British troops well outnumbered the French and knew victory would soon be theirs. What they didn't know was the French, along with the Indians, didn't wait for them to get to the fort. Instead, they went into the woods and waited for the British there. They were so well hidden that when they opened fire, none of the British troops could see them, and in their state of panic, they started firing into the trees and bushes. Many of the officers and aids to Major General Braddock were shot. Many were killed, and Braddock himself was badly wounded.

'With no one in charge, the men didn't know which way to turn. In their panic, they were even shooting their own men. Washington, an aide to Braddock, had been quite ill, so he was in the rear. When he saw the confusion, he rode up to the front and directed the battle. Washington had two horses shot out from under him, but each time he would look around and mount another that no longer carried an officer. That slaughter lasted for about two hours; Washington and his men were barely able to get away. Braddock died from his wounds shortly after and had to be quickly buried. After they were out of harm's way, Washington took off his coat to shake off the dust. In the light of the fire, he found four bullet holes, yet he was unharmed. Washington led many battles during the Revolutionary War, right out front on his horse but was never hit. It's believed that about fifteen years later when Washington met an old and respected chief who told him what happened that day . . .'

"TJ hesitated. I looked at him. 'What did the old Indian chief say?'

'I could tell you, Sir, but you'd probably laugh at me.'

'Why would I laugh?'

'Because, Sir, I can only tell it the way my father taught it to me. He made up Indian sign language so I could recite it as a child, but as an adult, it's a little embarrassing.'

"I assured him I wouldn't laugh, but TJ wouldn't tell it unless I followed along with him and learned the motions. I was reluctant, but I wanted to know the story. The ceiling of the cave was too low for us to stand, so TJ and I knelt. After about three times, I had it down. TJ approved. 'Very good, Sir. Now try to do it without my help.'"

James started to go on to his next story, so I stopped him. *"Wait a minute; you're not going to leave me hanging? What did the old Indian chief say?"*

"Nikki, my dear, if you want to know, you'll have to learn as I did. The story of Washington not being shot is true, but I should tell you the story about the old Indian chief, from all the research I've done, I believe to be apocryphal, but I still love it."

I could feel my face blush. *"Okay, what do I do?"*

James stood and instructed me to do the same. "I'll tell the story, and you follow me with the gestures as I do them."

James cleared his throat: "I am a chief and ruler over my tribes. My influence extends to the water of the Great Lakes and to the far Blue Mountains. I have traveled a long and weary path that I might see the young warrior of the great battle. It was on the day when the white man's blood mixed with the streams of our forest that I first beheld this chief. I called to my young men and said, 'Mark yon tall and daring warrior? He is not of the red-coat tribe. He hath an Indian's wisdom, and his warriors fight as we do—himself is alone exposed. Quick, let your aim be certain, and he dies. Our rifles were leveled, rifles which but for him knew not how to miss—'twas all in vain? A power mightier far than we shielded him from harm. He cannot die in battle.

"We immediately ceased to fire at you. I am old and soon shall be gathered to the great council fire of my Fathers, in the land of shades; but ere I go, there is something bids me speak in the voice of prophecy. Listen! The Great Spirit protects that man and guides his destinies— He will become the chief of nations, and a people yet unborn will hail him as the founder of a mighty empire! I pay homage to the man who is the favorite of Heaven and who can never die in battle."

James took a bow and I applauded. I started to sit down but James remained standing. Obviously, it was my cue to do likewise. "My dear, now it's your turn." We went through it several times until James thought I could do it on my own. I have to admit, it was a lot of fun.

We sat down as James continued. "TJ applauded my efforts as well. 'Very good, Sir. The Chief would be proud.' I was a little embarrassed. I felt like I was on a stage performing, but I had to admit, it felt pretty good. I looked at TJ and pointed. 'You could have recited that without the sign language. You only wanted me to learn it so I wouldn't forget.'

"TJ grinned and nodded.

'Now you'll be able to teach that to your children and grandchildren.' TJ paused for a moment. 'Yes, Sir, that Indian Chief's prophecy obviously came true.' TJ yawned and stretched. 'That's enough for now. We really should be getting some sleep.' The small fire had gone out long ago, and not even a glow from a single ember remained, only the light from the candle.

'Good night, Sir. Remind me tomorrow to tell you about the Battle of Trenton.' TJ blew out the candle; it became pitch black. You couldn't see your hand in front of your face. As I was kneeling in the dark thinking—no, pondering, about everything TJ had talked about, and in a silent prayer, I gave thanks for everything I had and for the blessing of being a United States citizen. I asked God to please let me be able to see my wife and son Jimmy, if it was to be His will."

THREE

THE SUN WILL ALWAYS RISE

"In the morning when TJ awoke, it was predawn. I was already up sitting on the ledge, my feet dangling over the mountain, as I waited for the sun to come up. There was enough light to read by when TJ came up to me and sat down.

'Is that John's Bible you're reading?'

'It is. He gave it to me before we parted. He called it a map. I guess he thought I was lost and could use it.'

'That sounds like John.'

"We sat there enjoying the moment. When the sun broke the horizon, it was like—Nikki, it's hard to describe, I've never experienced anything like it before or since. It was like an explosion and it was breathtaking. I heard myself say, '*Wow!*'

"TJ looked at me. 'You know, Sir, it doesn't matter how many times I see that sun rise, it always amazes me how everything in this universe is put together. God is in control, and no matter how dark it gets, the sun will always rise. Another thing a sunrise reminds me of is something Benjamin Franklin said after the Constitution was signed. During the Convention, there were times when things weren't going so well, and it looked like it might all fall apart. It was a long, hot, muggy summer, and George Washington, at one point, wished he hadn't come. It was about this time that Benjamin Franklin made his famous plea for prayer.

'He stood and spoke: "I have lived, sir, a long time, and the longer I live the more convincing proofs I see of this truth—that God governs in the affairs of men. And if a sparrow cannot fall to the ground without His notice, is it probable that an empire can rise without His aid? I therefore beg leave to move: that hereafter prayer, imploring the assistance of heaven and its blessing on our deliberations, be held in this assembly every morning before we proceed to business, and that one or more of the clergy of this city be requested to officiate in that service."'

"TJ told me it was voted down because there wasn't any money allocated for a clergyman to come in and give a prayer, and also because it was a closed-door meeting, but calling for a prayer seemed to calm things down, and the members of the convention started to work together and came up with that beautiful contract called *The Constitution.* Once the Constitution was signed, it was written that the old man wept, referring to Franklin. TJ also told me that on the back of Washington's chair was carved a sun on the horizon. Benjamin Franklin made the comment that while he had been sitting during the long summer looking at that sun, he wondered if it was a rising or setting sun. He was pleased to say he knew it was a rising sun.

"As we sat on the ledge looking at the morning sun, TJ said, 'You should congratulate yourself, Sir. The only ones that get to see this view are those who go through the effort to make the climb. Go ahead and finish reading while I heat up some water.'"

The Climb Down

"After we ate and put on our packs, TJ showed me the route we were going to take. He pointed out where the halfway mark was, and from there we would go to the other side of the mountain and start our way down. It was a difficult climb, but I kept up, and before long, we found ourselves going around the side of the mountain that had areas of vegetation, with water coming off from the snow melt. It was the best-tasting water ever. We gathered what branches we could for a fire later. When we reached our next rest stop, it was still early. TJ gave me the choice to stay there for the night or to press on. He thought we could be off that mountain by nightfall and make it to another spot that would be nicer, but we wouldn't have much light toward the end. But with a little help from the light of the moon, he thought we should be alright. I looked at TJ and told him I was feeling up to it if he thought it would be safe.

"We took the branches from our packs that we had collected and added them to the small pile that was already there. TJ took out his last two candles and added them to the pile.

'We won't need these, where we're going, we'll be able to light a fire. Hope they come in handy for someone else. Let's get going.'

"I smiled and said, 'We're burnin' daylight.'

"The sun was going down when we came off that mountain. TJ took the climbing gear and hid them. 'We won't be needing these anymore.'

"We crossed a dirt road and together walked into camp about an hour or so after the sun had gone down. TJ was right, it was a very nice spot. It had a small stream nearby so we had all the water we could drink and enough wood to build a small fire to keep ourselves warm. I looked around. 'This is nice. Too bad we can't build a fire.'

'I think we'll be okay. The trees are thick. They don't call it the Black Forest for nothing. So if we keep it small enough, we should be safe.'"

Fast Sunday with TJ

"TJ picked up my pack and took out the blanket. 'Get some rest, Sir. We should be safe here, but I'll take the first watch. Keep the fire small if you need to, but if you hear me come running, take the water and douse it quickly. Then take that mound of dirt next to it and cover it. We have no gun, so we'll have to hightail it.'

"TJ let me sleep for about five hours before it was my turn to stand guard. In the morning, I woke TJ by taking a strand of grass and lightly moving it over his face. TJ, not quite awake, kept brushing it away, and my laughing woke him up. 'Good morning, sleepy head.' TJ stretched and rubbed his face. When his eyes focused, he saw me with the biggest grin, holding up a jackrabbit by the scruff of the neck.

'Where'd you get that?'

"I couldn't help but laugh. I was having so much fun. 'At the rabbit store over the hill.' TJ shook his head.

'Yeah, that was a dumb question.'

"I told him, 'While I was standing guard as it was getting light, I saw what looked like the entrance to a rabbit's den. I wanted to reach in to find out, but for all I knew, there could have been a badger inside waiting for me. So I went behind it and waited. About thirty minutes later, this big guy poked his head out. I thought we'd invite him for dinner after we broke our fast!'

"TJ smiled. 'That's right, today is the first Sunday of the month. Thanks for reminding me. So both John and Hart got you doing this fasting thing too.'

'Yeah, when John first said we were going to rest on Sunday, I wanted to keep going, but taking a break and resting once a week to recharge the old battery did feel good. I really think that's why we can keep going farther in the week; at least, it feels that way. I'm not too sure about this fasting thing yet, but I figure it's worth trying.'

"That day, TJ shared with me different stories about fasting and prayer. There was one I really liked. TJ was always quite animated whenever he told his stories, so I knew I was in for a treat when he stood up.

"TJ cleared his voice. 'It was in the mid-1700s at the beginning of the French and Indian War. The French Fleet was coming up the East Coast and they had orders to burn all the coastal cities—Charleston, New York, Boston, all were to be burned. America had no way to protect themselves, so a day of fasting and prayer was called. Toward the end of the fast, everyone was to meet at the Old South Church in Boston, which still stands today.

'The Reverend raised his hands and called upon the Lord, "We need Thy help, Oh God." Everyone in the congregation pled for the Lord's help. They say the prayer lasted over an hour of pleading for some kind of intervention. All of a sudden, they noticed the room was getting darker and the windows started to rattle. The bell in the belfries began to ring, but the Sexton, was sitting right there in the congregation. He looked at the Reverend, as if to say, *Don't look at me, I'm not ringing the bell.* A mighty storm arose and the Reverend raised his hands again and called out, "Oh God, we hear Thee. We hear Thee. Thou hast answered our prayers. Thou hast sunk those frigates to the bottom of the sea."

'About a week or so later, they received word that on that very day, a hurricane came from out of nowhere in the Atlantic and sunk nearly every one of those French frigates, and what was left, limped back to whence they came. The cities on the East Coast were saved. Yes, Sir, things looked pretty dark, but because of their faith they were able to see another sun rise.'

"I was going to give a soft clap, but TJ's face turned serious. He held out his hand in a stopping motion, his other hand pointing to his lips. I didn't hear anything, but took his cue. While he covered the fire with dirt, I covered the area with debris to blend in. We went about twenty, maybe thirty feet into the woods when we came across a perfect place to hide. That's when I could hear them. Motors—what kind, we couldn't tell, but we knew they weren't tanks. They had to be coming from the road we crossed after we came off the mountain. The sound lasted for hours as we stayed in our hiding place. I didn't know about TJ, but for me, this day of fasting was spent praying we wouldn't get caught."

FOUR

MIRACLES HAPPEN

"The next morning, we came out from hiding. We felt it was safe enough to build a small fire to roast our rabbit. Before we ate, we thanked God for watching over us. When it was time to get going, I thanked TJ for a very enjoyable Sunday and for looking after me.

"We didn't cover a lot of ground that day, and I wasn't sure which was harder—the mountain or the dense woods. When we finally came to a stop for the night, I thought the mountain was easier.

"After we ate and were enjoying the warm glow from the small fire, I reminded TJ he was going to tell me about the Battle of Trenton.[ix] TJ smiled, and I knew it was going to be good. He stood up and I leaned my back up against a tree to enjoy the show.

"TJ started, in a low voice: 'It was December 25, 1776, the coldest winter anyone could remember. The better part of the troops' enlistment was about to end, and they were looking forward to going home . . . a nice warm home. Washington had lost battle after battle and knew how vital it was to pull a miracle out of his hat. Perhaps a victory would give the men the willpower to stay and fight.

'There they were on the icy banks of the Delaware River, waiting to cross. The men were still inspired by the words that Thomas Paine had written, entitled *The American Crisis*. It was two days earlier when Washington pulled a paper out of his pocket and handed it to General Henry Knox, and asked him to read it to the men. With a loud voice, Knox read:

"These are the times that try men's souls. The summer soldier and the sunshine patriot will, in this crisis, shrink from the service of their country; but he that stands it now, deserves the love and thanks of man and woman. Tyranny, like hell, is not easily conquered; yet we have this consolation with us, that the harder the conflict, the more glorious the triumph."

'Those words of encouragement gave hope to the men; they would need it for what they were about to do.

'Time was of the essence, and it took longer to cross the Delaware than was planned. Washington had to cross over 2,000-plus men, along with horses and cannons on anything and everything that could float. Washington crossed over in a large canoe-type vessel. Some of the men had to stand for the lack of room. With their set poles moving the large blocks of ice out of their way, they struggled to make it across.

'Not a minute to lose or the element of surprise would be gone. They had to be at Trenton before the sun came up or all would be lost, and so would the lives of those men who were depending on him. I'm sure Washington was concerned, but he never let his men see it.

'The plan was to have General Ewing with his men take and secure a bridge opposite Trenton so the Hessians couldn't retreat. General Cadwalader with his men was to take Bordentown, preventing them from assisting Trenton. They did everything they could, but it was no use—there was no way they could cross the Delaware from where they were. Washington didn't know he would have to go it alone with the few men he had.

'When all the men, horses, and cannons were finally across, Washington looked at his watch, four hours behind schedule. Was all that work they did going to be in vain? Everything had to go smoothly from here on out if they stood a chance. Trenton was only eight, maybe nine miles away; if it were a month earlier or a few months later it could be made easily, but this was in the dead of winter. The road was covered with ice that felt like broken glass with every step. So many men had no shoes and were walking in rag-covered feet. The soles of the ones who were fortunate to have shoes were so thin it was as if they, too, were in rags.

'The next day, when Major Wilkinson was coming up from the rear, the trail was easy to follow. All they had to do was follow the bloodstains left behind in the snow. It was so bitter cold it was a miracle Washington only lost two men on their march to Trenton. When they finally came to the outskirts of Trenton, the sun was coming up. No longer did they have the cover of night.

'Once again, the hand of Providence came to the aid of Washington and his men. The storm was so severe Washington couldn't see Trenton. Washington knew if he couldn't see Trenton, then Trenton couldn't see him. Any hunter will tell you, always hunt your prey with the wind in your face. With the sound of the men and cannons being blown away from the town and the white-out from the storm, perhaps, just perhaps, Washington could still pull out a victory.

'God answered his prayers; not a single soldier was lost during the battle. General Washington addressed his men and thanked them for their service. He put out a plea for the men, whose time was up, to stay. They could now go home with honor, not like the thousands who had deserted and abandoned him. Washington's plea went unanswered; they were only a stone's throw away from home and a nice hot meal from their mother's stove. For the married men, a warm bed with their wife. Again, the call to serve went out; just a little longer was the plea from their General. History doesn't say who the first was that stepped forward, but whoever it was, this country owes a great debt of gratitude to him. His example of courage and selflessness gave others the courage to step forward. Washington's heart was full of gratitude. He thanked them and God.'

"Nikki, I sat there humbled, thinking of their sacrifice. TJ could see I was in deep thought. 'Sir, when I told that story to John and the others, John told us how that reminded him about Gideon's army in the book of Judges. God had Gideon send 22,000 of his men home, leaving 10,000 to fight, but the Lord wanted still fewer. Gideon led his men to water to drink; those who drank by kneeling down and lapping the water like dogs were sent home while those who cupped their hands and brought the water up to drink, keeping themselves on guard, were chosen to fight. Gideon counted them: 300 were all that were left. They were so outnumbered their enemy could easily defeat them, but God wanted to show when you are in a righteous cause, being led by a man of God, He will be on your side and victory will be yours. Only be sure to give God the credit.'

"I opened John's Bible and asked where I could find that story. TJ told me it was in the Old Testament, Judges Chapters 6 and 7. It took a little while, but I found it and folded down the corner. I was curious as to why the Founders used the word 'Providence' instead of 'God' and asked TJ if he knew why. Nikki, I don't think I ever came up with a question that he couldn't answer.

"TJ told me that there are those who say the Founders were not Christians, but they couldn't be any more wrong if they tried. When the Founders read the Ten Commandments and it said not to take God's name in vain, they wanted to make sure they obeyed that commandment, so they would refer to God as 'Providence' or the 'unseen hand.' They had other names as well, but mostly they used Providence."

God's Hand at West Point[x]

"Nikki, I'm sure you were taught in grade school about the winter of 1776 at Valley Forge. But I'll bet they didn't teach you about that same winter as it went into '77 and how West Point was saved. I remember one night after we ate, TJ was getting ready to tell another one of his stories, and I was ready for another show. He stood and pointed at me.

'Many people would look at you like you were crazy if you were to say God was helping during that horrible winter. So how could God be helping, you ask? I'll tell you. Remember, God works in mysterious ways. The Hudson River played a vital role for both the British army and for us. If the British army could take control of the river, West Point would surely fall into their hands, and Washington would not be able to move his troops. To prevent that from happening, a plan was put together. If they could put a heavy chain across the Hudson to impede the movement of the British ships, it might work. I'm not talking about some chain you could get at a hardware store. We're talking huge, weighs-a-ton kind of chain. I believe there is a God, and He placed everything on this earth, knowing far in advance when and where it would be needed. Only a few miles from West Point, there was a mine of the purest iron ore the world has ever known.'

"TJ was moving his arms in a big round circle as he said *world,* and once again I was enjoying the show as much as TJ was telling it.

'Because the iron ore was so pure, they didn't have to make the laborious effort to refine it. In less than three months, they put together a chain that went four, maybe five hundred yards across the Hudson. It may have been miserable for Washington and his men at Valley Forge, but for the men making that vital chain, it required massive amounts of heat, and the cold weather made it possible for the men to do just that.'"

The Constitution and the Founders[xi]

"Nikki, TJ told me more stories that I'd never heard of before, more than you can count. I asked him, 'What is it about the Constitution that gets you so fired up, anyway?'

"TJ leaned forward and looked me right in the eye. 'I see the Constitution itself as a miracle. So many times I see how God's hand played a part in helping the Founders in so many ways. For example, in the nick of time there was a Scotsman by the name of Adam Smith. He wrote *The Wealth of Nations,* in which there were ideas that had never been tried before, but the Founders knew that under the right circumstances, his ideas could work.

'There are those who think the Constitution was put together by a bunch of uneducated farmers and that it may have been fine for their day, but not for a modern society like ours. They want the Constitution to be a living, breathing document so it could change whenever it was needed to fit their needs. I once played a game of poker with a guy who thought that way, so every hand I changed the rules so I could win.

'Since he didn't know the rules very well, it was easy to do, until it was so obvious what I was doing, and he got mad. I looked at him and said that the rules of poker were like the rules of a living breathing Constitution, and I could change them to my liking. He still thought that it applied to the Constitution and not poker, but at least I tried to get my point across.

'The Founders made it possible for the Constitution to change, but it has to go through the states for ratification. Those who think the Constitution doesn't apply to us today have no idea of the work that went into the framing of that work of art. It's important to remember that it took the Founders a hundred and eighty years, from the start of Jamestown in 1607 to the signing of the Constitution in 1787, to come up with their success formula for freedom and prosperity. Yes, Sir, the Constitution wasn't written for their time period, it was written knowing human nature, which never changes. Let me tell you, they studied history and not just any history, no, Sir. They studied government history, what worked and what didn't.'"

FIVE

THE WISDOM OF THE FOUNDERS

"Nikki, I'm going to share with you something that TJ brought to my attention, a trend I've noticed over my lifetime, and it's not a good trend. When he shared with me an experience he had in one of his classes, I made note of it. One night, we were talking about the men the Founders studied when TJ told me that there are those who want to change the government and they come from all walks of life. Back home, one of his professors was one of them. The professor was subtle in his teaching, but TJ could see right through it."

Plato's Republic

"One day, the professor was talking about how great the philosopher Plato was, and how we should pattern our government with what he had in mind, and that the Framers must not have been very educated to have overlooked Plato when starting a new government. TJ always thought we go to school not only to learn what the teachers have to tell us, but to question, to reason, evaluate, and yes—to challenge. Whenever TJ would study with his parents, if he made a statement, they would challenge him to support it. Even if it was something they had taught him. They sure liked playing the devil's advocate. So, when the professor went on about Plato, TJ looked around, and not a single hand went up. So he figured he would raise his hand and challenge the professor, as his parents did with him."

"Why do I get the feeling the professor ended up wishing he didn't call on TJ when he raised his hand?"

"Nikki, my dear, your feelings are spot on and I asked him what he said, he smiled, 'I was respectful, I assure you. I asked the professor if he thought it would be all right if I, along with a few of my classmates, destroyed his classroom in order to rebuild a new classroom in its place, the way we would like it? Of course, he said he wouldn't allow it. Why? I asked. Plato advocated rebuilding on a clean canvas, which required revolutionary destruction of a whole society before a new one could be built. So you should be fine with us destroying your classroom.'

'Then I asked, "Do you believe all men are created equal? Or do you think there should be different classes of people? Perhaps because you're a professor, those of higher learning belong in the upper class while those of lesser education should be in a more fitting lower class, and minorities like me should be even lower still, because Plato did."'

"I looked at TJ, 'So you used your minority status to put him in his place, did you?'

'I know—a little below the belt, and I shouldn't have, but I did.'

'What did you do then?'

'I asked him if he had any private property and he said he did. I shook my head and told him he would have to give that up along with his children who would now be raised in public nurseries, financed by his tax dollars, of course.'

"Nikki, I couldn't wait to hear what the professor said to that, so I asked TJ his response.

'I don't think I gave him a chance to reply. I kept going down the list. I said, I don't know if you have a traditional religion or not, but

I do, and I'm sure most of us in this classroom do as well. If we were to follow Plato's plan, that would be taken away from us and replaced with a political religion. Tongue-in-cheek, I told him there was one thing that I did like of Plato's government, and it was this: that no one would be allowed to tell lies. It's Plato's caveat that I objected to, which is that only the government would be allowed to tell lies. You should have heard the class laugh at that one.

'The professor stopped me and said, "The problem with you, TJ, is that you think people are and should be responsible. I, on the other hand, don't think they are capable of being responsible, and they need more intelligent people to guide them."

'I stood, I could feel my blood pressure rising, but I kept my cool. I looked at him and said, "That's Plato, all right, government by rulers, not by rules." Then I quoted Plato himself. "Nobody, whether male or female, should be without a leader. Nor should the mind of anybody be habituated to letting him do anything at all on his own initiative." I could have left it at that, but I didn't.'

"Nikki, I shook my head and chuckled. 'Put a little salt on the wound, did you?'

"TJ also chuckled. 'A little, but when someone tells me how uneducated the Founders were, I couldn't stop myself. I told him the American Founders did an in-depth study of Plato, and they called his ideas *utter nonsense.* The professor told me and the class that Jefferson wasn't that well-read.'"

Thomas Jefferson's Schooling[xii]

"Nikki, what I learned about Thomas Jefferson's schooling was beyond extraordinary. TJ very calmly let him have it with both barrels and told the professor a thing or two. I guess he didn't know what the initials TJ stood for. Let me tell you I was on the edge of my seat. This is what TJ told the professor. 'Let me give you a little taste of Thomas Jefferson's study habits. At the age of nine, he was studying Latin, Greek, and French. At sixteen, he entered college as an advanced student and graduated by the time he was nineteen. Then he put in another five years of even more intensive study with George Wythe, the first professor of Law in America. It wasn't uncommon for him to put in twelve to fourteen hours of study every day. When he went before the bar for his examination, he knew more than the examiners.

'He could speak five languages. He had studied the Roman and Greek classics. He had studied European history, and he had undertaken a thorough study of British history. He was a student of ancient Israel and the Anglo-Saxons, and was well-versed in science and mechanics. If you were to talk to him about theology, you would think you're talking to a trained minister. He knew the Bible inside and out. He studied Polybius, Cicero, Thomas Hooker, Coke, Montesquieu, Blackstone, John Locke, and Adam Smith, to name a few of the philosophers. When I finished telling him about Jefferson's schooling, I reloaded and let him have it again with John Adams.'"

John Adams's Education

"I have got to meet TJ."

"My dear, perhaps one day you will. Would you like to hear what TJ told the professor about John Adams and his education?"

I nodded my head. "TJ held nothing back. He looked at the professor.

'John Adams, whom you also have very little regard for, also studied Plato, and for no less than thirty years, with the help of two Latin, one English, and one French translation. Comparing some of the most remarkable passages with the Greek, Adams said, his disappointment was great, his astonishment was greater, and his disgust shocking. Plato's laws and his republic, from which he expected most, disappointed him most. I asked the professor if his studies could come even close to Jefferson or Adams, and to name for me one society at any time in the history of the world where Plato's ideas worked for any extended length of time. The Founders knew this, and that's why they came up with the balance of government that they did. They knew the most efficient form of government was one of *Representation*.'"

"What happened then?"

"Since TJ was already standing, the professor pointed to the door and invited him to leave. As he was gathering his things, he told the class it was a pleasure to have met them and that he was going to join the army because of the love he had for this great country. Then he turned to the professor and said, 'I go to protect the Constitution that gives you the right to say the things you say, no matter how ignorant they may be.'"

The Five-Thousand-Year Leap[xiii]

"I can see TJ giving the professor the What For."

James started to laugh. "The 'what for'? I haven't heard that expression in ages."

"Don't forget, I hung around my grandfather."

James nodded and smiled. "TJ was always giving me something to think about. Nikki, have you ever thought about what things would be like right now if we hadn't won the war with England and there never was a Constitution?"

"I haven't given it much thought."

"Think about this: when Adam and Eve were kicked out of the Garden of Eden, how did they travel?"

"How did they travel? I have no idea." I smiled. *"I wasn't there."*

James smiled back. "When TJ asked me that very question, I had no idea either. TJ smiled and told me, 'It was a trick question. The scriptures don't say, but it's a safe bet they either walked, or rode on some kind of animal. When George Washington left his home in Mount Vernon to go to Philadelphia for the convention, he traveled by horsepower, most likely a team of four.'

"I looked at TJ and told him I didn't understand. 'What I'm saying is this: from the time of Adam and Eve, mankind was using animals to help them get around. From the time of the Constitution to the time you were shot down, you had over a thousand horses in your P-51 as you flew over the skies of Germany. Think about it, for five thousand years nothing changed, and then the Constitution comes into play, and within a short time in history, you're flying through the air. You can't tell me that's a coincidence. As fast as things are progressing, I wouldn't be surprised if in the next fifty years we're flying to the moon.'

"Laughing, I said, 'That sounds a little crazy even for you.' But on July 20, 1969, Commander Neil Armstrong became the first man on the moon. I was glued to the TV when I heard: 'That's one small step for man, one giant leap for mankind.' TJ only missed it by twenty years or so."

Free Enterprise

"After I made the crack about TJ being crazy, he said, 'I know history and I may be stretching it, but you get the idea. Think about this: why didn't anything progress for five thousand years? Could it be because there was no real freedom, or free enterprise for someone to invent something and receive the profits from it? The King would only confiscate it anyway, so why bother? The only law up until that time was Ruler's Law. The King Giveth and the King Taketh away—and I do mean 'take it away.' But when the Constitution came into play, everything changed, and we now have People's Law. If we don't like the way our representatives are handling things, we can send them on their merry way. The Constitution binds men's hands from taking away our rights, at least it's supposed to.'

"I looked at TJ. 'What are you talking about? The Constitution is still in place.' He agreed. 'Yes, Sir, it is, and as long as we have men and women like you, both abroad and on the home front who are willing to fight for it, we always will. I'm afraid it's going to be hanging by a thread before enough of the people wake up.

'When some people get into office and get a taste of power, they look for ways to stay in power by bending the Constitution's meaning. One of the ways is when they offer the masses something for nothing, by taking from those who have and giving it to those who don't. Telling them it's only fair: "Vote for me and I'll make sure you get your fair share." If they can get enough people relying on the government for everything from food and shelter, the politicians know the people will never vote them out of office, that is, until someone comes along and offers them even more. Lord Acton once said, 'Power corrupts, and absolute power corrupts absolutely.'"

'My father had a way of explaining the Constitution this way: "Ten wolves surround one chicken and take a vote. How many say we eat the chicken? How many say we don't? Sorry chicken, ten to one, let's eat." The Constitution comes in and makes the one vote equal by protecting the chickens' rights. There's something about power that goes to a person's head when they get it. I think that's why the Founders wanted those who served to do so for a short amount of time and then get out and let someone else serve.'"

100%
0%

SIX

THE BALANCED CENTER

"Nikki, you've played on a teeter-totter before, haven't you?"

"Of course."

"I'm going to teach you something about a teeter-totter that TJ taught me. The Founders studied all kinds of governments throughout history; they boiled it down to two kinds, Ruler's Law, where all law comes from the King or Ruler, and People's Law, where all the law comes from the people. Each has its pros and cons. The Framers of the Constitution wanted to blend the two into one.

"TJ moved over to my left and sat down, clearing the ground of debris. With a stick, he drew a straight line about three feet long above the small fire, then looked at me and asked, 'If you were to measure the two laws, it would look something like this. The far left is Ruler's Law and the far right is People's Law. Let me ask you, Sir, what do you think we call these two laws today?'

"Nikki, I had to think about it for a moment. What would be your answer?"

"Let's see, I remember one of my teachers telling the class that the far left of government is Communism and the far right is Fascism."

"Nikki, that's what I said. TJ looked at me and shook his head.

'Sir, both of those systems fall under Ruler's Law; they're both very similar police states. For a simple definition, under Communism, the government owns and controls everything, whereas Fascism doesn't own the businesses but controls what the businesses produce and everything in between, from what workers will get paid, to how long they'll work.

'Hitler, being a socialist, should never have been so anti-Communist, after all, his Nazi Party and the Communist Party are practically the same. Hitler would have the men in the factories working twenty-hour workdays, so he could be prepared for war. If the men complained, they and their families didn't eat.

'As far as Fascism being on the far right, those who believe and teach that never stop and think to break it down. The word *fascism* comes from the Latin word *fasces*. As for their symbol, a *bundle of sticks with an ax,* its meaning is life over death, and it comes from ancient Imperial Romans.

'Benito Mussolini, being the fascist dictator in Italy, got along fine with Hitler because of the similarities in government rule.'

"TJ looked at me. 'So, using this political spectrum I've drawn on the ground can be rather confusing, what with all the different names that can be placed on it. The Founders had another way of measuring government. Their political spectrum looked like this.'

"TJ put two hash marks on both ends. 'Sir, this mark on the left is 100 percent government, and this one on the right is 0 percent government. You can't get any more or less than this. A 100 percent government is tyranny and 0 percent is anarchy. Tyranny comes in all kinds of flavors: Communism, Socialism, Fascism, Militarism, or Monarchism, a King. Whatever "ism" you want to call it, it's still Ruler's Law and Tyranny, telling you what you can and can't do, so we know we don't want 100 percent of government.

'Anarchy on the other end of the political spectrum is where there are no laws or rules . . . can you imagine what life would be like without any laws? Both ends of the spectrum are where people suffer and die. With no laws in place to protect the individual is . . . well, Sir, for lack of a better word, insane. The French, in their Revolution, went through anarchy, and they guillotined anyone they felt had control over their lives. The history books say that the blood ran through the streets like water after a rainstorm, so we know we don't want anarchy, as well.

'One of the reasons we almost lost the war with England was because of the Articles of Confederation that the people were living under. Those laws were set up closer to the far right because they didn't trust the government. They knew from their experience with King George in England what happens when a man gets power.'

"Nikki, here's where the teeter-totter comes in. TJ drew a triangle, putting the small fire in the center of it with the point of the triangle right in the middle of the line between tyranny and anarchy. Right above that, TJ drew something on top of the line. I asked him what it was, and he told me it was an eagle. I laughed and told him it looked more like a turkey to me. TJ smiled, 'Funny you should say that. Franklin wanted the American symbol to be the turkey. At least that's the rumor because of a letter he wrote to his daughter Sarah.'

"TJ then pointed to the triangle. 'This triangle or pyramid is where the Founders set up the Constitution, right at the top of the political spectrum. I call this the balanced center of Liberty, with the power at the base of the pyramid in the hands of the people, telling their leaders at the top, whom they elected, what they can and can't do. With Ruler's Law, all the power is in the hands of the few on the top, telling the people what they can and can't do.'

"Nikki, ever since the Constitution was signed on September 17, 1787, there have been those who have been trying to pull that eagle to the left, even from those you wouldn't expect. They go by all kinds of names, Communist, Socialist, Statist, Progressionist, and Environmentalist, the list goes on and on. They like to hide in the dark by belonging to different organizations that sound so benevolent, so patriotic that one would never suspect they want to control your life. That list is longer than your arm.

"The same thing goes for the ones who want to pull the eagle to the far right toward anarchy. Each wing of the eagle represents the political sides of government; one wants more government and the other wants less.

"The left wing is the problem-solving wing, while the right wing is the conservation wing. Each wing is equally important. Without them, the eagle wouldn't be able to fly. The left wing could be called the compassion wing, always wanting to take care of everything."

I interjected, *"What's so wrong with that?"*

"Nothing, my dear, if you're on the receiving end and you want to be taken care of your whole life. John told me a scripture that says, 'If a man will not work, he shall not eat.' In other words, if a man is capable of working but doesn't, he doesn't deserve to eat. That's in 2nd Thessalonians 3:10. You see, Nikki, a little help is fine. Everyone needs help now and then. In fact, those who help others also receive a benefit for helping. You've helped others in need before, so how did that make you feel?"

I thought for a moment. *"I must admit, it felt good."*

"Ever help someone and find out later that they took advantage of you?"

"A few times."

"Nikki, those types of people have been around from the beginning, and I suppose they'll be around till the end. The trick is to figure out who needs a hand up and not a handout. Helping others in their time of need is something that we have an obligation to do, if we can. But taking care of those who can take care of themselves for long periods of time isn't helping but hindering them.

"When God kicked Adam and Eve out of the Garden of Eden, He told Adam by the sweat of his face he'll eat bread until he returns to the ground. In other words, when they were in the garden, everything was provided for them, but when God kicked them out, it was at that point God wanted man to work and appreciate what he was given. Everyone on this earth needs to grow and if all our needs are taken care of, do we really grow?"

"I never thought of it like that before, but since you put it that way, probably not."

"Nikki, have you ever seen a butterfly come out of its chrysalis?"

"Not to my recollection."

"Well, when it starts to emerge, it can take hours. If you were to help it out of its chrysalis, you'd be doing it more harm than good. It needs the struggle to strengthen itself, and its wings.

"TJ taught me that's where the right side of the eagle's wing comes in. Its job is to make sure we can afford whatever it is that the left wing has come up with; I suppose that's why the right wing gets accused of being heartless. It's only trying to protect the rights and freedom of individuals. If either wing grows bigger than the other, it won't fly straight. There must be checks and balances, so the body of the eagle can stay in the middle, with both wings staying the same size. When that happens, the eagle will fly higher and straighter than any country in the history of the world. It's human nature to want to help others, but we need to be careful and help them to help themselves, so they can be strong and independent. Otherwise, the very people we're trying to help become slaves to others, and they don't even know it.

"This country has lost hundreds of thousands of lives getting rid of the kind of slavery that came with chains we can see, but make no mistake, there is a kind of evil slavery that comes with chains we can't see.

"Each wing has within it political extremists. They hide within, like wolves in sheep's clothing, trying to get that eagle to the far end of the political spectrum. To them, it's like a religion.

"Putting the eagle in the balanced center where the Founders did, was designed to maintain a political equilibrium between the people in the states and the federal government. You've been on a teeter-totter before when the balance on both sides weren't equal, right?"

I nodded.

"Not much fun, was it? Nikki, you're either sitting on the ground or up in the air, so you make adjustments to balance it out. That's what the Founders had in mind when they put that eagle in the center. The idea was to keep the power base close to the people, with an emphasis on a strong local self-government. That's why there is a separation, both vertical and horizontal.

"Nikki, I have to be honest with you, I really didn't know what that meant at the time and I was embarrassed to ask, but I did anyway. TJ thanked me for the question and explained it this way: vertical separation was to divide the responsibilities and political authority between the States and the federal government. The Constitution is to coordinate, not consolidate the State into the federal government. You see, Nikki, the Founders wanted the States to be responsible for their own internal affairs, and the federal government would step in only when the matters couldn't be fairly handled by the individual States, not to take over the States.

"The Framers knew how important it was to keep things balanced because they knew Rome and Greece didn't. They thought their governments would never fail, yet they did, because of corruption and class warfare. They say the fall of Rome was complicated, but it can be boiled down to a simple cycle. The state slowly takes away freedom and demands more power. The people, not wanting to be responsible for themselves, want what they think are freebies from the government. Not realizing they are paying for it with their freedom. Taxes go up to pay for the freebies and the size of government grows until it can no longer sustain itself. The economy slows to a snail's pace and sooner or later collapses. The laws of economics, like the law of gravity, can't be ignored."

SEVEN

THE THREE BRANCHES OF GOVERNMENT

"TJ then drew two more heads on the eagle, and I couldn't help myself and told him, now it really looks like a turkey. TJ tilted his head . . . Looking at it, he said, 'It really does, but it's still an eagle, only one with three heads.'

"Nikki, this is where the horizontal separation of power comes in: each head is a branch of government with separate powers and one neck, so they can't function without the support of each other. This is how our government is set up and it's brilliant. TJ pointed to the central head. 'This is the legislative branch. They make the laws. It has two eyes, one for the House and one for the Senate and they have to see eye-to-eye, so to speak, before any law is passed. The Constitution in Article 1 Sections 8 and 9 only gives these guys about twenty powers. I wish someone would remind them of that. This branch of government was set up with a lot of thought. The House of Representatives, which is the Congress, is elected every two years by the people and could all be voted out if the people in their district didn't like what they were doing. The senators are in office for six.

'Two things I think are brilliant about the legislative branch and the way it is set up; first, the Founders staggered the terms of the

Senate, so every two years, one-third are elected by someone new or re-elected. That way, if the people ever got so fed up with the legislative branch of the government and wanted to vote them all out at the same time, there would be at least two-thirds in the Senate that would be left behind for a smooth transition. Someone who knows what's going on must be left in charge.

'If things didn't change the way the people wanted, in two more years, another election and another third could be voted out. I would love to see that happen if only once. I think that would put the fear of God into them and they might straighten up. I doubt it will ever happen, but it's nice to dream.

'The second thing I think was brilliant was how the Senate was elected: They were put in by each State's legislature. That is, until 1913, when the Seventeenth Amendment came along and had the people vote them in. 1913 really wasn't a good year for the Constitution.'"

"James, I'm confused. I remember my teachers in school teaching how good the Seventeenth Amendment was and how it made it more democratic, that the people should be the ones to decide who represents them in both the House and Senate."

"Nikki, I was taught the same thing even way back then and I asked TJ why. TJ cocked his head, 'More democratic? Maybe, but it was set up the way it was so there would be less politicking. You see, Sir, the Founders knew human nature and how easy it would be for a congressman, who is elected by the people, to want to give things away in order to be re-elected, buying their vote so to speak. That's why the Senate was put in by each State's legislature.

'When Jefferson returned from France, he asked Washington why even have a Senate and why it wasn't chosen by the people. Washington answered him by asking why he poured his hot tea in the saucer. Jefferson said, "to cool it." Washington told him that's what the Senate is for, to cool things with the house when they wanted to start giving things away. You can't give something to someone you don't have, unless you take it from someone else.

'The Senate's job is to look out for property and State's rights. By being elected from their state's legislatures and not the people, it removes the temptation of telling the people what they can do for them, instead of watching out for property and State's rights. It was to be more of a checks and balances, but not anymore, the Seventeenth Amendment took care of that.'

"Then, TJ pointing to the second head on the eagle, 'This head was put in for the President. It's the Executive branch and he only has six responsibilities, at least that's all the Constitution has granted him in Article 2. It's unbelievable the laws that come out of the Executive branch that usurp authority that it doesn't have with Executive orders.' TJ could see that he had lost me with this one, so he backed up. 'The President can only give executive orders to those who work for him. In the beginning, Presidents would give maybe forty or so executive orders that pertained to the executive branch. But, when Teddy Roosevelt came into office . . . you want to talk about usurpation, he actually said, "I can do anything as President that I feel is right for the Nation, unless the Constitution forbids me doing it." Nothing like getting things 180 degrees off. During his administration, he passed over a thousand executive orders, and for some reason, Congress let it slide by as laws of the land. Somebody should have told him and the legislatures, *we don't work for you, you work for us.*

'George Washington warned us about usurpation, taking authority they do not have. In his farewell address, he said, "But let there be no change by usurpation; for, though this, in one instance, may be the instrument of good, it is the customary weapon by which free governments are destroyed."

'When Roosevelt finished two terms, he recommended William Taft for President. As you know, he won and took office in 1909.

Roosevelt and Taft were good friends, but when Teddy got back from his safari in Africa, he wasn't happy with Taft and tried to run for a third term under a new party. President Roosevelt was the founder of the Bull Moose Progressive Party and split the vote, which let in another progressive for president, Woodrow Wilson. Between him and the two Roosevelts ignoring the Constitution, I can't tell you how much I feel they turned the Constitution on its head. They each placed their hand on the Bible, and took an oath to uphold the Constitution, not to walk all over it, doing whatever they wanted.' TJ gave a slight pause. 'Someday they will be held accountable for that oath they made to God.'

"TJ pointed to the third head. 'This is the Judiciary. Their job is to make sure the Constitution is interpreted in the way the Founders meant it be, and to make sure the laws passed by Congress are in keeping with the twenty-eight principles of liberty the Founders put in place. The Judiciary branch only has eleven types of cases assigned to them in the Federal Courts and that's in Article 3.'"

Principles of Liberty

"Forgive me, James, but the twenty-eight principles of liberty? I've never heard of that term."

"Don't beat yourself up. Neither had I. They're the principles that the Framers used to form the Government with. TJ told me when he was about eight, he was studying with his father when they started coming across what they felt were principles the Framers used to form the Constitution. By the time he was fourteen, they had about twenty. His father must have gone over 150 volumes of the Founding Fathers' writings to come up with the list.

"Nikki, when I was building this house, I knew I had to have a firm foundation and a strong frame to withstand the elements of nature. The Founders also knew to build a strong nation, they would also need the same. The foundation is the Constitution and the frame is made from the Principles of Liberty. Once they were put in place, amazing things started to happen."

"Like the five-thousand-year leap you were telling me about?"

"Precisely. The Constitution allows us to govern ourselves. When we follow the correct principles, we grow stronger together as a Nation. When we don't, and we start to go astray, that's when we find ourselves in trouble.

"Nikki, did you know there was a Constitution about a hundred years before Thomas Jefferson was even born?"

"Once again, my teachers failed to mention that as well."

"Mine, too. Now you can start to see why I'm so beholden to my mentors. TJ told me he was sharing the list of the principles of liberty with the guys one night and how he and his father found some of them in the first written Constitution America had. It was written by Reverend Hooker. The Reverend Hooker gave a sermon on ancient Israel and the principles of government that they lived by. If it was good enough for God's people, it was good enough for them, was the Reverend's attitude. John wanted to know where in the Bible the good Reverend got his ideas. TJ told him it was in the first chapter of Deuteronomy. When John turned to it, TJ said you should have seen his face. He looked like a kid opening a present on Christmas morning. John said he had read that chapter many times and never noticed it. He even underlined those principles in that chapter.

"When TJ told me that, I reached into my pocket and took out John's Bible. TJ helped me find Deuteronomy, sure enough, just as TJ said, was where John underlined the principles. I noticed a piece of paper folded in half stuck in between the pages. As I opened it, TJ said, 'That's the list of the twenty-eight principles that John wrote down as I told them to him.'

"It was good to see John's handwritten notes and I thought of it as a treasure as I reflected back on John and the things he taught me as I read through the list."

Liberties List[xiv]

1. The only reliable basis for sound government and just human relations is natural law.
2. A free people cannot survive under a Republican Constitution unless they remain virtuous and morally strong.
3. The most promising method of securing a virtuous and morally stable people is to elect virtuous leaders.
4. Without religion, the government of a free people cannot be maintained.
5. All things were created by God, therefore upon Him they are equally responsible.
6. All men are created equal.
7. The proper role of government is to protect equal rights, not equal things.
8. Men are endowed by their creator with certain unalienable rights.
9. To protect man's rights, God has revealed certain principles of divine law.
10. The God-given right to govern is vested in the sovereign authority of the whole people.
11. The majority of the people may alter or abolish a government which has become tyrannical.
12. The United States of America shall be a republic.
13. A Constitution should be structured to permanently protect the people from the human frailties of their rulers.
14. Life and liberty are secure only so long as the right to property is secure.

15. The highest level of prosperity occurs when there is a free-market economy and a minimum of government regulations.
16. The government should be separated into three branches; Legislative, Executive, and Judicial.
17. A system of checks and balances should be adopted to prevent the abuse of power.
18. The unalienable rights of the people are most likely to be preserved if the principles of government are set forth in a written Constitution.
19. Only limited and carefully defined powers should be delegated to government, all others being retained in the people.
20. Efficiency and dispatch require government to operate according to the will of the majority, but Constitutional provisions must be made to protect the rights of the minority.
21. Strong local self-government is the keystone to preserving human freedom.
22. A free people should be governed by law, and not by the whims of men.
23. A free society cannot survive as a republic without a broad program of general education.
24. A free people will not survive unless they stay strong.
25. Peace, commerce, and honest friendship with all Nations, entangling alliances with none.
26. The core unit which determines the strength of any society is the family. Therefore, the government should foster and protect its integrity.
27. The burden of debt is as destructive to freedom as subjugation by conquest.
28. The United States has a manifest destiny to be an example and a blessing to the entire human race.

"When I was finished, I looked up and TJ added, 'I wish more people and Congress knew about that list. Maybe then they would stop passing counterfeit laws that weaken the Constitution.'

"I asked him what he meant; TJ shook his head. 'I mean, Satan always has counterfeits.' He stood up and stretched. 'It's late; we'll pick up where we left off tomorrow and I'll tell you about the counterfeits. Get some rest; I'll take the first watch.'"

Doom and Gloom[xv]

As James leaned back in his chair, I could see him go into deep thought. His hands were clasped over his stomach. Then he leaned forward, resting his arms on the desk and in a calm voice said, "I was thinking about everything I've seen in my lifetime and how fast things are going downhill. If TJ were here, he could put it on a graph and chart it better than I ever could. I'm concerned about what the future may look like. I've seen so many corrupt politicians in my lifetime; it's amazing this great country is still standing. That eagle has been pulled so far to the side of tyranny; I wonder if it can ever be brought back to the balanced center? If you were to read the Communist Manifesto, you'd think we were following it instead of our Constitution.

"This nation is in so much debt, I don't see how we'll ever climb out of this hole. If Congress were serious about paying it off, or getting things under control, they would do what Andrew Jackson did.

"He is the only President who paid off the National debt, and he didn't do it by raising taxes either. He increased the tax money coming in by getting government out of the way. Jackson freed up the free market so it could grow. With less regulations and taxes on the ones creating and innovating, it meant more people working. The more people working, the more the American economy grows.

It's simple math. Instead, I see our government doing the same things that Rome and Greece did before they fell with more and more taxes. I shake my head and wonder.

"Why do we keep putting the same people in office over and over, expecting different results? Don't we know that's the very definition of insanity, doing the same thing over and over, expecting different results? Maybe if the mainstream media were doing their job, to be the warning bell for the people like the Founders wanted them to be, maybe then the people would throw the bums out.

"Nikki, because I was told to always keep my eyes open and look for patterns, whenever Congress passes laws, I always ask myself, 'How does this fit with the Constitution and the principles of liberty?' I have to tell you, it's not very often that they fit. Both Republicans and Democrats spend money they don't have. They spend it like it's going out of style. Whenever the government takes money from one and gives it to another, you know they're trying to buy votes so they can get re-elected. But, for some reason, either the people don't know it, or they don't care. If I ran my company like the government, two things would happen. I'd be out of business and I'd be in jail.

"When I think of all the money that is thrown out the window from all the different departments . . ." James shook his head in disgust. "They think they have to spend all the money that is allotted to them, because if they don't spend it, they won't get more the next year. It's a use it or lose it policy and one that needs to go. It makes my head feel like it's going to explode and don't even get me started on earmarks and baseline budgeting."

I looked at James, *"I know earmarks are the pork spending Congress likes to add in a bill, where they say they will sign it if they add a pet project for their state or district. So by the time the bill gets through both houses, billions have been added on. That's why President Reagan wanted the line-item veto, but I don't think I've ever heard of baseline budgeting."*

James loved teaching moments. "Oh, that's one of the many tricks they like to do to get away with pulling the wool over people's eyes. In their budget, they have a baseline that they start at and it has an automatic increase that goes up every year. In their negotiating, they come down from what was the automatic increase, calling it a cut, even though they still plan on spending more than they did the previous year."

I must have looked a little confused, so James explained it this way.

"Let's say you want to buy a new car, even though you don't need it and can't afford one. Let's say you plan on spending $50,000 on this new car, but you find one for $30,000. Did you cut or save $20,000?"

"Sure." I could tell by the look on his face I gave the wrong answer. I figured it out and I hit the side of my head. *"No, I spent $30,000 I didn't have."*

James gave me a smile of approval. "Now, Congress can go around either complaining or bragging that they cut or saved $20,000 from the budget, when in essence, they spent $30,000. I can't tell you how many times my company had to tighten the belt to make things balanced. I wish the government would do the same. Here's an idea, freeze spending until things catch up. But, for some reason, either the people don't know about it, or they don't care."

James sat there for a moment shaking his head. "I wonder if we'll ever have a Congress and a President that will get the budget under control?

"I'll tell you another thing I'm concerned about and that's the things the schools are teaching our impressionable youth, and it scares me to death. There are those who want control and believe like Lenin when he said, 'Give me four years to teach the children, and the seed I have sown will never be uprooted.' Those who want control know if you want to change the people's behavior, change their beliefs. And the best place to start that indoctrination is in the schools, as Hitler did with his youth program. It was set up to indoctrinate them to hate, and pledge allegiance to him. I can't help but feel the same spirit from those who want to control our youth through the school system. I'm sure others feel it too. That's why more and more charter and private schools are popping up and home schooling is getting stronger and stronger.

"Trying to get anything done is next to impossible. There is so much red tape in the government, even when the troops need vital and basic supplies; they rely on outside help from nonprofit organizations to cut through all the red tape. Where the government should really be effective, they fall flat on their face. Things seem to be upside down where the government is concerned. Where we the people should be filling the void, the government steps in and takes over."

"What do you mean?"

"What I mean is, government should only do what's in the Constitution and protect us in the areas where we give them the authority to protect us. Then, we, the people, should help our neighbors when they need help to get back on their feet. We should be the safety net, not the government hammock it has become. God's plan is for us to take care of others that can't care for themselves. Satan's plan, I think, is for government to replace God and have the people be dependent on the government, by taking away our responsibilities. The more we rely on government, the more our taxes go up, putting more and more people on the dole. The more people that depend on the government, the more enslaved they become. No one knew this better than FDR. He said, 'Government handouts could be a narcotic, a subtle destroyer of the human spirit.'"

"When did he say that?"

"It was in one of his State of the Union Addresses." James, shaking his head, said, "That's our money that Congress keeps wasting to put the people under their control. In my opinion, it's downright evil."

James once again went to his bookcase. "I've told this story to the family more times than I can count." He took down a small paperback book. It was an old Reader's Digest. As he sat back down, he said, "Back in October of 1950, I came across this story called *Fable of the Gullible Gull.*" James turned to page 32 and began to read.

"*In our friendly neighbor city of St. Augustine, great flocks of seagulls are starving amid plenty. Fishing is still good, but the gulls don't know how to fish. For generations, they have depended on the shrimp fleet to toss them scraps from the nets. When it was time, the shrimp fleet moved on.*"

"The shrimpers had created a Welfare State for the seagulls. The big birds never bothered to learn how to fish for themselves and they never taught their children to fish. Instead, they led their little ones to the shrimp nets.

"Now the seagulls, the fine free birds almost symbolize liberty itself, are starving to death because they gave in to the 'something for nothing' lure. They sacrificed their independence for a handout."

James stopped. "Why can't people see they are giving up their freedom for scraps? Don't they see how dependent they've become? What's going to happen when the government runs out of freebies, and you know they will. You can't keep taking from those who produce it and give it to those who don't. There will come a time when there will be more takers than givers. There will be riots in the streets like never seen before.

"There are those who have been on the government dole so long they don't know how to survive. We need to reach out and help them to stand. Help them help themselves, by teaching them to first walk and then to run. It'll be hard, but nothing worth having is ever easy. I don't think they even realize they have been bought and paid for.

"When I first started putting up buildings, I could build them at a reasonable price. But as time went on with all the regulations they kept adding on . . ." James paused. "I mean, really, do we need someone to come in and stop the whole project because the light switch is one inch too low or too high? Office buildings are one thing, but now they're in my home telling me what kind of toilet I can and can't have. Even the kind of light bulbs are being dictated. The government controls so much of our lives in areas that most people don't even realize.

"I think total control has always been Satan's objective. I believe John was right and that's what got Satan and his angels cast out from heaven in the first place. With so-called help, we lose more and more of our freedoms and become dependent, controlled, and miserable without even realizing it. And you know what they say about misery liking company. We're like crabs in a bucket."

James paused with a slight grin and I looked at him with puzzled eyes.

"Okay, James, I'll bite. How are we like crabs in a bucket?"

James winked. "When I was a little boy, my father took me to the ocean to catch crabs. When we caught our first one, Dad put it in the bucket and had me put the lid on. After we caught our second one, Dad told me the lid wouldn't be necessary because whenever one tries to get out, the other will pull it back down. Sure enough, that's what happened. People are the same. They want you to be as miserable as they are and they'll try to pull you down if you try to get out of that proverbial bucket.

"I also think this political correctness is another form of control. They may say it's a way of being polite, but it's not. It's control. Satan would love to control how we think. The first time I heard P.C., I couldn't figure out why they were using 'personal computer' in that sentence."

I couldn't help but smile at that one.

"I once heard there was a Canadian minister who was arrested for hate speech because he quoted the Bible. I wonder how long before that happens in America? Satan has been trying to remove God from our lives for a long time and he has come a long way. In cities all across America, if there was a copy of the Ten Commandments on public property such as courthouses and the like, they had to be removed because of the perceived lack of separation of church and state."

James took a deep breath and slowly let it out. "Ignorant fools. Don't they know if they take God out it leaves a vacuum, and Satan is all too happy to fill the void? For example, no longer are Nativity scenes allowed on any government property; Christmas songs that have any thought of Christ can't be sung in our schools; No longer can a prayer be uttered at a graduation; Easter is now a celebration of spring; we don't want to offend anyone now, do we? What about me? I'm offended, don't I count?

"I was listening to the radio a while back and heard someone complain about a lemonade stand in the neighborhood. A lemonade stand, can you believe it? The cops shut it down because the kids didn't have a permit. What's this world coming to? I think it's a way to start training those youngsters that they need to ask Big Brother first.

"The mainstream media should be sounding the warning bell of freedom about this kind of stuff, but they don't. I gave up on them a long time ago.

"Nikki, I've given this a lot of thought and I may not have all the answers, but I think I have a few. The Founders never expected, nor intended for politicians to make government a lifetime career. In the beginning, they were paid very little so they would do their patriotic duty and go back home to work on their farm, or whatever their profession was.

"Politics was meant to be a service to the community. So let's put term limits for both houses. After all, we put one in for the President. Let's also make it so they can't go from one office to another, or become a lobbyist. They need to go home and let others serve. We need more common everyday people who understand freedom.

Someone who has had to meet payroll and understands what a real budget means. We need Frank the farmer and Joe the plumber. When the opposition says, 'Only lawyers should serve to pass laws,' we need to remind them the Constitution only delegates Congress about twenty powers. Surely anyone can be brought up to speed and learn twenty things."

"What about a third party?"

"A third party? It's been tried several times and it only splits the votes. No, a third party isn't the answer. You'll never find someone that meets all your expectations. No two people think exactly alike. Find those who come as close to the Constitution as you can and support them and keep their feet to the fire. Don't send them to Washington and forget about them. It doesn't take long before all the trappings of that town can snare them.

"I've always said, America gets the government it deserves, but it deserves so much better. When I look at most of the politicians, not all, but way too many, I see a bunch of educated ego-maniacal, what's-in-it-for-me type of politicians. I don't think they started out that way, but after a while, I think they fall into that trap. People telling them how special and wonderful they are with all the special privileges they get. I think they get to the point where they believe their own hype. It's like the heat has been turned up on them slowly and they don't even notice the water is now boiling."

James looked at his watch and apologized for going on one of his rants, and I knew we were done for the day. I tried to get him to tell me about the counterfeits, but it was no use. He knew his grandson Ray and I were going out again that night and he didn't want to be the reason I was late.

EIGHT

COUNTERFEITS

In the morning when we met, I turned on my recorder.

"Nikki, where did we leave off, before I got so sidetracked?"

I didn't even need to look at my notes. *"You were telling me about counterfeits."*

James smiled and I could see him go back in time. "I remember TJ leaving me hanging by the seat of my pants when he took first watch. The next day, we covered a lot more ground. A little before dusk, TJ spotted a trail that was used by small animals to get to a stream nearby. We set up a snare and set up camp about fifty feet away.

"That night after we ate, I asked TJ about the counterfeits. TJ shook his head. 'Satan always has counterfeits. Lust for love, greed for desire, there is a whole list. The *Communist Manifesto* for the *Constitution* is also one of them. I truly feel anything that is contrary to good is evil and evil can only come from Satan.

'The night John wrote down the principles of liberty list, he told us about when Israel wanted a King to rule over them. Not even Samuel the Prophet could change their minds, even after he told them what would happen if they chose to have a King. The people at that time were no longer following God, so God told Samuel to let them have a King. They looked around and found the best man for the job. His name was Saul. Saul was a good king for a while, but like Samuel warned them, the power went to Saul's head, and he became a ruler and not a leader.'"

Washington as a King?[xvi]

"Nikki, did you know George Washington could have been crowned a King?"

"What, a King? I'm beginning to think my school years were a waste of time."

"Don't feel bad, you're getting additional education as I did. It turns out one of the counterfeits Satan would have loved was a king instead of a president. TJ told me when the war was over and before the Constitution was hammered out, the men who served under Washington were still not getting paid. They were ready to take over the government and make George Washington a King. Make no mistake about it, all Washington had to do was say the word and it would have been done, but he didn't.

"Washington met with the men who wanted to take over the government and asked them to be patient and give Congress more time. He reminded them they had given so much to rid themselves of a King and to not throw it all away to put in another. Some were moved and agreed, but most were not.

"Washington thought maybe a letter from Joseph Jones, a Congressman from Virginia, who, in a letter, expressed deep sympathy for the army and pledged his help and support, would sway the rest.

"Congressman Jones wrote quite small and Washington had a hard time reading it, so he reached into his coat pocket and took out a pair of glasses. Only his closest aides knew he wore glasses. He had difficulty putting them on because his hands were shaking. He tried to read it again, but again he couldn't. After a moment, he stopped and spoke. His voice cracked, as his throat tightened, 'Gentlemen, you must pardon me. I have grown gray in your service and now find myself going blind.' Those battle-hardened men softened their hearts to see their Commander in Chief whom they loved, humbly asking them to give Congress more time . . . and they did.

"The men no longer talked about overtaking the government and making Washington a King. I'm sure Satan was disappointed that day, but I'm also sure he's satisfied with the way things have turned out. So many today rely on the government to take care of them. Instead of a father at home helping a wife to raise their children, government has taken his place."

James caught himself. "I'm sorry, I got a little off track with one of my rants. Now, where was I? Oh yes, Washington as a King.

"Nikki, things were so bad after the war; George Washington said, 'If any person had told me that there would have been such a formidable rebellion as existed at that time, I would have thought him a bedlamite, a fit subject for the madhouse.' You see, Nikki, during the war they all had a common enemy which united them, but after the war, they started fighting amongst themselves. King George didn't even bring his troops home. He left them on the Canadian side of the border waiting for us to fall apart.

"Luckily for us, after the Constitution was in place, George Washington wrote in a letter that said, 'The United States enjoys a scene of prosperity and tranquility under the new government that could hardly have been hoped for.' He also said in a letter to David Humphrey, 'Our public credit stands on that high ground, which three years ago, would have been considered as a species of madness to have foretold.'

"Nikki, over the many years, I've watched as our government has stepped outside the bounds of the Constitution and in my opinion, things are going downhill fast, but I have faith. If Washington was amazed at how quickly things turned around in three years, then I know if those we send to Congress would follow the Constitution the way it was intended, then I'm sure our Nation would once again be on solid ground."

Keep the Fires Burning Within

"The next morning, TJ and I checked the snare and found we caught a raccoon. Nikki, that night we had it for dinner."

I had to ask, *"What does raccoon taste like?"*

James smiled, "A little like chicken, but I wouldn't serve it for Sunday dinner."

I loved his sense of humor. *"So, what did TJ teach you that night?"*

"That night, TJ continued his lesson on the balance of good government. Once again, he cleared the brush and drew out what he had before. The eagle still looked like a turkey, but I kept my mouth closed. With the small fire in the center of the triangle, I looked down and noticed the fire was going out, so I put on a few more small sticks to keep it going. TJ looked at me and said, 'Sir, what you did right there, is something every American needs to do. We need to keep the fire burning within us to keep that eagle in the balanced center; otherwise, we can kiss our freedoms goodbye. I believe complacency is another counterfeit that is the kiss of death.'

"TJ paused. 'It seems like America has always been able to be divided in thirds. One-third for, one-third against, and one-third sitting on their butts.

'During the Revolution, John Adams, from the best he'd been able to gather, looked like one-third were for freedom and put their lives on the line. While about a third were on the side of England, and the other third were somewhere in the middle, they could go either way. They mostly sat it out and waited to see who was going to win before taking a side and whoever won they could say, "I was behind you all the way."

'There will be a time in the future when the one-third that believes in the Constitution will have to stand up for what they know to be true and work together to bring those in the middle over to the right side of freedom. The other third, don't even waste your time with them, their minds are made up. They want the government to take care of them from cradle to grave. All you can do for them is love and pray for them. The day will come when there will be no fence-sitters; you're either hot or cold. I told that to John and, of course, he was reminded of a scripture in Revelations.'

"I found myself, again, reaching into my pocket to pull out John's Bible, at least this time, I didn't need help finding Revelations. 'What chapter and verse?' I asked. He told me, 'Chapter 3, verses 15 and 16.'

"I read it out loud. 'I know thy works, that thou art neither cold nor hot: I would thou wert cold or hot. So then because thou art lukewarm and neither cold nor hot, I will spue thee out of my mouth.' I looked at TJ. There's no fence-sitter there.

"He smiled and said, 'The problem is, when that eagle gets closer to the far left with the one-third who wants more handouts, the more violent they become with those who want to follow the rules that the Constitution lays out.'"

"James, it sounds like handouts are another counterfeit for freedom."

James nodded sadly.

"Nikki, TJ asked me if I ever thought about what government is. I thought it might be a trick question; with TJ, you never knew. So, smiling I said, 'Sure, but why don't you tell me what you think it is, and I'll let you know if you're right or not.' TJ couldn't help but laugh.

"TJ had such a way of explaining things so anyone could understand. He asked me if I had the right to stand on the top of my house with a 45 strapped to my hip to protect it from intruders? And did I also have a right while I'm up there to hold a garden hose, waiting for a spark to land on my roof so I could put it out? Nikki, what do you think?"

"Of course you do, but why would you do that when you can call the cops or the fire department?"

"Right you are, my dear, and that's what a government is. It's giving to others what we have the right to do for ourselves and giving to them that right for efficiency. If we didn't have that right, then how could we give it to someone else? TJ liked the way John Locke put it. 'The only authority to govern oneself is with oneself, individual authority is all the authority that exists.' Now let me ask you this. Can I go to one neighbor and take his spare car without his permission and give it to another neighbor because he needed it?"

I looked at James. *"I believe that's called grand theft auto and you can go to jail."*

"Nikki, I couldn't agree with you more. If *you* don't have the authority to do it, then how could the government? They may not take your car and give it to someone else, but they take your money through income taxes, which was against the Constitution up until 1913 with the passing of the Sixteenth Amendment.

"I wish our legislators would be reminded they can only delegate with the authority that we have as an individual. If we don't have the authority to take from someone, then they shouldn't either.

"I asked TJ how he knew all this stuff. He smiled and said, 'Having a name like Thomas Jefferson wasn't easy. My parents wanted me to study like he did. I tried to live up to the legacy, but I know I fell short.'

"After what TJ told me about Thomas Jefferson's study habits, I'm sure most, if not all, today would fall short.

"Nikki, the men of that time were a special breed and TJ believed they had a burning desire put inside them to study history. He and his father knew throughout history there were and always will be changes. When TJ and his father studied civilizations that had freedom and then lost it, they noticed that there was a pattern with their rise and fall. The one thing that remained constant was human nature. It was usually little things at first, so people didn't even notice when it was happening to them. One thing leads to another and then another until one day you wake up and you no longer have the freedom your parents or grandparents once had. The counterfeit was complete, and another civilization had fallen.

"Nikki, are you familiar with the story of the frog in the pot of boiling water?"

"I am. Put a frog in a pot of boiling water and it will jump right out. But put it in cool water and turn up the heat slowly, it won't notice and it will boil to death."

"Right you are. TJ told me he looked at history in that way and he saw over and over again the rise and fall of man, war after war. For some reason, man doesn't learn. Oh, he might, from time to time have what you would call a season of peace, but before long Satan puts it in the hearts of men to control one another and it starts all over again as the water gets hotter and hotter. Leaders promise the masses security in exchange for a little of their freedoms and rights. For the people of Germany, one day they woke up with Hitler and that was the beginning to their end."

NINE

EARLY AMERICA AND COMMUNISM

"The problem is that most people look at history as what they experience in their lifetime, and they don't notice the boiling water all around them. I think Satan doesn't want us to study history in depth so we can put the pieces of the puzzle together. For example, one night around the fire, TJ was warming his hands.

'I'll bet that like most people, you think of America as starting around 1776 with the signing of The Declaration of Independence, and technically they would be right. But if you think about it, it started long before that.

'In 1585, Queen Elizabeth tried to stop the Spanish from colonizing north Florida by having Sir Walter Raleigh establish a colony on Roanoke Island. You might say that was a trial run, because they starved and the survivors went back to England. Three years later, they tried it again, and we don't know what happened to them. They simply disappeared, and they were known as "The Lost Colony of Roanoke." It's believed they were either killed by the Indians or they went and lived with them. That little adventure cost Sir Walter Raleigh his fortune.'

'In 1607, King James the First tried to stop the Spanish again by letting some businessmen from London finance a colony. They were the ones who set up Jamestown. Those who financed the colony thought it would be profitable if the colonist lived under a secular communism kind of lifestyle.'"

"Wait a minute, James, are you telling me America had communism?"

"Nikki, that was the first time I ever heard it too, and I told TJ so. 'Yes, Sir,' he said, 'twice actually, and twice it failed. Jamestown almost went under until they divided up the land and began to fend for themselves.'

'What was the second time?' I asked. TJ always had the same look before he was about to impart wisdom.

'That would be the Pilgrims in 1620. The same group of London businessmen who financed Jamestown put up the money for them as well. And like before, they thought it would be profitable under this communal lifestyle. You see, Sir, those businessmen believed in Plato's *Republic,* and I guess they thought it would work this time because these colonists were Christians, and as Christians, everyone gets along, right?'"

"TJ said that with a little sarcasm in his voice. 'After all, they believed in brotherly love and share and share alike. I guess you could call it "Christian Communism." It doesn't matter what you call it, it doesn't work. Oh, it worked for a little while, but it wasn't long before human nature set in, and there were those who wouldn't pull their own weight. The ones who didn't do much of the work thought they should have equal amounts of the harvest and it drove poor Governor Bradford crazy. After nearly starving to death because of the lack of work that wasn't getting done, Governor Bradford finally had enough. He threw up his hands and said, "That's it, you have made me a tyrant trying to get you to do your work. We left England to get away from tyrants! I'm dividing up the land, the seed corn, and the tools according to the size of your family, and you can do with it what you will. You can starve to death, for all I care." Maybe those weren't his exact words, but you get the point.'"

"James, I can't believe what I'm hearing; this is all new to me. What happened then?"

"Nikki, my dear, what always happens when ownership, pride in accomplishment, and the free market comes together? Governor Bradford couldn't believe the difference in the people's attitude, and more corn was planted than ever before."

Religion Taught in Schools[xvii]

"TJ thought he'd thrown me a curve ball. 'Sir, I'll bet you didn't know that the Founding Fathers wanted religion taught in schools?'

"Now I knew that was a trick question and I was quite arrogant when I told him that we had left England to get away from that kind of thing, so we could have freedom of religion. Besides, what about separation between church and state? There was that smile again.

'Well, Sir,' TJ explained, 'the Constitution does say that *Congress shall make no law respecting an establishment of religion,* meaning that England had the *Church* of England, and this provision would make it impossible to have a *Church of America*, where everyone would have to pay taxes to the Church whether they belonged to it or not.

'The term *separation between Church and State* came from a letter that Jefferson wrote to the Danbury Baptist Association. Jefferson was putting their minds at ease when he told them the Constitution had created *a wall of separation between Church and State.* Leave it to the courts to use this metaphor and twist it all to heck.

'Religion in America has always been very important. George Washington, in his farewell address, said, "Of all the dispositions and habits which lead to political prosperity, Religion and Morality are indispensable supports. It is substantially true, that virtue or morality is a necessary spring of popular government."'

"You see, Nikki, the religion the Founders wanted taught in the schools was what some called the *American Religion*, which covered five points. Benjamin Franklin said the five points were what all sound religions believe in.

"First, the Founders wanted religion taught to recognize and worship a Creator who made all things. Second, the Creator gave us a moral code of behavior to distinguish right from wrong. Third, the Creator holds mankind responsible for the way we treat each other. The fourth is that all mankind will live beyond this life. The reason that was so important is because of the fifth fundamental point, which was that there is a next life, and we will be judged for what we did in this life.

"The Founders knew how important it was for everyone to embrace these principles, because they knew people tend to behave according to the way they believe. No one knows this better than Satan and those who have that kind of evil in their hearts; Hitler is only one of a long list. Hitler, and those like him, knew that if you control what people believe, then you can control their behavior. And where better to start than with the youth going to public schools? As the teachers in America would lead their students in the Pledge of Allegiance with their hand over their heart, in Germany, teachers would lead their students with their pledge of allegiance to Hitler with their arm held out.

"Adolf Hitler is our Savior, our Hero.
He is the Noblest Being in the Whole Wide World.
For Hitler we Live. For Hitler we Die.
Our Hitler is Our Lord, Who Rules a Brave New World."
(1934 The National Archives of The United States)

"Hitler would take young boys out of their homes and teach them what he wanted them to believe. He wanted to brainwash them. In one of his booklets, he had the youth taught that *Christianity is a religion for slaves and fools. That the New Testament is a Jewish lie written by four evangelicals*. Or how about this one, *There is no Christian culture*. One of my favorites is that *Christianity had spoiled the German people because it taught them ideas such as adultery and theft which they had never known before Christianity came along*. Can you believe that?"

I looked at James while scratching my head with the most puzzled look: *"What?!"*

"Nikki, not only did he brainwash the boys, but the girls as well. By the time the girls were of childbearing age, they felt it was their duty to have children for the fatherland. Hitler took a page right out of Lenin's playbook: indoctrinate the children and it will never be uprooted. I can't prove it, but I think that's what's going on in our schools today and why true history is being left out."

Alexis de Tocqueville's Discovery

"Nikki, the Founders knew that without religion, the government of a free people could not be maintained. You see it throughout their writings. In 1831, a gentleman by the name of Alexis de Tocqueville came over from France and stayed for a few years. When he returned to France, he wrote a book called *Democracy in America*."

James went to his bookshelf, took down a book, and sat down. As he opened it, I could see it had been well-marked. "Nikki, this is one of TJ's favorite quotes from de Tocqueville: *I sought for the greatness and genius of America in her commodious harbors and her ample rivers, and it was not there; in her fertile fields and boundless prairies, and it was not there; in her rich mines and her vast world commerce, and it was not there. Not until I went to the churches of America and heard her pulpits aflame with righteousness did I understand the secret of her genius and power. America is great because she is good, and if America ever ceases to be good, America will cease to be great.*

"When TJ told me that, I sat pondering about what he had told me. Then he looked me in the eye. 'Sir, you probably didn't know that before the signing of the Declaration of Independence, there were heated and sometimes violent debates over the issue of morality and whether or not the people were sufficiently virtuous and moral enough to govern themselves.

'You see, Sir, they knew that self-government could never take hold if the people were corrupt and selfish. Even Benjamin Franklin said, *"Only a virtuous people are capable of freedom. As nations become corrupt and vicious, they have more need of masters."* Sir, because my ancestors were slaves, they had to call another man master, but it'll be a cold day in hell before I do and I'm sure you feel the same way. After all, isn't that why we're here in Germany, to protect our freedoms?'

"Nikki, TJ was right. I'll be damned before I call anyone master."

America Foretold in the Old Testament

"Thomas Paine was quite the writer in his day. He saw a dilemma and wrote *Common Sense*. He laid out the need to break off from the British Crown. Paine assured Americans that they were ready for independence, that they were industrious, frugal, and honest. He also pointed out that few Americans had been corrupted with riches the way people had been in Europe, where all they wanted was luxury, indolence, amusement, and pleasure.

"But leave it to the New York newspapers, along with Boston and other big city newspapers, to point out America's weakness, trying to make them self-conscious about their lack of public virtue. Lucky for us, not everyone believed the papers.

"There were those who knew America was destined to be great. I like the way John Adams saw America when he said, 'I always consider the settlement of America with reverence and wonder, as the opening of a grand scene and design in Providence for the illumination of the ignorant, and the emancipation of the slavish part of mankind all over the earth.' Adams wasn't the only one. Back then, many leaders in Europe spoke of America as the hope of the world. One of these leaders was a famous philosopher by the name of Bishop George Berkeley. He wrote a poem about the destiny of America, and the last verse really tells it all."

James stood up. With facial expressions and gestures, he could hold your attention. He cleared his throat for a dramatic effect and began.

"Westward the course of the empire takes its way; the four first acts already past, A fifth shall close the drama with the day; Time's noblest offspring is the last."

"James, I really enjoyed that, but I don't have a clue as to what that meant."

James laughed. "Neither did I when TJ told it to me. Turns out, John was the only one TJ ever met who knew what that poem meant. You see, Nikki, ever since the Europeans were able to read the Bible in their own language; they noticed that from Daniel to Revelations, it tells about the four blood-thirsty kingdoms that would follow one after another.

"John knew the four tyrannies were Babylon, Persia, Greece, and Rome. The fifth act the poem talks about would prepare humankind for God's kingdom of universal peace and prosperity and establish freedom of religions. Bishop Berkeley felt that America would lead the way. It was a common consent among the people, and that's why they knew what Bishop George Berkeley was talking about at the time.

"TJ knew a lot about the meaning of the poem, but leave it to John to go much deeper. John taught that in the book of Daniel, the King of Babylon, Nebuchadnezzar, had a dream and he wanted his magicians, astrologers, and sorcerers to reproduce the dream and then interpret it. The penalty for failure was death. They tried to convince the King that no man could bring back the dream and its interpretation. Needless to say, the king, now unhappy, was about to execute them, until Daniel stepped in and asked the King for a little time, and promised that he would interpret the dream, which he did.

"Daniel tells the King that his dream was a portrayal of what was going to happen in the history of the world. He saw a great image with a head made of fine gold, and its breast and arms were made out of silver, the belly and thighs of brass, while the legs were made of iron, and the feet of iron and clay. Daniel tells the King that he represents the head of gold and that he is a King of Kings.

"I'll bet that made the King feel pretty good. Daniel went on to tell King Nebuchadnezzar, after his kingdom, other kingdoms not as great as his would come and go. Daniel saw a stone cut out of the mountain without hands, and that stone, which symbolized God's kingdom would never be destroyed. The stone rolled down and smashed the image into many pieces and consumed all the other kingdoms. That was what Bishop Berkeley's poem was talking about."

TEN

MORALS REMOVED FROM SCHOOLS

"When TJ shared all that with me, he could tell I was a little overwhelmed, so he let me think about it for a moment. Then he broke the silence.

'One night when all the guys were together, we were talking about morals, religion, and government. I shared with them that I liked the way John Adams put it when he said, *"Our Constitution was made only for a moral and religious people. It is wholly inadequate to the government of any other."* After the Constitutional Convention, the people wanted to know what kind of government they were given. When someone asked Benjamin Franklin, he said, *"A republic, ... if you can keep it."* He knew it would depend on the people electing virtuous leaders.'

"In amazement, I shook my head. 'Why haven't I ever heard any of this before?'

"TJ shook his head. 'It's because it was taken out of the curriculum a long time ago. There are those who don't want the population to have morals and beliefs. It's the old philosophy, *"Eat, drink, and be merry, for tomorrow we die, and when we die there is no more."*

'With that kind of attitude, it's no wonder things are going downhill fast, or as John would say, "To hell in a handbasket."

Morals are the guardrails for a strong society, and unfortunately, the guardrails are slowly being taken down. Sir, I'll give you three guesses who's behind it all and the first two don't count.'

"I looked at TJ and took a guess: 'Satan?' TJ, in his best W.C. Fields voice said, 'Bingo, give that man a cigar.'

"I couldn't help but chuckle. With that, he told me, 'Satan will tell a hundred truths, to get you to believe one lie.'"

"Nikki, there was something else Alexis de Tocqueville discovered when he walked the streets of America. He found that the children not only knew their rights but also where their rights came from and how the Constitution applied in their lives. It was because they were being taught the Constitution the way the Founders meant it to be taught. In the schools, they were using *The Catechism on the Constitution.*

"I asked TJ, 'When did the slippery slope of morals and beliefs start to go downhill?' He paused for a moment.

'It was about a hundred years after the Constitution was signed, when you start to see a real change in education. Sir, know this, the adversary wants to remove morals and anything wholesome from society and what better place to start than our youth.'

"Then he said something that was quite a shocker, 'I wouldn't be surprised if they try and take prayer out of schools.'"

"I'm sorry, what did you say? That they would take prayer out of schools? That has never been part of the schools."

"Nikki, my dear, I forget that you never knew what it was like to have prayer in school. Every morning, we would take turns with the Pledge of Allegiance and a prayer to start off the day. It helped quiet down the children and get them ready for the school day. I wasn't that religious, but I liked seeing how my classmates prayed. But in 1962, those who wanted prayer banned, finally won. I can't prove it, but I think you can trace the slippery slope to the proverbial hell in a handbasket of America when prayer was taken out of the schools.

"It's funny you stopped me, because you couldn't believe there was prayer in school, and I stopped TJ when he told that to me because I couldn't believe prayer would ever be taken out of schools. I told him that would never happen. I remember him rubbing his neck while telling me, 'I don't know, Sir. I hope not. I really hope not, but when you look at the pattern of what was in the schoolbooks then and compare them to today's, I wouldn't be surprised.'

"I asked TJ what he meant. 'I mean, if you were to take a look at a textbook from the early 1800s, you would find about sixteen moral lessons woven in about every twenty-five pages—morals teaching the youth of America right from wrong, how to treat each other. And, you know, don't lie, don't steal, and don't cheat, things like that. If you could get your hands on other textbooks, say about every twenty years after that, you'd see a drastic pattern in how these stories of morals kept dropping off.

'In the 1930s, you'd be lucky to find one in every twenty-five pages. I don't know what it'll be like by the end of the 1940s, but I wouldn't be surprised if all you could find is one moral story in the whole book. You see, Sir, back then they were being taught morals at home and also in the schools. I shudder to think what we'll find in the next twenty years. Without a moral compass, it's easy to get lost—just ripe for the picking, so to speak. Like I say, pieces of the puzzle. Once you're aware there's a bigger picture, you'll start to see it too.'"

"It sounds like what TJ was describing is a conspiracy theory."

"It does, doesn't it? And I told TJ as much. Sadly, he said, 'It would be a conspiracy if those who were doing it weren't out there admitting to what they wanted.'

"I asked him who these people are. TJ sighed. 'From the beginning of time, they have been with us and they have gone by all kinds of different names. It doesn't matter if they're on the left or right side of the swing of the pendulum, if what they want is to pull that eagle past the center, either way, society becomes out of balance. One of the tricks they like to use is to try and make the word *Constitutionalist* a bad word by ridiculing anyone who talks about the Constitution in its original state. Others like to use words that have one meaning and change it to mean something else.'"

I was a little confused. *"What kind of words? Can you give me anexample?"*

"Of course. If I were to ask you if the American government is a democracy, what would you say?"

James stretched out his hand to indicate for me to answer, and I said, *"Of course, it is. Everyone knows America is a democracy."*

"Nikki, that's what I said when TJ asked me that very question. Could you do me a favor and recite the Pledge of Allegiance."

I wasn't sure if James wanted me to stand or not. After all, he did have a flag in his office. I started to stand, but he gestured I was fine to sit. *"I pledge allegiance to the flag of the United States of America and to the Republic for which it stands . . ."* James quickly raised his hand to stop me, "And to the Republic for which it stands? Why didn't you say, and to the democracy for which it stands?"

I couldn't believe it; I had walked right into that one.

"Nikki, we're a constitutional republic, because we have representatives of the people. Don't feel bad. TJ got me on that democracy question as well. I told you he was tricky."

James could tell I was a little embarrassed. "My dear, I have found, as TJ had, that only one out of ten could get that question right, and you could thank the ISS for that."

"James, what and who are the ISS?"

"That's what I wanted to know when TJ told it to me and of course, he knew the answer. I learned that the ISS stands for 'Intercollegiate Socialist Society.' Back in 1905, about one hundred or so people got together in New York and organized the ISS. It started somewhere in the neighborhood of sixty chapters from coast to coast on college and university campuses. One of the leaders, a guy by the name of Harry W. Laidler, said, 'The ISS was set up to throw light on the worldwide movement of industrial democracy known as socialism.' They even had a snappy slogan: *Production for use, not for profit.* If they had ever read Adam Smith's book *The Wealth of Nations*, they missed the part about how important profits play a vital role. They obviously forgot that America had already tried socialism, starting with Jamestown.

"By the time the 1920s came around, they had to change their name because when the Union of Soviet Socialist Republics, better known as the USSR, came along, it gave the term *socialism* such a bad name. The ISS had to change its name to *The League for Industrial Democracy*."

"What happened after they changed their name?"

"Good question. There were hundreds of men and women in the ISS who became big names in government, in the press, and on the radio. They kept referring to the United States as a *democracy*—even in the school books. President Wilson surrounded himself with a lot of the ISS. He contributed to the confusion when he said, 'World War I was the effort of the allied forces to make the world safe for democracy.' By the end of the 1920s, the schools had been gutted to teach anything important about our heritage. By the 1930s, they were everywhere—in publishing houses, academic circles, teacher-training colleges, and about every other major center of opinion-molding influence you can think of. So don't feel bad you couldn't answer the question about America being a republic.

"John Adams best put it this way when he said, "Remember, democracies never last long. It soon wastes, exhausts, and murders itself. There never was a democracy yet that did not commit suicide."

"James I'm starting to understand what's happening, not only in the schools, but in social media as well."

ELEVEN

GIVERS AND TAKERS

"I was amazed not only by TJ's knowledge, but how he could quote things off the top of his head. I've been able to memorize a few things he said, but TJ could quote all day. When I asked him how he did it, he told me he reads a lot from a variety of sources, and then puts the pieces together. It also helped that he had a near-photographic memory.

"Nikki, do you remember when I told you about the types of people who want to, for the lack of a better term, create anarchy?" I nodded.

"At the time of the Founders, there were two groups who went by the names Tories and Levelers; The Founders did everything they could to keep their ideas out of the Constitution. It turns out even Hamilton favored some of their philosophies. The Levelers wanted the government to redistribute the wealth so everyone would be equal. The Tories were no better; they took their name from an Irish phrase, *Ta a Ri*, which means 'Come, O King.' Whenever there was a problem, they wanted the King to fix it. Let's just say that self-reliance wasn't their thing.

"You have to take your hat off to the Founders. They also had a colorful name; they called themselves *Whigs*."

I laughed. *"Wigs? James, that had to be the dumbest name ever. Was that because they wore those white wigs?"*

Now James was laughing. "No, not wigs, Whigs! It comes from the Scottish word Whiggamores. The Whiggamores were the drivers of horses, and they were a very independent group of people who didn't want a king or a government to help solve their problems, unlike the Tories.

"TJ found the more he studied history, the more he found there have always been givers and takers, and the takers are never satisfied. They're like a tick that sucks the blood right out of the host. A few ticks, and the host can survive, but if there are more ticks than the host can handle, they'll suck the host dry until it dies."

"So you're telling me that Alexander Hamilton followed the philosophy of the Tories or Levelers? I thought he was one of the great Founders."

"Oh, he was. He fought right alongside Washington. He even helped write some of the Federalist Papers, along with Madison and Jay! He didn't consider himself one of the Tories or Levelers, but he did have some of their philosophies in him. He was a Federalist.

"Hamilton was the first Secretary of Treasury; he had a few ideas that Jefferson didn't agree with that caused quite a rift among the people. One of which was to let the bankers from England get a foothold in America so we would become indebted to them. Jefferson tried to convince President Washington not to do it, putting Washington in quite a quandary.

"You see, Nikki, he loved and respected both of these men, but they couldn't both be right. I suppose with the major debt America was in, Hamilton convinced Washington to bring in the bankers from England. Jefferson went along with it, but he had the first session of the First Congress put on a twenty-year charter so it would have to be renewed at that time if it was working. So in 1811, after twenty years, it wasn't renewed. I'm sure it was only a coincidence that we went back to war with England again in 1812. The more TJ studied history, the more clearly he saw that most, if not all, of the conflicts between men have been over religion, land, money, and power."

"What other differences did Hamilton and Jefferson have?"

"Hamilton thought the clause in the Constitution talking about the General Welfare of the United States was a general grant of power which allowed Congress to tax and spend money for any good cause. Jefferson told him that was not what the Welfare Clause meant, reminding Hamilton that it had been discussed in great length at the convention. Tax revenues could be used only for the General Welfare of the nation as a whole and not for individuals, special groups, or some senator's pet project.

"Hamilton thought like TJ's professor, that the common man was incapable of self-rule and needed the government's help. Jefferson believed in the right and ability of the people to rule themselves. Up until 1936, the Supreme Court took the side of Jefferson, but after FDR filled the court, they changed their minds and took the side of Hamilton. Nikki, that act alone opened up the floodgates of the treasury to be looted, and another guardrail to our personal rights came down."

TJ and Slavery

"Over the next few weeks while we traveled through the Black Forest, TJ would give me a taste during the day of what he would go into more detail that night. I always looked forward to each night. TJ shared with me each of the major battles, along with their victories and defeats. How the final battle at Yorktown was won with Cornwallis trying to escape with his men in boats to row across the York River; when a hurricane suddenly arose and blew the boats back to the riverbank and how Cornwallis said, that it 'even looked like God was on Washington's side.' I learned about how the Founders searched for the ideal society and expressed their basic beliefs on how

America got its roots and how slavery came about. Only Satan smiled with how that got started and how tens of thousands lost their lives trying to end slavery.

"One night, when TJ was talking about slavery, he told me that the Founders knew slavery was wrong, even in the Southern States. The States that had slavery, asked at the Convention for twenty years to phase it out. Unfortunately, cotton was the main source of income, and with the invention of the cotton gin, the Southern States couldn't see how they could afford to let the slaves go. Some say because the Constitution mentions each slave as three-fifths of a person, it was meant to be demeaning, but it was a compromise between the States for representation and taxation.

Jefferson and Slavery

"Nikki, did you know that ten years before the convention, Jefferson wrote three constitutional drafts for Virginia, but they were all rejected except for a small section in the third draft?"

"I'm sorry to say I've never heard of that."

"It's true. Jefferson wanted to get rid of the weaknesses existing under British rule and one of the weaknesses was slavery. He called it an *ugly institution*. He had a way to gradually ease out of slavery in one generation by simply declaring every person born would be free at birth. But Virginia said, "No." There are those who call Jefferson a hypocrite for saying that, because both he and Washington owned slaves. Neither one approved of slavery; they inherited them from their father and father-in-law. At that time, it was against the law to free slaves.

"When Washington came home from the war, he was quite strapped for money. The farm was in great need of repair, and he had more slaves due to their offspring than were needed for his farm. Slaves needed to be fed and clothed. Back then, slaves were looked upon as a commodity, and if they're not producing more than the cost for their upkeep, most slave owners would sell what they considered surplus. Washington could have sold one slave and taken the financial burden off his shoulders, but the very thought of selling another human and splitting up a family was more than he could bear. So he found other ways to make ends meet.

"TJ told me he was glad that once all the slaves were free, their ancestors stayed in America. I asked what he meant. TJ, in turn, asked me what I knew about Liberia, and of course, my answer was 'not much.' I did remember reading something about President Roosevelt going there a few years earlier and that Liberia was somewhere in Africa.

"TJ explained, 'It's in West Africa and it was colonized in 1820 by freed slaves with the help of a group of people who were called the American Colonization Society. They believed ex-slaves would have greater freedom in Africa. Unfortunately, it was impossible to return them to their families, they needed a place they could call their own. By 1847, the colonists founded the Republic of Liberia, and you'll never guess what they named the capital city.'

"I looked at TJ with a blank face."

'Go on, guess.'

"The way he was smiling I guessed, 'Jefferson City?' That made TJ smile and chuckle a bit."

'You're closer than you think, but no. It was called Monrovia, after the fifth president James Monroe, a strong supporter of the colonization. The colonists became known as Americo-Liberians.' TJ loved their motto."

"James, what's their motto?"

With a wink, James smiled, "*The love of liberty brought us here.*" *Liberia* means 'liberty.' Their flag even looks like ours, but instead of multiple stars, it has only one. After the Civil War, former slaves, if they wanted to, could also go to Liberia and start a new life. Many did, but TJ's family had been treated very well by their master, and stayed in the United States, as did the majority."

I shook my head. *"Once again, I've never heard any of this either."*

"Nikki, it's one more thing that doesn't get taught in schools. I asked TJ what he knew about his family line. 'More than most, Sir. My great-great-grandfather earned the trust and respect of his master, who had him educated to carry out many of his business affairs. He could even travel with his family. If anyone stopped him, he carried with him letters of introduction from his owner, stating that he was not to be interrupted in his travels. This meant he could not be accused of being a runaway slave.'"

"I don't understand. If they had those papers, why didn't they keep on going to another state where slavery wasn't allowed?"

"TJ explained it this way to me. 'There were many cases where the slaves and their master's families were very loyal toward each other; and of course, there were others who did not have that type of good relationship. Like all other areas of society, there are all varieties of human nature, even in the case of slave owners. My ancestors, however, were treated well. They were given an income, days off from work, their own house with land, and a few livestock to start with. My great-great-grandmother, on the other hand, was one that was treated rather inhumanely. Now there is a love story that would compete with the best of love stories.'

"TJ told me about how his great-great-grandmother was treated and how she was rescued with the help of his great-great-grandfather and his master. I told TJ he should put that story to paper to share with others, at the very least, a sonnet.

"TJ smiled. 'Perhaps one day you can do that for me.'

"Nikki, I don't know how much time I have left; perhaps you could take on that challenge."

James told me the story of the rescue, and I have to tell you, it is a love story to end all love stories.

TWELVE

THOSE WHO MADE A DIFFERENCE

"Other nights, TJ explained the Constitution and the Bill of Rights, line by line. One night, he asked me, 'Sir, did you know that there were three delegates who didn't sign the Constitution because it didn't have a Bill of Rights?' I remembered something like that, but couldn't remember the details. Of course, TJ could."

I raised my hand like a little schoolgirl. I was excited, finally something I remembered from my high school civics class. *"The ones who did sign felt the Federal Government wasn't given that much power, so there really wasn't a need for a Bill of Rights, right?"*

Three Would Not Sign[xviii]

"Very good, Nikki, go to the head of the class. TJ reminded me the Constitution only gives about twenty powers delegated to Congress, with six responsibilities granted to the President and eleven types of cases assigned to the Federal Courts. James Madison tried to convince the three by telling them the Constitution didn't give that much power that they could assume. George Mason of Virginia said, "But they will. They always do." He knew they would try to grab more power whenever they could; it's only human nature to do so. Good thing the three so insisted. I hate to think what things would look like without it. It was agreed that one of the first things Congress would do when in session would be to work on a Bill of Rights."

Congress Gives Washington a Title[xix]

"One night, TJ had that look on his face, and I knew there was something on his mind. 'Come on,' I asked. 'What is it?'

"TJ smiled. 'I was thinking of the First Congress and the titles they came up with for George Washington. The Senate favored the title'—TJ cleared his throat, and in a rather pompous tone replied—'His Highness, the President of the United States of America, and Protector of Their Liberties.' We both started to laugh. 'Let me tell you when Washington heard about that one, he was mortified. He was glad when they came up with the simple title, *President of the United States.*'"

Hansen Learns About Music

"Nikki, I didn't know it then, but it was on our last night together when TJ asked me if I knew that when Thomas Jefferson was writing the Declaration of Independence, he would often take a break and play the violin. Of course, I didn't know that, like so many other things he told me I had never heard of.

"Nikki, I'm going to teach you another trick TJ taught me. Sometimes, when we have a lot on our minds or we're stuck on a problem we need to solve, we step back and relax, to get our mind off the problem. For Jefferson, it was playing the violin."

"I'm seeing a pattern as to where you got your ideas, like playing a game, or exercising, or taking a nap."

James smiled and gave me a wink. "Nikki, you can add playing an instrument to that list. I asked TJ if he played the violin; after all, he was named after Jefferson. He said no, but he did play the trumpet.

"TJ said something I couldn't agree with more. He said, 'Sir, I'd rather be carrying a trumpet than a gun any day of the week.' I nodded my head in agreement and asked him why the trumpet. 'I wanted to be the next Satchmo.'

'Louis Armstrong?' I asked.

"TJ took out a handkerchief from his pocket. With a big toothy grin and squinting his eyes, while wiping his forehead, he gave a very good Satchmo impression. 'Ooooh, yeah.'

"Nikki, I'll bet you don't even know who Satchmo is."

In my best impression of Satchmo, I started to sing "Hello Dolly." It wasn't very good, but we got a laugh out of it.

James looked at me. "I keep forgetting about you and your Grandfather Vince.

"TJ wanted to know if I played any instruments. I shook my head no and told him I always wanted to, but we could never afford lessons, let alone any instrument. He suggested when I get back home to start out with the piano. That way I could learn the notes and measures, and from there, I'd be able to learn other instruments more easily."

James was giving me more pieces of the puzzle that shaped his life.

"That night TJ asked me if he ever told me the story about the signing of the Declaration of Independence. No, I told him, don't believe you have. TJ's eyes lit up.

'I haven't? That's one of my favorite stories.'

"He stood up. I loved it when he stood. I knew this was going to be good. TJ cleared his throat.

'There they were on a typical hot, muggy Philadelphia July day, with the doors and windows locked. Inside the room stood fifty-six men, discussing quietly what to do about King George the Third.

Things had gotten so bad they were ready to break all ties with England. The doors and windows were locked, and all were talking low because what they were discussing was high treason.

'These were mostly wealthy men and they had a lot to lose. Not only their wealth, but their lives as well. If they had lost the war, they would have been stripped of their wealth. There would be no inheritance to pass down and they would be sentenced to death, but not by anything as kind as a firing squad. No, they would have been hung. Something not too many people know about hanging, depending on where you place the noose, death can be a quick snap of the neck or a slow suffocation. If a person was too light, sandbags would be added to the job.

'For those who had committed treason, they would have been hung until they became unconscious, then cut down, and revived. Then, when they became conscious and aware of what was going on, they would have been disemboweled, beheaded, quartered, boiled in oil in four separate kettles, and then their remains would have been spread in different parts of the land so they wouldn't have a final resting place for their loved ones and others to pay homage.'"

"James, that's terrible!"

"Yes, it is. Let me ask you what TJ asked me. If you were in that room, would you have signed that Declaration of Independence? Before you answer, let me tell you what TJ did before I could answer. He raised his hand to stop me and gave me something to think about."

'Remember, Sir,' he said. 'You're going up against an army that never loses. Every country they went into, they took control. The saying *The sun never sets on His Majesty's Kingdom* was real. What did we have in America? Only a bunch of misfits and farmers trying to defend their land.'

"Nikki, we didn't stand a snowball's chance in hell, going up against the King's army. So let me ask you again, do you think you would have signed it?'"

"I've never heard it put that way before. Knowing that, I doubt I would have."

"Nikki, I told TJ the same thing. He told me not to feel bad, because he doubted he would have signed it either. Lucky for us, we weren't there. The ones who were, however, were a special breed of men. But don't think they, too, weren't scared, because they were. They truly showed courage to have signed it."

The Old Man From the Back Of the Room[xx]

"What I'm about to tell you, neither TJ nor his father could find written anywhere. It's one of those stories handed down from generation to generation that feels true. TJ's father told it to him, and his father heard it when he was a young man, who heard it from his father, who heard it from his father.

"As the Founders were discussing this act of treason, you can only imagine the fear that was going through their minds, when in the back of the room an old man spoke, 'Gentlemen, I perceive a hesitation in this room. Wilt thou allow me to speak?' The men turned, and all eyes fell on the old man. The men in the room stepped aside, making a path for the old man. It was like Moses parting the Red Sea as he walked to the front of the room.

'He turned to face the men. When he spoke, it was in a low and soft voice, a voice that pierced deep into each of their hearts: "Gentlemen, the fear that ye feel was planted there by the adversary. Divine Providence has brought you here for a reason. Each of you was placed upon this earth for this Divine calling. This is thy destiny. Placing thy name upon said parchment is indeed the signing of one's own death sentence. Rest assured, brethren, your sacrifice will not be in vain.

"Your time upon this earth is but a grain of sand in the hourglass, but what ye do with this time will forever influence the fruits of your loins. Behold, this is the time that young Daniel spoke of to King Nebuchadnezzar when he interpreted his dream. Ye are a part of that stone that was cut with no hands, rolling down the mountain. Sign this Declaration of Independence. Send a message to the King, and more importantly, to your fellow patriots, and to those who are yet to inhabit the earth. Mutually pledge to each other your lives, your fortunes, and your sacred honor.'"

"Everyone in the room felt the Spirit of the Almighty and signed. When all had signed, they turned to the old man to sign, but he was nowhere to be found. The doors and windows were still locked, and all knew they had witnessed a manifestation from Divine Providence."

Goosebumps filled my arms as the tears rolled down my face. James stood and walked around his desk, handing me a box of tissue. Lovingly, he put his hand on my shoulder.

"Ray had the same reaction when I told it to him. I know he's been waiting for me to tell it to you. The two of you can now discuss it tonight when you see him.' With that, he kissed the top of my head and left me to compose myself.

BOOK FOUR

FOR LOVE OF MONEY

ONE

A SOLDIER NAMED RICHMAN

The next morning after breakfast, we walked into James's office and sat down. With a smile on his face, he asked, "How was your date with Ray last night? Did you talk about anything interesting?"

I couldn't help but play along. *"Nothing that I can think of."* We both smiled. *"It seems like you always give us something to talk about. Ray told me he couldn't wait for the ending. I tried to get him to tell me more, but it was no use."*

"As it should be, my dear, as it should be." James always waited until I sat down before he took a seat. I noticed some time ago that whenever James was about to start his story, he would pause as though he were going back in time, reliving that moment. James began:

"TJ and I were finishing breakfast when we heard someone coming. Quickly, we doused the fire, covered it with dirt, then hid ourselves. As we waited, my heart was pounding in my chest. I closed my eyes and uttered a silent prayer. '*Father, we've come so far. Please let us get back to our families.*'" Off in the distance, we could hear someone calling out in a stage whisper. 'TJ, are you there?'

"Both TJ and I gave a sigh of relief. TJ called back in a low voice, 'We're over here.'

"In a few moments, we were joined by another soldier, who walked into camp with his rifle over his shoulder. He was not as tall as TJ, but had the same slender build and was about the same age. His countenance was bright and his smile wide. I heard him say as he gave TJ a hug, 'You made good time.'

'Hansen here picked up climbing rather quickly, a real mountain goat. We've been on a pretty good clip ever since.'

"That was quite a compliment, coming from TJ."

'Sir, I'd like you to meet Sergeant William Richman.'

"He gave me a salute, which I returned. 'Pleased to meet you, Sergeant Richman, any relation to the billionaire William J. Richman?' I thought I was making a joke, something that he had probably heard a thousand times. But the joke was on me."

'Yes, Sir. That would be my father.'

'William J. Richman, the billionaire, is your father?'

'Yes, Sir, only he's not a billionaire. The press exaggerates.'

"I couldn't believe it and had to ask, 'Sergeant Richman, what on earth is someone like you doing in a war like this?' He looked at me like that was the dumbest question he'd ever heard."

'The same as you, Sir, serving God and country. Our family comes from a long line of patriots, and Dad couldn't be more proud of me.' I was embarrassed for asking and apologized.

"I asked, 'Sergeant, what's our game plan?'

'To get you home, Sir.'

"Let me tell you, Nikki, I sure liked the sound of that. I picked up my pack, slung it on my back, and cinched up the straps. I turned to TJ. I could see it written all over his face: 'You're not coming with us, are you?'

'No, Sir.'

'I know, I know. You're needed elsewhere.'

'Yes, Sir. This section of the Black Forest can get pretty tricky. In some ways, you'll find it harder than the mountain we climbed. My specialty is in climbing; Sergeant Richman's is in hiking this part of the forest. But we'll meet up again, I promise.'

"I pointed my finger at him and replied in a stern voice, 'I'm going to hold you to that.' We gave each other a hug and I turned to Richman, 'Lead the way, Sergeant.'"

Peaks and Valleys

"It was indeed a very tiring day. Up and down the peaks and valleys, with a lot of traversing. By the time we stopped for the night, I felt like I had that first night with TJ on the ledge. After catching my breath, I helped gather a few branches for the fire, and we sat down to eat. After dinner, Richman took out his map and showed me how far we had gone and the route we would be taking. It looked like we had covered only a few miles, but we were mostly going straight up and down, and with the traversing, it felt more like twenty or better."

'Sir, what we went through today is something you'll experience your whole life.'

"I didn't understand, which the expression on my face must have told him.

'You probably think that because my family has money, we don't have any downs, only ups. That's where you would be wrong. Everyone has their own personal peaks and valleys, their own mountains to face. What you do with them will determine your character. When you're at your low point, look for something good, something you can look forward to. If you're down, it doesn't mean you have to bring others down with you. When you're on that peak, be careful there, too. You'll have to learn what to do to stay there without, as my father would say, "looking down on others, thinking what they're going through isn't that hard." Also know, even on the top of the mountain, you'll have your own valleys to deal with. What goes up must come down. How long you stay on that peak or down in the valley will depend on you.'

"Richman, seeing how worn out I was, told me to get some sleep, and he would take my watch as well. I told him no, I'd take my turn. 'I'll let you go first. Besides, tomorrow is fast Sunday, and we can both rest, and that's an order.'

"Richman smiled back, picked up his gun, snapped to attention, and gave me a salute.

'I'll wake you for your shift.'"

Getting To Know Each Other

"The morning was cool and crisp. I was standing guard a few feet away when Richman woke up. He tells me that since this is a day of rest, I should lie down and catch up on some much-needed sleep. 'It'll be kind of like sleeping in on Sunday back home.'

"I was having a hard time keeping my eyes open, so I took him up on his offer and got a few hours of shut-eye. When I woke up, Richman was smiling. 'I'd ask you how you slept, but by the way you were snoring, I don't need to.'

"I stretched as I lay there. 'Pretty loud, was I?'

'No, Sir, having a little fun with you.'

"We spent the day getting to know a little about each other. I asked him what it was like growing up with all that money. He looked at me and asked, 'What was life like growing up without a lot of money?'

"Not a question I was expecting. I pondered, and then replied. 'Never really thought about it—let's see, normal, I guess you would say. I went to school, did my homework, and messed around with my friend, who always seemed to get me in trouble. I worked wherever I could to make a buck or two.'

'Did you always get whatever you wanted, Sir?'

"I chuckled. 'Far from it. Mom and Dad both worked, and we knew there wasn't money to waste. I'm sure they worried about not having enough, but they never let it on to us kids, and we got by fine.'

'I can relate with you more than you may think, Sir.'

'I doubt that.'

'No, really, Sir, when I or any of my brothers or sister wanted something that my parents thought was, let's say, frivolous, we had to work for it. Of course, there were exceptions on birthdays and special occasions, but for the most part, there was no way my parents were going to spoil us. They taught us by example and experience what the real world was like.'

"I couldn't believe it. You could have knocked me over with a feather. I told him, 'If I had your dad's money, whatever my kids wanted, I'd get it for them, and that's for sure. What's the point in having all that money if you can't spend it? I know life sure would have been easier for me, and I would have been a lot happier.'"

Money Doesn't Equal Happiness

"Richman tilted his head. 'Money doesn't determine if you're happy or not, Sir. I've been all over the world with my parents and I've seen destitute, and yes, my heart goes out to them. Some people are miserable, yet many are happy, truly happy. I discovered that happiness is a mindset. I once saw a mother sweep her dirt floor. At first, I thought it was a joke. Why bother sweeping dirt off dirt? But I noticed she was getting great satisfaction from a job well done, and afterward, she would sprinkle water on the floor and pack it down. Believe it or not, that floor almost had a shine to it. The spirit those mothers brought into their homes and the love they showed to their children—Yes, Sir, they were truly happy doing what they could to provide for their children. You could see it in the children's faces, the love they had for their mothers. They didn't have money, yet they were happy.'"

Know Thyself

"Richman added, 'My father always has his eyes open, looking for places to open up new areas for expansion and to grow the business. And yes, to make more money for the shareholders and for himself as well. There are those who call him greedy, only looking out for himself. He's been called everything you can think of under the sun, and then some. I know my father's heart, and he doesn't let it bother him. There's something very few know about my father. He took a page out of the playbook from Andrew Carnegie and is one of the most generous people you'll ever know. He's at peace with himself because he knows he's doing the best he can. Not only do the wealthy invest in my father's business, but also those whom you would call the *Moms and Pops of America.* They too have faith in my father and would like to retire with a little, if not a lot extra, so they won't be a bother to their family, or a drain on society. I've seen firsthand the good that comes to areas that need what my father provides.'"

Tax, Tax, Tax

"'When people know you have money, they will do everything they can to separate you from it. They'll try to make you feel guilty, wanting you to apologize for working harder and smarter. Those in power will stir up the masses, saying the rich need to pay their fair share. I guess they have forgotten that the tax structure was made to go after the rich. If you want to talk about fair, how about a fair tax or consumption tax, or a national sales tax, even a flat tax, so everyone has some skin in the game. Pick one, but only one. As I was talking to John about this, he interrupted, "If the Lord only asks for ten percent, then that should be a guideline for everyone else." But I guess class warfare is easier to sell.

'The poor and middle class forget that if it wasn't for the wealthy who sign the front of the check, they couldn't sign the back. They're taught that there is only so much money in the pie, and if the rich don't get it taken away from them to spread the wealth around, it's simply not fair. I wish someone would tell them there's plenty to go around; all you have to do is make more pie. There are those who think the rich should help everyone so no one will be poor, especially themselves.'

"I cut in, 'That's the communist way of thinking. John told me that Jesus said, "There will always be the poor among us," when his disciples were chastising a woman for anointing his feet with very expensive oil. They felt it should have been sold and the money given to the poor. John added, "The poor serve a purpose for all of God's children to help one another. Even the poorest of the poor can minister to others with love, if that's all they have. You help those you can and pray for those you can't." At least that's what John told me.' Richman nodded."

Make a Difference, If Only for One

"'That reminds me of a story I once heard about a young boy and an old man who were on the beach. There was a high tide, and when it receded, there were thousands of what some call starfish, but they were sea stars, and they were all over the beach. The young boy would pick one up at a time and throw it back into the sea.

'When the old man saw what he was doing, he walked up to the boy. "Young man," he said, "what you're doing is useless. It won't make a bit of difference." The young boy picked up another sea star and threw it back into the water. "It made a difference to that one." The old man thought for a moment, then reached down, picked up a sea star, and tossed it back into the sea.'"

TWO

SPEND WISELY

"I remember asking Richman, 'So if I understand you right, your father invests money to make it grow so it can help others? Doesn't that kind of prove my point? Money makes the world go round, and if I have it, I should spend it. Right? So if I buy my kids whatever they want, it puts money into the economy, then that's also good. Right?' Richman smiled, while shaking his head. 'Spending can be good, no doubt, Sir. But spending money only to spend it is foolish, and spending money you don't have isn't only foolish, it's downright—well, let's say, not very wise. Know the difference between needs and wants. Take your kids, for example. If it's something they need, then by all means, it's your responsibility to provide it for them. But if it's something they want, save that for a special occasion. Otherwise, let them earn it. They'll appreciate it a whole lot more, and they'll take care of it.

'Something else the rich do that most people don't think about. When a new product comes out, it usually costs more, because the company has to make up for the cost of research and development. The prices will eventually drop, because the rich spend their money on the newest items. That gives the companies the resources to make more products so they can lower the price. The more profits they make, the more people they can hire.'"

What is Wealth?

"'Money isn't everything. You could have a house full of gold, but what good is it? You can't eat it. Gold doesn't keep you warm. It needs to be working for you. Money is power, no doubt, but it can be like fire. When controlled, it can be of service by keeping us warm. It can cook our food, or it can burn down our house. I think Andrew Carnegie understood this best, because he once said, *A man that dies thus rich dies disgraced.'*

"Nikki, did you know that before Andrew Carnegie passed away, he gave away 90 percent of his wealth, leaving only 10 percent to the family? I guess he figured that if 10 percent was good enough for the Lord, it was good enough for the family. I don't know that for sure. I'm guessing. But I digress.

"Richman continued, 'Sir, when my father spends money on, let's say, a large project, he knows it will be long-term before he sees a profit, but there is an immediate return that he loves to see. It puts a lot of people to work in the communities and a lot of contractors who spend money on supplies and services needed for the project. They pay their workers, which allows them to purchase things of comfort for their families in their community. The stores now have money to hire workers to stock the shelves, sweep the floors, and so on and so on. Everyone receives a benefit directly or indirectly. With a free market, it trickles down, even if they had nothing directly to do with the project. It may take a while before there is a return for the stockholders, but with my father's team, there is always a return that benefits many more.'"

Assets and Liabilities[xxi]

"'So when you spend, make sure you know the difference between an asset and a liability. Assets make you money and liabilities cost you.'

"I thought for a moment, and then, chuckling, I said, 'I've seen a picture of your father's house. That is one mansion of an asset.'

'Actually, Sir, you're wrong on both accounts. It's not a house, it's a home. And it's not an asset, but a liability.'"

"James, if I may interrupt, your home is what I too would call a mansion, but certainly not a liability. When your son Jimmy gave me a ride to your home, as we pulled up the driveway, I commented on how beautiful it was. Jimmy told me how the home was built. That you built it in stages, paying for it as you went so you wouldn't get in over your head. Also, it was paid for, so how can it be a liability?"

"A very good question, my dear. It may be paid for, but since it doesn't bring in any money, it's a liability. There are still costs for the upkeep, along with the property taxes and such, so it definitely falls under the liability category. Only when I sell does it become an asset."

"James, please forgive me, but with that understanding, what about those jets? I know they cost a lot of money, not to mention the upkeep."

"That's true. What you've observed does cost a lot of money and upkeep. I look at things in a different light. You've heard the term *time is money,* and in business, time is very expensive. We can always make more money, but we can never make more time. Wasn't it nice to be able to have Ray stop what he was doing and fly you home so you could get things done so you could come work for me, instead of going to a hotel and hope there was a flight out of town the next day?"

"That was nice, and I'm starting to understand. Because your home doesn't produce income, it falls under a liability. But because your company jets produce an income, then it falls under assets."

James nodded. "Most of what we have are business expenses that keep the business growing. There are, of course, what some people call *toys*, I call *blessings*, and I truly do enjoy my blessings. One of which is my old P-51 Mustang. But let me assure you, the money

I use for those toys comes from the extra that the assets produce. I learned that from Richman, who learned it from his father. It took his father a long time to learn delayed gratification, and he had to learn it the hard way, but he did learn it."

"James, I'll be honest with you. I think if I had a lot of money, I'd want to spend it on whatever my heart desired."

James smiled. "Something you may want to investigate when you're finished with this project. Take a look at the ones who win the big lottery jackpots. So many do just that, and before long, they're right back where they were, only worse off because they didn't know how to manage money. Money managed them. Nikki, would you like to hear an old Chinese proverb that Richman told me?"

I nodded my head.

Delayed Gratification

"If you want to wish misery on your enemies, wish for them to have whatever their hearts desire and that they may receive it immediately."

I laughed. *"James, you can give me that misery anytime. That would be great."*

"Be careful, Nikki. That's how greed takes hold. Think about it, if you got everything your heart desires, without any effort, would there really be any joy in that? Think about the joy you get out of accomplishing something that requires hard work. What about all that hard work you went through to get where you're sitting right now? Your schooling, the hard knocks you went through learning your trade, or your trip to Germany, tracking down the old commandant and then tracking me down! That was your mountain you had to climb, one of many, and many more to come. Tell me, Nikki, how does it feel, knowing you have accomplished such a great task?"

"I never thought of it like that. Looking back, I have to admit, it really felt good."

"I know pride is a sin, but you should be proud of yourself for such an accomplishment. Let me ask you, with each challenge and struggle you went through, was it out of your comfort zone?"

"I'd be lying if I said no. At first, I was really out of my comfort zone, but after a while, it got easier." I had a thought flash through my head. *"James, it's something like the butterfly and the chrysalis, right?"*

James smiled and nodded. "You took a risk in going over each one of those mountains. Taking risks helps us to grow. It gets us out of our comfort zone. Another name for comfort zone is *rut*. As a kid, did you ever ride a bike when the wheels went into a rut?" I nodded. "If the rut was deep, do you remember how hard it was to get out of it?" I nodded again. "Life is the same way. Never find yourself in a rut. If you do, take a risk and stretch yourself.

"Get out of your comfort zone and grow. Richman's father would tell him when he did something for the first time he was green. 'Better green and growing than ripe and rotten,' he would tell him. Another thing he would tell him, 'If you're not moving forward, then you're going backward.'

"Nikki, those who have been blessed with money may have a bad reputation for wanting all the money for themselves, and for some, that's true. I know people like that, and they're not pleasant to be around, very self-centered. Be very careful if you find yourself around them; their thinking can rub off on others. They think the world revolves around them. I call it stinkin' thinkin'. They usually have to hire public relations people to help change their image. They do things like handing out dimes to the people in the street and having their pictures taken for the newspaper for all to see. I prefer to follow the Sermon on the Mount and let my offering be done in secret.

"Nikki, money can change a person, and usually not for the better. I look at money as a tool; it can be used for good or evil. That's what I learned from John and Richman."

The Law of Giving

"Now let's get back to the story, shall we? I remember Richman asking me, 'Sir, have you heard that money is the root of all evil?'

'Sure!' I told him. 'Everyone knows that.'

'Actually, Sir, money isn't the root of all evil; it's the *love* of money that's the root of all evil. People that seek for wealth can never have enough money, like those who seek for fame can never have enough. I think that's one of the reasons why my father gives; it keeps him grounded. Some call it the law of giving; others call it the law of tithes and offerings.'

"Nikki, I have to admit it, I wasn't sure what he was talking about. I knew what giving was, but tithes and offerings? Richman told me tithing had many meanings in different times, but basically it meant ten percent. I looked at him and said, 'Your father gives ten percent? That's got to be a lot of money.'

'My father gives more than ten percent when it comes to offerings or contributions. He knows there is much debate regarding the law of tithing, that believers are no longer under the Mosaic Covenant. Others feel that since Abraham and Jacob both lived before the Mosaic covenant was in place, when they gave a tenth, the law still stands. My father gives, not because he feels he has to, but because he wants to.'

'Yes, but ten percent! That's a lot of money. I could never do that.'

'Let me ask you this: if I gave you a dollar and I asked for ten cents back, would you have a hard time giving it to me?'

'Of course not, it's only ten cents.'

'What if I gave you a thousand dollars and asked for a hundred back, would you have a hard time giving that back to me?'

'Not at all. It wasn't mine in the first place, so why should I have any trouble giving back a hundred? I'm still up nine hundred.'

'And that, Sir, is how my father looks at it. He truly feels that all he has wasn't his in the first place. Yes, he worked for it and earned it, but all the riches of the world were here before he came and will be here after he's gone.'

"I didn't get it at first, so Richman sat there staring at me, not saying a word. Then it was like a light that came on and I understood. 'My father knows a lot of wealthy people who are Jewish, Christian, and non-Christian, who know that the law of giving or law of tithing is as real as the law of gravity.'

"I looked at Richman. 'I'm not sure I can believe in this tithing thing. Ten cents is one thing, but when you're talking about thousands, if not hundreds of thousands, that's another thing.'

'Just because you don't believe it doesn't mean it isn't true. If you didn't believe in gravity and you fell off the mountain you and TJ climbed, would what you believed make any difference?'

"I grinned, 'Not likely.'

'The law of giving or tithes and offerings is like the law of attraction. Try it and find out for yourself.'

'What the heck is the law of attraction?' I asked.

'When you want something, give it away first. Start off with something simple, like a smile. If you want to receive a smile, try giving it away first and see what comes back in return. Or kindness! Be kind to a stranger and see what kindness comes back.'

'I can see a smile and even kindness, but money?'

'Why not? The trick is to give with a giving heart. It will take faith, but exercise that faith and see if God doesn't open the windows of heaven to pour out his blessings to the point where there won't be enough room. That's in Malachi 3:10.'

"I reached for John's Bible. It took a while, but I found it. "Bring ye all the tithes into the storehouse, that there may be meat in mine house, and prove me now herewith, saith the Lord of hosts, if I will not open you the windows of heaven, and pour you out a blessing, that there shall not be room enough to receive it."

"Once Richman felt I understood, he threw me for a real loop. 'My father's mentor taught him the law of giving as found in the

Old Testament and challenged him, after he believed in that law, to stretch his faith and increase it by 1 percent each year until it was 50 percent. My father gives 10 percent to his church because he knows there is a cost in building, maintaining, and running a church. The other 40 percent goes to different charities around the world.'

"Nikki, I was shocked. I looked at him, '50 percent? Your Father gives 50 percent of his income?' Richman smiled.

'I knew that would get your attention. Yes, 50 percent of his profits from the last time he gave.'

"I looked at him. 'Why on earth would your father do that?' Again, Richman didn't say anything; he let me think about what I said. I was embarrassed when it hit me, I said, 'It's obvious that it works for your father.'

'Giving or tithing works for everyone, and God only asks for 10 percent. Think about it. God doesn't need money. He doesn't need yours, mine, or even my father's. He asks of His children to have faith, to give something we perceive to be of value to see where our heart is, and to see if we are willing to sacrifice to help our fellow man. Yes, Sir, "Cast your bread upon the water that it might come back tenfold," is one of my father's favorite sayings.'"

Wants and Needs

"'Sir, it's important that you know the difference between wants and needs. It seems the more money people make, the more their wants become needs, and that's normal. You must stay focused on the difference between desire and greed. Desire is good; it motivates us. Greed, on the other hand, blinds us. Remember, everything in this life is temporary. It's your heart and your love that are eternal. I'm sure John shared with you the eye of the needle story?'

"I actually found myself excited to recite the story John taught me. Richman sat down as I started the story.

'There was a young man who came to Jesus and asked how he could have eternal life. Jesus told him to obey the commandments, to which he replied that he had, from the time he was little, but he wanted to know if there was more. That's when Jesus told him to sell all he had and give it to the poor and then follow him. The young man left in sorrow, because he was wealthy. Jesus then told his disciples, "It's easier for a camel to go through the eye of a needle, than for a rich man to enter into the kingdom of God."

'When John told me this, I must admit my heart sank because I went to school so I could learn to make money. Truth be told, I wanted to be wealthy. I asked John why God would bless someone with wealth if that meant he couldn't have eternal life. John told me that at night, the gates to the city were closed, but there was a small opening in the wall for travelers who came after the gates were closed. It was called *the eye of the needle.* It was difficult for a camel to get through, but it could be done. The camel would have to have everything removed from its back and get on its knees to go through. John felt Jesus was giving the young man a test, to see if he, like the camel, would be willing to remove all he had. For this young man, it was more than he could do. He loved his money more than he loved the Lord. John told me we all have tests throughout our lives. Some are harder than others.'"

The Sacrifice of Abraham

"'John had also told me, "Let's hope you never have to go through a test like Abraham did. God gave Abraham a commandment to sacrifice his only son Isaac. Abraham had waited so long for a son, and now he was asked to sacrifice him for God. Abraham loved his son, but he loved God more and was willing to do what he was asked. As he was about to sacrifice his son, God stopped him at the last possible moment. God, knowing Abraham's heart, provided a ram for the sacrifice." John told me he felt the test was also giving Abraham a taste of what God would have to go through when His only begotten Son would be sacrificed.'

"Richman nodded a smile of approval, stood up, and stretched. 'I'll take first watch.'

As I sat there thinking about Abraham, I noticed a grin on James's face, one I've seen many times. *"Okay, spill it."* His face became serious. "Nikki, have you ever wondered how old Isaac was when Abraham was asked to sacrifice him?"

"I don't think the scriptures say."

"They don't, but I think I've narrowed it down. Isaac had to be, twelve and under, or twenty and above."

"Why's that?"

"Because, if Isaac was a teenager, it wouldn't have been much of a sacrifice."

James almost said it with a straight face, which made me laugh even harder.

THREE

WELL-ROUNDED AND BALANCED

"The next day after dinner, and from out of nowhere, Richman said, 'As long as you keep things in perspective, by keeping things well-rounded and balanced in your life, you'll be fine.'

"I must have had a puzzled look on my face. 'Sir, let me try and explain it the way my father did.'

"Richman picked up a stick and drew a circle in the dirt about three feet in diameter with a small circle in the center. Then he made a bunch of little hash marks all over inside the large circle. Some were close to the center of the circle and some farther out. 'Okay, Sir. Let's suppose this large circle represents your life, with the small one in the center representing your birth. As an infant, you started out in the center learning things day by day. These hash marks represent life's experiences. Name off, in order, what you think you learned as you grew.'

'All right! Let's see. First, I learned to crawl, then walk, then run.' As I was naming off a list of things, Richman drew a circle over the smaller one, about four times bigger, encompassing some of the hash marks. Richman stopped me. 'Now, make a list of things you learned in school, starting in the sixth grade.'

"I thought for a moment and went through another list, all the while, Richman made more circles. 'Thank you. That will do, Sir. Did you notice as you went through your list, the circle got bigger, encompassing the hash marks? Those marks represented each item you named.'

"I looked down at the ground. 'That, Sir, is a well-rounded person. Now you'll notice that there are still hash marks on the outside of the smaller circles, and they could be anything, things you have yet to experience. Since we're talking about money, let's say this hash mark way over here to the right, outside the circles is money, and this one at the other side to the left of the circles is family. Since you already have a family, I'm going to make the next circle bigger, to encompass your family. Now let's say you have a home, a job, and you want to have more money—lots and lots of money.'

"Richman then took the stick and drew the circle so it only encompassed the hash mark that was money. 'What do you see, Sir? Do you see a nice round circle?'

'Not anymore.'

'Now let's imagine this circle is a wheel. Would it give you a nice, smooth ride down the highway of life, or a difficult, if not impossible, ride?'

'I'd say that wheel is out of balance.'

'Sir, if you were to put all your energy into one thing, no matter what it is, you could lose your family. No amount of money or success in this world could ever compensate for losing your family. Everything we learn, even finance, must be learned step by step. There are no shortcuts.'

"I sat looking at the oblong circle in the dirt, thinking of those I knew who were out of balance. I never thought of life that way. I thanked him. I stood up and stretched. 'I'll take the first watch. I'd like to ponder this one for a while.'

"In the morning when I woke up, Richman already had the water on the fire, ready to pour into the C-rations. 'Good morning, Sir. Breakfast is served.'

"I laughed. 'How about that? The son of a billionaire is serving me breakfast in bed! It can't get any better than this.'

"Richman couldn't help but play along. In a butler-type voice, he said, 'I took the liberty of shining your shoes, Sir. Can I bring you your morning paper?'

"Not missing a beat, I replied, 'Thank you, my good man, that would be fine. Is my suit back from the cleaners?'

'It arrived while you were sleeping. Would you like me to bring it up?'

"It sure felt good to laugh, and I thanked him for that. 'You're welcome, Sir. Sometimes a good laugh can be a great diversion, like playing an instrument, exercising, or even having a good game of stick pulling.'

"I lit up. 'John taught you stick pulling too?' Richman nodded. 'I couldn't beat him for the life of me.'

'You should have challenged him to Indian leg wrestling, Sir. Your legs are longer, and you could have beaten him every time.'

'Thanks. I'll keep that in mind if I ever see him again and get the chance.'"

Have a Desire

"After breakfast, we broke camp and resumed our trek through the Black Forest. As the days went by, we were able to snare a few small animals to add to the C-rations. The terrain was in some ways as difficult as the mountain was with TJ, but we faced the peaks and valleys together.

"Each night, I had questions for Richman. 'I have to tell you, I have never met anyone as young as you that had such a business mind.

You don't look old enough to have more than one year of college under your belt.'

'Well, Sir, you're right. I finished one semester before I enlisted.'

'So how is it you know so much?'

"Richman smiled. 'Because I had a desire. Anything in this life that's worthwhile is worth going after. My father would invite each of his children at the age of fourteen to start sitting in on the board meetings and begin to learn the business. He made it perfectly clear; he was not about to turn over the keys to the car until we knew how to drive, so to speak.

'I'm the fourth and the youngest in the family. I wanted to be like my dad. So, when each of my brothers and sister turned fourteen, every time they came home from the board meetings, I would pump them for information. By the time I was fourteen and it was my turn to sit in on the meetings, I already had years of knowledge from my siblings. I knew my father, after about an hour or so, would ask his green, wet-behind-the-ears kids a tough question, to keep them humble. You should have seen the look on his face and the board members' when I answered. They didn't know I had what you would call *insider information.*'

"I laughed. 'I sure would have liked to have seen that. What else did you learn?'"

Mentorship and the Power of the Mind

"Richman thought for a moment.

'Let me ask you, Sir, have you given much thought about what you want to do when you get home?'

'Ever since I went through the barn door and met you guys, I'm more than happy to listen to any suggestion you can give me. As John put it, "The teacher will appear when the student is ready." And Richman, I'm ready.' He smiled and nodded.

'That's one of John's sayings, all right. I don't know how much of a teacher I might be, but I'll tell you what I know. I remember a couple of lessons my father taught us. I couldn't have been more than six, but I remember it like it was yesterday. He took the family to the circus. As we were walking around, we saw the elephants behind the tent. There were three, two rather large and one quite young. My father pointed out the small chain around the two large ones and a small stake that went into the ground. I remember thinking that those elephants could break loose with barely any effort.

'Then my father pointed to the smaller one, which was held with a large, heavy chain attached to a thick stake driven deep into the ground. It didn't make any sense to me. I thought it should be the opposite. That's when my father told us, "If the younger one had the same chains as the older ones did, that young elephant would break loose and cause all kinds of damage. Once it's learned that it can't break free and its brain has been trained that it's no use to try, then all that will be needed will be a smaller chain. Why even try?" Our mind, he told us, is a very powerful tool that we must train and exercise. He pointed his finger at each of us kids. "Don't ever let someone say you can't do it, or don't even try." He looked us in the eye, "Never, never sell yourself short. You may fail, but at least you tried, and it's from our failures that we learn and grow." Then he put his hand on our heads and messed up our hair, which our mother had taken so long to get just right, and challenged, "Race you to the tent!"'

Hansen Learns About Service

"'There under the big tent, he told us to look around. The place was packed with people. Dad told us that one of the secrets to making money was to serve as many as you can. This tent can only hold so many, so you can only make so much money. But if you could have a bigger tent, and more that were set up all over the world, you could serve more people. I shared that with John and the others one night when we were together around a campfire. John shared with us the story of Jesus washing his disciples' feet and how he served others. John pointed out that no job should be beneath anyone when they are serving others. I know my father would agree.'

"A few minutes passed in silence. Richman broke the silence. 'I remember another thing my father taught us that day. When the clowns came out to juggle, first, there was only one. He started out with three eggs, while another clown came out and tossed him another and another. He got up to about five or six when in walked another clown. It was then the clown that was tossing in the eggs added another. We were all waiting for him to start dropping eggs.

'After all, that would have been funny. Then my father said, "Watch this." The clown that was juggling all the eggs started to toss them to the other clown who had just walked in. They started juggling them back and forth, while the other clown still added eggs until all three were tossing them back and forth to each other.

'Of course, in the grand finale, they all tossed the eggs high in the air which landed on their heads. Dad told us, "No matter how good we think we are at juggling, we can't do it all. We must have help. Don't be so proud as not to bring in help, and be sure to find those who are the best in their field. You want someone smarter than you, especially in areas where you're weak. Everyone has areas in which they're better than others are. So what's wrong with learning from each other?"

'My father unfortunately had to learn that lesson the hard way. I have a half brother from his first marriage, who I've only met a few times. He wants nothing to do with our father.'

'What happened?'

'It's an all-too-familiar story. Dad had tunnel vision; all he could see was his work. He was so focused on money that it was all he could see. He was definitely getting out of balance. He started out as an employee and put in a lot of overtime, even though his boss encouraged him to go home and spend more time with his family. His boss was a well-rounded man and knew what was important. He told Dad that when he goes through his front door at home, to mentally leave office work at the office. Of course, he didn't.

'Then my father started his own company. His wife and son saw even less of him than before. He was what you would call, "The Head Chef, and Bottle Washer." As he was juggling everything by himself, he would say, "If you want a job done right, you have to do it yourself." Dad kept doing the same thing over and over, expecting different results. How insane is that? He hadn't learned to delegate to people better than he was at that point. Instead of asking his son if he would like to learn the business, he told him he was going to learn it whether he liked it or not. Yes, Sir, that cost my father his first marriage and his first son.

'He fell flat on his face, but at least he fell forward, so when he picked himself up and dusted himself off, he made a promise that he would never fall into that trap again. That's when he tried the law of giving, and he's since been true to his word.

'After being humbled, my father went back to his old boss, whom he had left on good terms, and asked for help. Before he fell flat on his face and lost everything, I don't think Dad had ever asked for help. His old boss became a mentor and took him under his wing. You see, he liked my dad and was really hoping he would make it, but he knew the odds were against him. He wanted to help him, but he wanted my father to ask. The problem was he was too proud and stubborn to ask.'

"I asked, 'What's the difference between a mentor and a teacher? Aren't they the same?'

'Yes and no. A mentor is someone who has gone through what you're going through. Take TJ, for example! He could have been a teacher and told you about mountain climbing, then sent you on your way. How far do you think you would have gotten?'

"Shaking my head, 'Not very far, that's for sure.'

'A mentor is more than a teacher. They are someone who is willing to take the time and walk you through step-by-step. A mentor can also be someone you've never met. They have left behind bread crumbs for us to pick up—bread crumbs or pearls of wisdom in their writings and teachings. Make sure it's someone who has gone through their own peaks and valleys and not some theoretician. Once my father was sufficiently humble, the first thing he and his mentor did was to sit down and lay out a plan together, a step-by-step plan. You see, Sir, you have to learn to walk before you can run, and you have to know where you're going if you want to reach a certain destination. A mentor is someone who can help you on that journey.

'He taught him about the power of thought. Think about what you want and then put it down on paper. If you feel good about it, then ask God for help and go out and do it. For those who don't have a belief in God, they can then put that thought out into the universe. John shared with me the biblical saying in Proverbs, "As a man thinketh in his heart, so is he." Thoughts can lead to either good or evil. Everything that is, or will be, was first thought of. Think about this, do you really believe that God created the earth and everything on it, even though he was God, without any forethought? Of course, he thought about it all first. At least that's what John told me, and it makes sense.'

"I sat pondering over this concept, and it made sense to me, too."

FOUR

TIME TO SHARPEN THE AX

"Richman taught me to slow down and smell the roses, to keep my mind clear and keep things in perspective.

"One night, Richman said, 'Let me tell you a story about two lumberjacks: one young and the other one much older. The younger was always bragging about how good he was until one day the older lumberjack challenged him to a race. Whoever cuts the most trees by thickness at the end of the day, he, and only he, can brag. The young man puffed up his chest, stuck out his hand, and said, "Deal." At the end of the day, the old man won by a clear margin, yet the young man complained. He couldn't see how it was possible. Every time he looked, he saw the old man taking a break with his back to him. How is this possible? The old lumberjack picked up his trophy and told him, "It's because of what you didn't see. While I was resting, I was taking the time to sharpen my ax."

'Even though my father was no longer married, his boss insisted that he learn to take time for himself and sharpen the ax, so that when he met someone else, that habit would already be in place.'

"I gave Richman a light punch in the arm. 'Lucky for you, someone came along.'

'Yes, Sir. She was a secretary who worked for one of the team members. After they were married, his mentor wanted him to be part of the inner circle. That's when he told my father that T.E.A.M. stood for "Together Everyone Achieves More." Think about it. No matter what kind of team it is, baseball, basketball, football, it doesn't matter. That acronym fits all teams. My father's mentor knew that with what he had taught him, it was time for him to go into business again, and this time he would do it right. When a person was ready, he would help set up an entirely new business. He told my father he would rather get a small percent of his efforts than none at all. The mentor showed him how to pick his vice presidents on down, and how to pick a team, or what he called a *Mastermind Group*.'"

Mastermind and Moses

"'The same night that John told us about service, I told him about how my father had set up his company. It was similar to the way Moses set up the Israelites. Come to find out, Moses and my dad were somewhat alike in that they both tried to do it all themselves! Moses was trying to solve everyone's problems by himself. John said there were probably two, maybe three million people, and trying to solve everyone's problems was virtually impossible. Before the Israelites were freed, they lived under Ruler's Law. They were told by their rulers what to do in every facet of their lives. If you never knew freedom, then chances are you wouldn't know what to do, so you'd be looking to Moses to solve your problems. His father-in-law, Jethro, saw what Moses was trying to do and knew it wouldn't be long before Moses would wear himself out. Jethro took him aside and counseled with him, telling Moses what he was doing, and showed him a better way.

'Moses then broke things down into smaller, more manageable groups. Moses took more than 600,000 families and put each family into groups of ten families. They would elect a leader to preside over them. Any problems in that group would be taken to their leader. Next, Moses took five groups of the ten and combined them to make a fifty-family group. They elected a leader out of each larger group to help solve problems that were too hard for the other leaders in the smaller groups to solve.

'Out of the larger fifty-family groups, he combined them into groups of one hundred families, each electing leaders that were capable of solving even tougher problems. But Moses wasn't done yet. Next groups of one thousand families, with more elected leaders. And if they couldn't solve the problem, that's when they took those to Moses. You might say he was the Supreme Court because he only dealt with the hard cases, and he, of course, could take even the harder cases to God. Moses had two vice presidents; he put Joshua in charge of the military and Aaron in charge of spiritual matters. He had a council of seventy that was like a senate and elected representatives that would be like a congress. They were kind of like his *Mastermind Group*.

'John added, "They were set up as a commonwealth of freemen." Then he quoted Leviticus 25:10: "Proclaim liberty throughout all the land unto all the inhabitants thereof." You should have seen TJ when John shared that with us. You know how excited he can get.'

'I sure do.'

'TJ stands up all excited, raising his hand as if John was his school teacher, waiting to be called on.'

"I found myself smiling; I could imagine it all too well. 'So there he was, his hand in the air, and John couldn't help himself. He looked at TJ and asked, "Is there something you'd like to share with the class?"

"Richman and I both started to laugh. 'We tried to keep a straight face, but it was no use. Hart started to laugh, which made me start to laugh, and John couldn't hold it back any longer. TJ got a little embarrassed, but he soon got over it and laughed along with us.'

'Let me guess, TJ told you that scripture from Leviticus is inscribed on the Liberty Bell, and how the Founding Fathers set up the government the same way Moses did.'

'He sure did. We already knew that, and I was about to stop him, but John nudged my knee with his, so TJ wouldn't see. That was my cue to shut up and let TJ talk and enjoy the story. Even though I knew what he was going to say, I enjoyed the company and his story.'

The Four Quadrants[xxii]

"'Say, did Hart tell you about the four different personalities and putting the different combinations together?'

'He sure did.'

'Did you know that there are also four different areas in which to make money?'

"I looked at Richman, 'Only four ways to make money?'

'No, there are many ways to make money, of course, but you can categorize them into four quadrants. Actually, it's a good idea to make money in as many areas as you can and have multiple sources of income. Sometimes, we need patience in some of these areas. Remember the bamboo tree. Nothing happens for a long time after you plant it, then all of a sudden; it grows so fast, if you hung your hat on it, the next day you wouldn't be able to reach it. My father has been in every quadrant. First, he started out as an employee, and then he moved into the self-employed quadrant. He thought he was in the world of business, but he was only fooling himself. It was his old boss who became his mentor and he taught him the world of business.'

"Nikki, I didn't understand so I asked. 'What's the difference between being in business for yourself and the world of business?'

'One is when you have a system that makes money without you hovering over it. The other is when, if you don't work, you don't get paid. Which one would you like?'

'I'll take the system that you don't have to hover over, thank you.'

'Good choice, Sir. So, you would rather sign the front of the check, instead of the back?'

'I never thought of it that way, but yes.'

'Having a good system in place doesn't guarantee that your business will be successful. Always look for trends and cycles, and if the government wants to get involved, be very careful. Always be willing to bend and change as necessary. Don't be so set in your ways that you miss an opportunity. I'll give you an example. There once was a company that made a lot of money selling buggy whips and carriages. A friend saw a new trend coming and wanted him to go into business with him. His shop, his workers, along with his system of assembly-line workers, would be perfect for this new adventure. But his friend turned him down. He was content making money the way he always had and didn't see why he should change.'

"I raised my hand to stop him. 'Let me guess. His friend went into automobiles and put his friend out of business?'

'You guessed it. Of course, spotting a trend is easier said than done. Always keep your eyes and mind open and you'll spot them. Remember, the more you can serve, the more you'll make.'

'You said there were four quadrants. What's the fourth?'

'The fourth quadrant is the investor quadrant. This is where you can make a lot or lose a lot. You really need to know what you're doing in this quadrant. It can be very risky if you don't take the time to learn. Think of it this way. You remember what it was like in flight school, how it was both exciting and scary at first, but with a lot of study and practice it got easier? When you were ready to climb into the cockpit for the first time with an instructor, your heart raced, but you knew you'd be all right, because the guy in the airplane with you was experienced and could help you if you needed help.'

"I reflected back. I could see it all too well. 'And when you were ready to fly solo, that excitement once again came over you, but you knew you were ready.'

"I asked, 'Are you sure you didn't attend flight school?' Richman smiled. 'No, Sir. I do know what it's like to try something new and exciting. Investing can produce that same kind of excitement. Like it was in flight school, when it comes to investing, you'll want to get an instructor and start off slow. I would suggest starting off by getting yourself out of debt.'

"Richman went through an exercise on how to pay off those I was indebted to and to never become enslaved again. He taught me to pay myself first, to build up a safety net of about six months to a year. 'Know this,' he said, 'those who understand interest receive it. Those who don't, pay it. Always use your intelligence.'

"Richman got that look in his eyes and started to chuckle. I knew he had something else on his mind. 'Come on, spill the beans. What is it?'

'I remembered a joke my father told me, that's all.'

"I motioned with my hand as if to say, let's hear it. 'There were two guys digging down in a pit. Their boss was up on top enjoying a nice cool beverage. Finally, one of the diggers turned to the other and asked, "Why does he get paid more than us and we do all the work?"

"Good question, I'll go ask him." So he climbed out of the pit and asked. His boss told him "Intelligence."

"Intelligence?" he asked. "Yes, intelligence." Not understanding, the boss said, "Let me show you." So the boss put his hand up against a wall and told him to hit his hand as hard as he could. "If I do that, I'll hurt your hand."

"It'll be fine, go ahead."

"Okay." As he went to hit his hand, the boss, of course, moved his hand, causing great pain to the worker. As he was shaking off the pain, the boss asked, "Do you understand now?" Still shaking his hand, he said, "I think so. I'll get back to work." When he got back down, the other worker asked, "Well, what did he say?"

"He said he gets paid more because of intelligence."

"Intelligence?"

"Yeah, intelligence. Let me show you." He then put his hand up in front of his own face and said . . .'

"Richman started to laugh, and I said, 'Hit my hand.'

"After a good laugh, Richman told me, 'There are countless numbers of ways to leverage and grow your money. It will take time and effort on your part to keep up with the laws.' He went on to tell me, 'If you don't get that same kind of excitement when investing as you did in flight school, then it's best you do what my father does and put together a team that finds investing fun and exciting. Be sure you keep on top of it while you tend to what interests you. Find something you love, and you'll never work a day in your life. Life is too short otherwise. Knowing trends when investing is also very important. Not only knowing when to get in, but when to get out.'

"Richman looked at his watch. 'It's not that late, but we pushed ourselves pretty hard in some of those ravines. By turning in early, we'll get some pretty good sleep. I'll take the first watch and wake you at 0300.'

"I took my shift at three o'clock. A little before daylight, Richman was awake and ready to go. We quickly heated up some water, ate, and took off. By the time we made camp that night, Richman calculated we had traveled over twenty miles that day."

First Impressions

"Over dinner, I asked Richman what his dad looked for when hiring someone. 'Everything. It depends on what he's looking for, but first impressions are very important. Confidence and eye contact are very important clues. A smile, a firm handshake, and I don't mean one of those vice-grip type handshakes. I've had a few of those, and I've never been impressed. They're almost as bad as a limp-fish handshake. You know, with no grip at all. Whenever I get one of those, I feel like telling them to put it back in the water.'

"I laughed. I've had a few of those myself. 'What else?' Richman thought for a moment. 'It takes time and study, but when you put people together on a project, you'll need to know the different kinds of personalities that work best for the project. Not only what Hart taught you, but what comfort zone people fall into in the four different quadrants. My father, unfortunately, hasn't interviewed someone for the regular type of work for some time. He leaves that to the project managers.'"

Taxes and Congress

"'Why is that unfortunate?' I asked.

'Because for some time now, he has had to spend a lot of money on lawyers and accountants to keep up with the changing laws that come out of Congress instead of spending time on the people who do the labor that makes the company grow. If you had to go down a dark alley and you knew you were going to get mugged, would you hide most of your money and leave a few bucks in your wallet, or would you put it all in your wallet?'

'I'd hide it, of course.'

'And that's what the rich do; only they hide it legally. When Congress passes laws, businesses react. They keep their money where it will do the most good, out of the hands of politicians who line their pockets and buy votes. Though, I'm sure not all politicians are that way. At least, I hope not.'

'Sir, TJ told you about the Sixteenth Amendment, didn't he?'

'He did.'

'Did he tell you how it came about?'

'I don't think so. He did tell me it was an income tax that was a redistribution of wealth. He said it wasn't the first time, either. It seems that during the Civil War, Congress passed an income tax measure, and the Supreme Court, you might say, squinted its legal eye and let it go through to help pay for the war. Later, the Court reversed itself and called it what it was, a direct tax, ruling that it was unconstitutional.'

'That's true, but when the direct tax passed again in 1913, the precedent had been set breaking the Tenth Commandment.'

"I jerked my head back. 'You mean the Tenth Amendment, don't you?'

'No, Sir, I meant the Tenth Commandment; however, the Tenth Amendment has also been trampled on. But the Tenth Commandment, simply put, means, do not covet other people's things. If you want what your neighbor has, go out and work for it. It's the Lord's way of telling you to get up off your fanny and earn it for yourself. It looks like getting something for nothing was a problem even back in the times of Moses. By the time the 1900s rolled around, class warfare had picked up a pretty good head of steam. The cry "Let the rich pay for the programs because they can afford it" was so loud that a Democrat senator from Texas introduced an amendment to a simple tariff bill. That bill would introduce an income tax of 2 percent to those who earn more than $5,000. That was a lot of money back then. The senator introduced the amendment to embarrass the Republicans. He forced them to openly oppose a measure that seemed to be gaining popularity among the people.

'There were liberal Republicans back then as there are today who wanted it to pass. When it looked like it was going to, the conservative Republicans quickly put together an income tax bill as an amendment to the Constitution.

'They thought it would put egg on the faces of those who wanted a 2 percent tax only for the rich, because everyone knew it was unconstitutional and it would never pass. The plan backfired on them. The Democrats couldn't vote against it because it was their concept in the first place, and the Republicans couldn't vote against it because it was their bill. All they could do was hope the House would kill it, but it sailed through as well. Now, it was up to the states to stop it, but there was such an outcry from the lower classes to punish the rich that in 1913, it became the Sixteenth Amendment.

'Congressman Payne of New York, who introduced the bill in the House, admitted that they were trying to defeat the first bill the Democrats introduced. He even said that an "income tax makes a nation of liars." Richman shook his head. 'I don't know what the people were thinking. Once you start to feed the government money, it's like drugs to addicts. They always want more, and more is never enough. It didn't take long before more and more people started to find themselves in the rich category, not because they were making more, but because the top income bracket started to become lower and lower.'"

FIVE

THE REUNION

"Over the next few weeks, Richman went into greater detail in each of the quadrants—what to look for when talking to employees and where they would be best suited in the company. What was more important was how to spot someone he too could mentor when the time was right.

"It was a Saturday night when we heard someone coming. I grabbed the water and was about to douse the fire when Richman stopped me. 'That won't be necessary, Sir. That will be the other guys. This is our rendezvous place.'

"In walked John, Hart, and TJ. I jumped to my feet. I couldn't believe my eyes. It was so good to see them.

"TJ smiled, while pointing his finger. 'I told you we'd meet up again.'

"I gave him a big hug. 'You sure did.' I gave each a hug and turned to Richman. 'You could have told me we were going to meet up.'

"Nikki, Richman threw out his arms and said, 'Surprise!' We all had a good laugh."

"Is that why you like to give surprises?"

"I suppose so."

"As we sat down to eat, John and the others pulled out of their backpacks enough food for a Thanksgiving dinner. All I could say was, 'Now I'm really glad you guys came around. This is a great meal to start our fast.'

"I saw John smiling. 'I'm glad to hear that. What shall we fast for?'

"I asked the guys if it would be all right if we fasted for hearts to be softened so we could all go home. All took their canteens and raised them in approval. After dinner, John asked if I would do them the honor and open our fast with a word of prayer. To which I replied, 'It would be my pleasure.'

"That Sunday, they went over the key points they had taught me and told me to write everything down the first chance I had.

"Before we turned in for the night, John told us one of his father's favorite parables. 'A woman saw three old men sitting on her lawn. They appeared to be hungry, so she invited them in to eat. One thanked her for the kind offer and explained that only one of them could come in. Confused, the woman asked why. He explained, "I am Love, and my companions are Wealth and Success. Only one of us can fill your home. Go discuss with your husband which one of us you would like in your home."

'The husband was elated and wanted Success to come in. The wife, on the other hand, wanted Wealth. Their daughter, knowing the kind of spirit that was in their home, asked if Love could please come in. The parents, looking at their young daughter, knew she was right. The woman went out and asked if Love would like to come in and be their guest. Love stood and started to walk in. Success and Wealth also arose and followed. The woman, rather surprised, asked, "I invited Love. Why are *you* coming in?" Love answered, "Had you asked Wealth or Success, the other two of us would've stayed out, but since you invited me, wherever Love goes, Wealth and Success follow."'

"We all nodded our heads in approval and thanked John for the parable. John took the first watch, and with the others taking turns, they were able to let me sleep through the night. I felt bad that I didn't do my shift, but John said it was a gift the four of them wanted to give, and I accepted the gift gratefully.

"That morning, we were on our way once more. In less than an hour, we walked out of the Black Forest and came upon a road. I was surprised to see all four walking down the center. 'What are you guys doing? We're out in plain sight.' John smiled.

'It's all right. This is our road. Remember when we first met, I told you I was part of a team for search and return?'

'I remember.'

'You're on that road of return. A few miles from here is an army base. Would you like to lead the way and take point?'

"John stretched out his arm, pointing down the road. I couldn't believe it! Could this be real? With tears in my eyes I said, 'I would be honored.'

"As we walked down the road, John let me get about ten feet in front of them. Then he asked, 'Could you do us a favor, Sir?'

'Anything, ask and it's yours.'

'Could you find our folks and let them know we're fine, and we couldn't be happier and how grateful we are for them?'

"As I was turning around, I said, 'Sure, but you can tell them yourself.' It was then that I saw them dressed in the whitest uniforms I'd ever seen, their countenance so bright I had to shield my eyes. Behind them were countless other soldiers. That's when I noticed there were Germans standing alongside them, all showing great love for each other. More and more was revealed before my eyes. They were dressed in all kinds of uniforms from all periods of wartime, all uniforms bright. It came to my mind that even though they were enemies, at one time, they had been brothers. I was so overwhelmed with that love that I wanted to join them. John, knowing what was in my heart right then, shook his head. 'It's not your time, Sir.' I looked at John with tears in my eyes. 'I'm never going to see you guys again, am I?'

"John said lovingly, 'Course you will. It'll be awhile is all.'

"Richman stepped up; 'Sir, when you see my father, hand him your resume and tell him you're not looking for a job. You're looking for a mentor.'

'Thank you. I'll do that.'

"Hart reached into his pocket to give me a sealed envelope. 'Sir, when you see my parents, could you give them this?'

"I was unable to speak; all I could do was nod my head. If I tried to say anything, I probably would have broken down, bawling my eyes out. What I didn't know was that it was a letter instructing his parents to give me his old violin.

"John walked up to me and put his hand on my shoulder for the last time. 'We took you the way we did to teach you what you'll need to know and apply it in your life. Everyone has fears to face, their own mountains to climb, and deep valleys to go through. When God banished Adam and Eve from the garden, he told them they would have to work by the sweat of their brows. Never be too proud to ask for help, or to help someone so they can help themselves. It's too bad there are those who don't want help; they have their comfort zone right where they are, so don't waste your time or energy. Believe me, Sir, they'll take both. All you can do for them is love and pray for them.

'Before we go, here's one last word of advice. Only share with your family what you have experienced, and then only when they are ready to hear it. If you don't feel they can keep it to themselves, then don't. The day will come when you'll know it's time to share it with the world.'

'How will I know?'

'You'll know. Sir. Trust me, you'll know.'

"They went into attention and saluted. 'It's been an honor to have served you, Sir.' With tears rolling down my face, I returned the salute. And with that, they were gone."

The Puzzle Comes Together

While James was telling me about the four whom he always referred to as his guardian angels, a wave of emotions washed over me. I sat with tears rolling down my face. James handed me a box of tissue. "So, my dear, Nikki, you can understand our excitement when you came into our lives. When Jimmy introduced me to you, we knew you were the one I've been waiting for all these years who John told me I would know when it's time to share it with the world."

As I sat there trying to compose myself, my mind was filled with memories. I remembered when I was a little girl going through Grandpa Vincent's treasure chest, my trip to Germany tracking down the commandant who held both James and my grandfather. It was as if my whole life flashed before my eyes. I could see how the pieces of the puzzle fit. How my grandfather was shot down, receiving a broken leg, making it impossible for him to try to escape. How he was taken to the very camp where he saw a young pilot being led into the woods, never to return.

My burning desire to become an investigative reporter and the story that caused me such great unrest, led me halfway around the world on an impossible mission to find their captor. I could see the hand of God through it all. My whole life was preparing me for this moment. I took a deep breath and composed myself. Wiping the tears from my face, I looked at James.

"We've been working these many months, daily from nine to five, breaking only for lunch. I had no idea these four rescuers were angels. Why didn't you tell me?"

James replied with a big grin. "I didn't know until the very end, so I felt it was only fair that you find out at the very end."

I sat there running through my mind everything I had learned. James told me he loved to watch me whenever I was in one of those—what he called pondering moments and asked what I was thinking.

"I'm looking back from the first time I met your son Jimmy until now. I see a lot of the pieces of the puzzle coming together, including where your family got their ideas. I thought we stopped at five because you were getting tired and needed to rest. You wanted me to, as you put it, 'Have a life.'

"Of course, my dear! You didn't think I would deny my only grandson the honor of your company, did you? By the way, how are things going with the two of you over the last six months or so?"

I leaned forward, motioning with my hand for him to come closer, and whispered.

"He's taking me to a fancy restaurant tonight. I think he's going to propose."

James whispered back, "I think so, too. What are you going to say?"

"How would you feel if I started calling you Grandpa James?"

"Nikki, my dear, that sounds like music to these old ears hearing you say that."

James wiped his eye before a tear could fall.

Hope

After a moment, leaning back into his chair, James took in a deep breath. "I know that Benjamin Franklin, at the Constitutional Convention, saw the sun carved on the back of Washington's chair as a rising sun, but I'm afraid I see it as a setting sun. I worry for the future, for you and my grandkids."

It was then James stared off in a way I had never seen him do before. After about a minute or two, I started to get worried. After all, it was getting close to the time the doctors said it could be the final time. I stood, not knowing what to do. James started to smile as tears streamed down his face. I walked around the desk, took a tissue from the box, and lovingly wiped his face. James took my hand and held it up against his face. Giving my palm a kiss, he said, "Thank you." Then giving my hand a loving pat, he asked, "Go get Ray, could you please? There's something you two need to hear."

I went to the double doors and slid one open. Sure enough, Ray was sitting right there waiting for me. I motioned for him to come in. The look on my face concerned him.

"What's wrong? Is everything all right?"

"Your grandfather wants to see us." I took Ray by the hand, and we walked in together.

James was finishing wiping his face when he smiled and said, "I'm fine, so get those worried looks off your faces."

Ray stood until I sat down. Then he sat in the chair next to mine and took my hand.

James looked at us both and then turned his attention to Ray. "Ray, you're my youngest grandchild, and I want you to know how much I love you. I told Nikki about the angels."

Ray exhaled. He didn't even realize he was holding his breath. "I love you too, Grandpa." Ray turned to look at me. "So, what do you think?"

I looked at him, but all I could do was nod and smile. It was obvious I couldn't speak. Ray took his other hand and caressed my face, and with his thumb, wiped away a tear.

James broke the silence. "I was about to tell Nikki my concerns about this great country of ours when I saw my old friend John. He stood there shaking his head. It came to me that all is going to be fine. The good Lord is in charge, and there's nothing Satan can do that is going to change the outcome. I saw that the battle between good and evil would continue. Now is the time for all denominations, all good men and women, to come together in the aid of their country.

"When I think of all those who have died over religion, only because they couldn't see eye-to-eye, it saddens me." James shook his head. "Satan loves contention, no matter who it's with—husbands and wives, siblings, family members, it doesn't matter. To him, it's all music to his ears. I think he especially loves it among Christians and politicians.

"We need to put aside our differences. Who cares what one believes, as long as they believe in good versus evil. We must all stand together, arm in arm, and fight for what is going to keep this country strong. Not with hate and violence, but with love. Satan uses hate, and it is very easy to fall into that trap, but we must stay clear of that. Yes, we need to fight for that freedom for which so many have paid the ultimate price, but we need to fight with the truth and get the message out in a spirit of love. When you turn on the lights, the cockroaches flee. Use the light of truth that God has given us in the Constitution to send those cockroaches back to hell.

"There is something I want you two to understand and never forget. I think few in the world realize or have taken the time to think about the principles I've taken the time to teach you . . . Satan seeks to enslave all men, to make them captive and miserable like him. His tool is fear.

"Jesus's mission, on the other hand, is to free all men, and all that he has ever done for humanity has been motivated by His love for us.

"I feel God has saved His most valiant to be on earth at this time, for this battle, just as God placed the Founders when he did for their mission. It is up to you to wake up those who will listen and stand up for what is right. For some, it will be like talking to a brick wall. Don't waste your time with them. Look for the ones who are like lost sheep, looking to find their way out of the wilderness. Show them the way.

"I always loved watching westerns; John Wayne and Jimmy Stuart were only a few of my favorites. Whenever the wagon train was pinned down, its members thinking all was lost, off in the distance you would hear the bugle call "charge," letting everyone know that help was on its way. It may feel like a losing battle at times, but know this: God is in charge and nothing is going to happen that He doesn't already know. Nikki, you and others like you need to sound that bugle with the call 'Help is on the way.' Remember, *'Failure will never overtake you if your determination to succeed is strong enough.'*"

I smiled. *"That's from one of the books you gave me, The Greatest Salesman in the World, right?"*

"It is, and it's definitely one of my favorites. I remember the first time I read that book back in 1983, and I wondered if Mr. Og Mandino had ever met John and the others. No matter how much time goes by, that book will always be relevant.

"Nikki, Ray, the eagle has been pulled so far to the left it can scarcely be seen, but I believe it can be brought back to the balanced center peacefully. The Founders set it up that way. It can be done if the people are informed, righteous, and willing to sacrifice.

"Be strong and have faith and know that you'll be watched over. It won't be easy. There will be those who will try to stop you at every turn. You'll be ridiculed and belittled, called every name in the book. They will try to stop you by reaching into that old bag of tricks and use everything they have, and yes, they will use violence. There will be balance and order once again, and Satan knows it. Stay close to the Lord, and he will protect you. Nikki, everyone has to face their fears and go through their own personal barn door. Remember, where there's faith, fear flees.

"You know, the more flak you fly into means you're getting closer to the target. Are you ready and willing to fly into the flak that awaits you?"

I paused and looked into James's eyes. As I contemplated everything, I felt that same overwhelming peace I felt when James first asked if I wanted to come work for him. I knew it was the right thing then, and I know it is the right thing now. Taking a deep breath, I answered. *"Bring it on."*

James smiled, then turned to Ray: "How about you?"

"Grandpa, you have been preparing the family for this fight for a long time. Of course, I'm ready."

James closed his eyes and nodded. There was a calmness about him that Ray and I hadn't seen before.

James took in a deep breath and slowly let it out. "I feel as though I can now meet my maker, and I can return home with honor."

Ray looked at me. "I wanted to wait for tonight, but I feel now is the time." He stood and moved his chair out of way.

Reaching into his pocket, he went down on one knee. Opening the small box, he held it out. "Nikki Brown, I've already asked your father for your hand in marriage. Now I'm asking you. Will you marry me?"

I stood, and as a queen would raise her knight in shining armor, I put my arms around him. *"Yes, I'll marry you,"* and I gave him a kiss.

James stood and went around the desk to give us both a hug. "I'm so happy for you two. This calls for a celebration." James slid open both doors and went down the hall, calling out, "Alfred! Break out the champagne. There's going to be a wedding."

Hearing that, Karen came in all excited. "I was wondering when that was going to happen! Let's take a look." I held out my hand so Karen could get a better look. Some would say it should have been much bigger, but Ray knows me and my taste. Were it any bigger, I would have been embarrassed to wear it. To me, it looked like the Hope Diamond.

NOTES

NOTES

Why This Book

My wife and I have enjoyed being members of different networking companies, best known as MLMs. Most stress the importance of God, family, and country, but all have one thing in common: they place a high value on self-improvement through recommended books.

These types of companies attract those who want to help others . . . to better themselves and get ahead in life. They are the many good people we have made lasting friendships with.

So why this book and why is it in story form? It's simple: books written this way hold my attention and I find I retain the lessons much more deeply. Thus, the story I was told at the age of thirteen became my first book, *From Fear to Freedom.*

How I Became an Author

It was a Saturday morning in November of 2012. My wife and I were listening in on a conference call from a gentleman by the name of Dan McCormick.

Somewhere in that counseling session, Dan inspired me to step out of my comfort zone and write the story I heard at the age of thirteen. It was going to be a short story about stepping out of one's comfort zone. Years later, my first novel, *From Fear to Freedom,* was printed. I planned for it to have a sequel, *My Dear Nikki;* and leave it at that, but I had so much fun I'm now thinking a series. Thank you, Dan.

Hooked

I have always considered myself a patriot, one who loves America. It was in the late '70s when my wife and I attended a three-day seminar called "Miracle of America," hosted by Dr. W. Cleon Skousen and the NCCS. He brought history alive, and from that point on, I was hooked; I couldn't get enough.

There are other organizations that teach the Constitution; Dr. Cleon Skousen was the first who really lit the fire under me to want to learn more. To honor his memory and the NCCS, I took that information and incorporated it in Chapter Five through TJ. Thank you, Dr. Skousen. Your legacy lives on.

The NCCS no longer carries the *Miracle of America* but has an updated study guide called *The Making of America,* and it is great. It comes in MP3 and DVD. Make sure you get the study guide to follow along. That's where I received my inspiration and information for *From Fear to Freedom.* Thank you, NCCS.

If you would like to learn more about the Constitution, or the 28 Principles of Liberty that came after going over 150 volumes of the writing of the Founders which made our world leap 5,000 years (That's what inspired Dr. Skousen to write *The 5,000 Year Leap.)* Feel free to contact them at www.nccs.net.

Years later, I met Larry P. Arnn, President of Hillsdale College, who was giving a talk in San Francisco. Hillsdale has incredible online courses that cover the Constitution, along with many other subjects. I highly recommend you check them out at: Online.hillsdale.edu

Acknowledgments

I'm sure there are those of you, as you read through *My Dear Nikki,* will recognize a blend of many different authors who go into great detail in their books that cover the complexity of relationships. One thing I discovered in my research was how so many said the same thing in their own way. Who copied whom? I don't think anyone copied from one another. Observation of facts is simply that.

To name a few: Dr. Gary Smalley, *Keys to Loving Relationships*; Dr. James Dobson, *Focus on the Family;* John Gray, PhD, *Men are from Mars, Women are from Venus;* Dr. Laura Schlessinger, *The Proper Care and Feeding of Husbands.*

If you're looking for information on relationships, two websites I highly recommend, www.laughyourway.com, or call 866-525-2844. My wife and I attended one of Mark Gungur's seminars, "Laugh Your Way to a Better Marriage," and we definitely did. It was there we also learned about the four personalities by citing four different countries. Look for the book *Discovering Your Heart with the Flag Page;* take the test and find out what country you're from. You'll recognize the information in this book where Hart is teaching Hansen about the four personalities. Years later after I finished my first book, *From Fear to Freedom,* I learned that Mark would be back in California, about two hours from where I lived. He was very generous to give me so much of his time. I told him about this book, and he gave me the names of his contacts.

Thank you so much, Pastor Gungur.

The other website is www.garysmalley.com, or you can call 800-848-6329. Gary Smalley has a different style than Mark, and I thoroughly enjoyed his insight. You'll find that they too have many ways that can help in all kinds of relationships. I like the DNA series. You'll see his influence in my book as well. Thank you, Gary Smalley.

Special Thanks

If it weren't for my editors, this book could never have gone to print. Katherine Anderson, Susanne Larson, Professor Don Norton, and my daughter Andrea Bai.

Thanks to all the record keepers throughout the world through all time. Think about it, we wouldn't have the Bible if it weren't for them. Nor would we be able to learn from others' mistakes. To the historians that dig through all the writing and sift out the pearls of wisdom, if not for them, where would storytellers like me be?

Check out some of the books that Dr. Skousen wrote, *The Real George Washington*, *The Real Thomas Jefferson,* and many more. They have a world of information, and the NCCS would love to help.

The National Center for Constitutional Studies puts on one-day seminars all over this great country. Check out their seminar schedule to see if they're in your area. If not, they are willing to come to your group as small as fifty people.

The stories I tell in *From Fear to Freedom* and *My Dear Nikki* about George Washington came from the book, *The Real George Washington.* Thank you, Dr. Skousen and to all those at the center for all your help, for letting me tell the story of *The Making of America* and the printing of *Principles of Liberty.* Thank You.

Recommended Books

Here are some of the books that I would like to share with you and recommend. Not in any particular order, but the first would have to be a book I received back in the early '70s, *The Greatest Salesman in the World* by Og Mandino. When I told my good friend Graig my storyline, a part of it reminded him about this book. I went back and reread it, and sure enough, this book definitely had some influence in my book. As you read it, you'll see it too. There is a line that I had to put in: *"Failure will never overtake you if your determination to succeed is strong enough."* Thank you, Mr. Og Mandino.

If you want to learn about finance, go to any bookstore and you'll find hundreds of books on the subject. I love many authors but two come to mind, Dave Ramsey, for the simple way he lays out a plan on how to get out of debt, and Robert T. Kiyosaki for the way he teaches in his *Rich Dad Poor Dad* series. Thank you, for the countless number of people the two of you have helped.

I was wondering how I was going to gather all the things I had learned over the years to put in doom and gloom in Chapter Seven, Book Three. The Founders had Adam Smith in the nick of time with his book, *The Wealth of Nations,* I have two authors who have a wealth of information in their writings. In alphabetical order, Glenn Beck with his book, *Brook* (also in audio). I don't think I have ever come across a book with so much detail and information that I had never heard of before, about why we are in such deep *doo-doo* (my word, not Glenn's). The book, *Brook,* is so well researched and documented that in my references for my book, when it comes to the matters he talks about, I will give Mr. Beck the credit. Thank you, Glenn.

The other author is Mark R. Levin. His book, *Liberty and Tyranny* (also in audio) says it better than I ever could. I didn't think Mark could do any better than this one, but as I was finishing up with *From Fear to Freedom,* he came out with *Ameritopia: The Unmaking of America,* a must-read (also in audio).

Of course, *How to Win Friends and Influence People,* by Dale Carnegie, is a must-read if you want to learn to do both. For some people, this comes naturally and with ease. Others have to learn it, and Mr. Carnegie teaches it better than other books I've read.

The Miracle Morning, by Hal Elrod. Hal tells his story starting with a head-on collision at 70 mph. Clinically dead for six minutes, Hal survived. After you read *The Miracle Morning,* you'll know why a loving Heavenly Father didn't bring him home. God knew Hal Elrod had a gift to give others.

Last but not least is *Think and Grow Rich* by Napoleon Hill. He teaches thirteen steps you need to know for your path to success.

Schooling Today

Something that really concerns me is what is being taught in our schools, or should I say *not* being taught. Now there's a topic that is a book all unto itself. I have talked with others about this and have been told it's an uphill battle. I remember when our oldest daughter was in high school, there was a course called C.P.M. Math. My wife and I couldn't make heads or tails what this math book was talking about. When we went to parents' night, we asked the teacher a few of our questions. We weren't alone; many other parents had the same questions. What was sad was that the teacher couldn't answer the questions. From what I've learned, it's ten times worse today. The schools don't want you to know what your children are being taught. It's as though they think they're the parent and we parents have no say in anything.

Why should we give up power over our kids to the schools? Seriously! Our kids should be taught to question everything and every source of information, and not be belittled or shamed for expressing an opinion. That's where charter schools and homeschooling have come in. I don't know enough about this problem to give any real answers, but I'm open to suggestions.

Author's Final Thoughts

I want to thank you for taking the time to read this story. I hope you enjoyed it and found it worthwhile. If you received any good thoughts from it, please share them with others. Like the sea stars on a stranded beach, we reach out to others one at a time, and now there are two who can help.

I hope you found that I was equally fair with both the Republicans and the Democrats. I feel they have both let down the American people. I truly feel there are those who want to destroy the very kind of freedom the Founders gave us. I find it sad that so many follow the . . . *what's in it for me? philosophy* or *what can government do for me? attitude.* Whatever happened to President Kennedy's speech, *"Ask not what your country can do for you, ask what you can do for your country"*? So where do we start? Let's start with ourselves.

Giving Credit Where Credit Is Due

I can't tell you how many times I've come across where someone has taken credit for work that is not theirs. I can only imagine they are using "public domain," meaning anyone can "borrow" from a text without noting the sources. There is a caveat to using "public domain," if you "borrow" from most sources written by a personal writer, then you have to give credit. Or as my daddy would say, "Give credit where credit is due."

★Unfortunately, this is the one section that was left incomplete before Gary's unexpected passing. Blank sections have been filled in as best as possible and other endnote sections have had to be deleted due to not knowing exactly which sources he used. Please be understanding and forgiving of this. It was fully his intention to give all the credit where it was due. Thank you.

ENDNOTES

Book One

Chapter 6

[i] The Funnel Story is a true story with permission from Matt Wright. Thank you, Matt.

Book Two

[*] Book Two could not have been written without the help from Mark Gungor, Dr. Gary Smalley, and Dr. Gary Chapman.

Chapter 1

[ii] Prelude to War: The National Archives of The United States

Chapter 3

[iii] Stradivarius and The Violin Story was inspired by two stories, Myra Brooks Welch's *Touch of the Master's Hand* and Dr. Gary Smalley's *Keys to Loving Relationships.*

[iv] Understanding the Different Personalities came from Mark Gungor's book *Discovering Your Heart*, a must-read. Thank you for letting me share a part of your book.

[v] Control Country, Fun Country, Perfect Country, Peace Country: The Four Personality Profiles as countries by Mark Gungor. To learn more about the different countries, go to www.laughyourway.com.

Chapter 5

[vi] The Wiring of the Two Brains comes from Mark Gungor in *Laugh Your Way to a Better Marriage* (www.laughyourway.com). Gary Smalley's *Keys to Loving Relationships* also covers this information beautifully.

[vii] The Five Love Languages is very well known from Dr. Gary Chapman's book, *The Five Love Languages,* highly recommended.

Book Three

Book Three could not have been written without the help from the NCCS (National Center for Constitutional Studies).

Chapter 2

[viii] Washington and the Indian Chief: Indian legend of George Washington's divine protection by Dr. Harold Pease

Chapter 4

[ix] The Battle of Trenton: Trenton Battle Facts and Summary: American Battlefield Trust (battlefields.org)

[x] God's Hand at West Point: The Great West Point Chain by Hugh T. Harrington Journal of the American Revolution.

[xi] The Constitution and the Founders: Foundations of American Government (ushistory.org)

Chapter 5

[xii] Thomas Jefferson's Schooling: Thomas Jefferson and Education (wikipedia.org) and various other sources.

[xiii] The Five Thousand Year Leap by Dr. W. Cleon Skousen

Chapter 7

[xiv] Liberties List: Principles of Liberty in Our Founding Documents from National Center for Constitutional Studies.

[xv] Doom and Gloom Information came from Glenn Beck's book, *Brook.*

[xvi] Washington as a King?: Newburgh Letter (wikipedia.org) and Newburgh Address 1783 (constitutioncenter.org)

Chapter 9

[xvii] Religion Taught in Schools: The Religion of All Mankind from National Center for Constitutional Studies (NCCS.net)

Chapter 12

[xviii] Three Would Not Sign: George Mason, Elbridge Gerry, and Edmund Randolph (constitutionfacts.com)

[xix] Congress Gives Washington a Title: A President By Any Other Name (mountvernon.org)

[xx] The Old Man from the Back of the Room story was told at one of the NCCS conventions by one of Dr. W. Cleon Skousen's sons. I asked where I might find the resource to have it verified. I was told it was one of those apocryphal stories, one that feels right but can't be verified.

Book Four

Chapter 2

Though there have been many books written about how to make money, in my opinion, none can compare with Robert Kiyosaki's

Cash Flow Quadrant; part of the Rich Dad Poor Dad series. (I can't recommend this series enough.)

[xxi] Assets and Liabilities: Robert Kiyosaki "Do I have Assets or Liabilities" (richdad.com)

Chapter 4

[xxii] The Four Quadrants: Robert Kiyosaki's *Rich Dad's Cashflow Quadrant: Rich Dad's Guide to Financial Freedom.*

Gary James Sumner comes from a long line of patriots starting in the 1600s. The most famous was Senator Charles Sumner of Massachusetts. Senator Sumner was nearly beaten to death for his stance against slavery. He and Lincoln were such good friends that when the President was shot, Senator Sumner was allowed to stay with him during the night while he lay dying.

Gary's grandfather, James, passed on to Gary his love for America. He remembers his grandfather expressing how concerned he was that the freedoms for which so much blood had been shed had eroded.

Gary James Sumner, a passionate patriot himself, has dedicated more than thirty years of research on the courageous lives of dedicated Americans and pivotal events in our country's history. Gary has uniquely woven history into an intriguing novel, leaving the reader wanting to learn more. Mr. Sumner hopes that through his books, one's love and appreciation for America will deepen.

In Memoriam

It is with great sadness that we inform the reader of the unexpected passing of Gary James Sumner. He was a beloved husband, father, grandfather, brother, author, and friend.

He was a hardworking and dedicated man, and one of the last things he had done was send this book to his publisher. We are so grateful that the tragic car accident that took his life didn't stop him from sharing his work and his final words to all of us. He was a passionate historian who had many life lessons that he wanted to share with all he could. Just as the character he created of Captain James Hansen didn't want his story to be shared with the world until he had passed away, we find it poetic that Gary's story is being told after his passing. This book is the last gift he gave to all. We hope you enjoy it and find it to be of value in your life. Thank you.